Thanos Vlekas

»»»»»»»»»» ««««««««««

Pavlos Kalligas

Thanos
Vlekas

A Novel

TRANSLATED FROM THE GREEK
AND WITH AN INTRODUCTION
BY THOMAS DOULIS

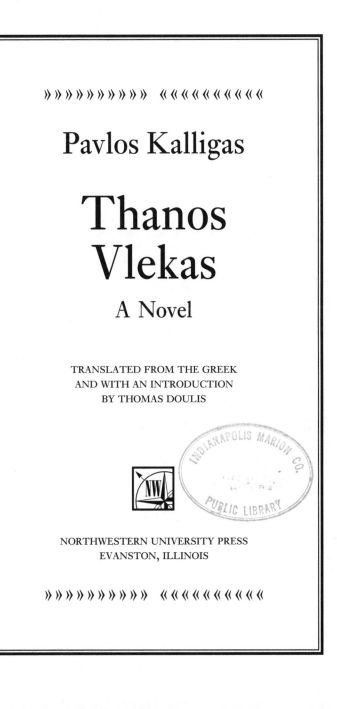

NORTHWESTERN UNIVERSITY PRESS
EVANSTON, ILLINOIS

»»»»»»»»»» ««««««««««

Northwestern University Press
Evanston, Illinois 60208-4210

Originally published in Greek in 1855 under the title *Thanos Vlekas*.
English translation, preface, introduction, "Historical Background," and notes
copyright © 2001 by Northwestern University Press.
Published 2001. All rights reserved.

Printed in the United States of America

10 9 8 7 6 5 4 3 2 1

ISBN 0-8101-1817-3

Library of Congress Cataloging-in-Publication Data

Kalligas, Paulos, 1814–1896.
   [Thanos Vlekas. English]
   Thanos Vlekas : a novel / Pavlos Kalligas ; translated from the Greek
and with an introduction by Thomas Doulis
     p. cm.
   ISBN 0-8101-1817-3 (alk. paper)
   1. Greece—History—Otho I, 1832–1862—Fiction. I. Doulis, Thomas. II. Title.
   PA5610.K237 T413 2001
   889'.32—dc21   00-012359

》》》 CONTENTS 《《《

Translator's Preface   *vii*

Translator's Introduction   *xi*

Historical Background   *xix*

1 The Cabin of Thanos   3

2 Political Thoughts of Hephaestidis and PapaJonas   9

3 The Captain   16

4 The Refugees   23

5 The New *Derven Aga*   30

6 The Crossing   39

7 Tassos Pursued   50

8 New Ordeals of Thanos   57

9 Ayfantis in Athens   68

10 The Trial of Thanos   83

11 The Sorrow of Ephrosyne   95

12 Hephaestidis Perplexed   102

13 The Symposium   111

14 Iapetos Caught in the Act   120

15 The Village Trivae   130

16 The Farewell   142

17 Thanos in Trivae   150

18 Return of Ayfantis to Thessaly   166

19 Tassos, Aide-de-Camp to the Leader   174

20 The Mediation of Ayfantis   183

21 The Final Events   195

Translator's Notes   *203*

Readers who wish to compare the original Greek of Pavlos Kalligas to my translation will probably remark on the occasional variation between the two.

I want to state clearly and at once that my first draft was an honorable attempt to render the Greek text with fidelity. The second draft, less than honorable, perhaps, was dedicated to keeping as much of the original meaning as possible while aiming the translation toward the modern, if not contemporary, reader. The third, fourth, and subsequent drafts were dedicated to making the reading of *Thanos Vlekas* as entertaining as possible, since I would not be doing Kalligas any favors by retaining his approach to the reader of the mid–nineteenth century, who was a product of the erudite school of Greek letters and welcomed classical more than popular references. Besides, the audience of the time had not resolved the issue of genre, believing that fiction was inferior to verse as well as to the more "respectable" kinds of prose literature such as political, scientific, and theological works.

Where I was puzzled by the exact meanings of phrases and encountered differing interpretations of classical and biblical quotations, I chose wording that made sense within the context. But, no matter how much I've tried to make Kalligas accessible, his prose style, witty, erudite, occasionally stiff, reminds one of a blend of Samuel Johnson, Henry James, and occasionally, alas, Thorsten Veblen.

The section "Historical Background" (page xix) presents historical information about major issues in the story that would otherwise require lengthy digressions. The translator's notes at the end of the book, arranged by chapter, contain information that the reader needs when puzzling references appear in the text.

Needless to say, I am interested in suggestions for improvement, especially in those quotations I have been unable to identify.

It is doubtful that I would have contemplated translating and preparing for publication a work as challenging as *Thanos Vlekas* if I could not count on the support of many scholars more qualified than I.

Though often out of my depth, I knew that colleagues and friends, Hellenists, Latinists, historians, and even botanists could be counted on to throw me a lifeline before I went down for the third time. I'd like to take this moment to thank Rod Diman, Wally Englert, and Sophia Denisi for the information they provided me about obscure matters.

To Athena Coronis I owe a great debt of gratitude for her careful reading of a late draft of the translation and for her willingness to provide advice when needed.

The facilities of the Gennadeion Library of Athens and the dedication of the staff have helped in inestimable ways by providing the most complete resources for the study of Hellenic matters, especially in light of the lack of comparable facilities in official Greece.

Nick Germanacos, director of the ITHAKA Program of Chania, Crete, has helped my endeavors by being a friend and colleague whenever I was able to spend extended periods of time in Greece. I thank him warmly.

Finally, during the decade I've spent on this effort I've had two sabbaticals from Portland State University, which generously allowed me to work on a text that did not immediately support my own teaching. With an enlightened institutional policy like this, one does not need the economic help of private or governmental foundations.

Pavlos Kalligas

Pavlos Kalligas (1814–96) was born into a merchant class in Smyrna. The family's real surname was Anninos, but his father wanted to distinguish himself from the others of that name and chose his origin, the Kalligata of the island of Cephalonia, for his new name. Sophia, Pavlos's mother, was of the Mavrokordatos clan of Smyrna.

At the outbreak of the Greek Revolution, the family moved to Trieste to avoid Ottoman persecutions, and Pavlos received his early education in Trieste, Venice, and at the famous Lyceum Heyer of Geneva. In 1832, after his father's death, he went to Munich for advanced work and, in 1834, studied philosophy and history at the university there. In 1835 he enrolled at the University of Berlin, studying law under Edward Gans and Friedrich Karl Savigny, then at Heidelberg, where he took his exams and graduated *insigni cum laude* in 1837.

In Greece, he taught law at the newly established University of Athens (Kapodistrian), beginning as a lecturer in natural law, international law, and on the Pandects (comprehensive digests of Roman law) and achieving full professorship in 1862. He was the rector of the university from 1869 to 1870 and the dean of the law school in 1845, 1872, and 1877. In his administrative capacity, he fought against the encroachment of the state on academic freedom and into university affairs. During his illustrious public career, he served on the Supreme Court of Greece and as a minister of justice, a minister of economics, a deputy of the city of Athens to the parliament of Greece, an adviser to kings and prime ministers, and the director of the National Bank of Greece, a position he held until his death, on 15 September 1896, at the age of eighty-two.

As an attorney, he argued against the extension of censorship (*Concerning the Law of Libel and the Press*, 1837) to include any criticism of royalty (*lesé majeste*) and for a more generous view of freedom of religion in the newly established kingdom of Greece, a point he made eloquently as the defense attorney for the Reverend Jonas King at his trial.

Besides *Thanos Vlekas*, his only work of fiction, Kalligas is known for his impressive studies of Byzantine history (*Vyzantinai Meletai*) and his five-volume synthesis of Roman law, wherein he systematized the Greek Civil Code, a project he began in 1839 and that, by the time of his death in 1896, had gone through four editions. "Roman Law will serve us as a school," he wrote, "as a series of introductory lessons; [adopting] the French Code, however, will forever bar us from the ability to achieve our own national legislation. . . . The reason is obvious. Roman Law, as a past system, will enable us to use and adapt it as we will. The French Code, on the contrary, is a living and flourishing thing. How could we possibly have French laws without blind obedience to French culture?"

Thanos Vlekas: *Mirror to a Flawed Society*

For reasons that are not hard to understand, little is known about nineteenth-century Greek fiction. Most novels of that time are written in a frosty archaic language and are remote from the attitudes and interests of today's reader. Even the one or two that continue to be read by literate Greeks have not aroused the interest of the academic community, and few studies, in any language, are available on the fiction and concerns of that era. *Pope Joan* by Emmanuel Royidis, *Loukis Laras* by Dimitrios Vikelas, *Andronike, Heroine of the Greek Revolution* by Stephanos Xenos, *The Beggar* by Andreas Karkavitsas, and the splendid *Murderess* by Alexandros Papadiamandis are among the few novels to have been translated into other languages. Recently, Johns Hopkins published Papadiamandis's *Tales from a Greek Island*, and the University of New England Press published Vyzinos's *The Sin of My Mother*, but these are collections of shorter narratives.

The inability to resolve the problem of language, certainly, is a major reason for the failure of the longer works. But the inaccessibility for contemporary readers of *katharevousa* (the purist language) is by no means the only obstacle to these novels attaining broad recognition: extra-literary objectives clouded the writers' judgments and marred their efforts. Spiridon Zambelios could not resolve the divergent objectives of novelist and didactic historian in *Cretan Weddings* (1871) and irreparably harmed what might have been a work in the grand scale. Despite its readable Greek, Alexandros Soutsos's *The Exile of 1831* (1835) was flawed by his sense of obligation to provide a historical, almost journalistic, background to the events of the Revolution of 1821. *Leandros* (1834) by Panayiotis Soutsos was a tour of postrevolutionary Greece and a prediction of better things to come under King Othon that for many reasons did not materialize. Similar weaknesses can be identified in most of the score or so novels written within the first half century of Greek independence.

The witty and ambitious *Thanos Vlekas* by Pavlos Kalligas (first serialized in the periodical *Pandora* in 1855 and published seven times thereafter but never translated) stands out among the rest. Contrary to the dictates of romantic spontaneity, its author constructed a plot that, while respecting the sentimental and genteel values of his readers, treated them to an examination that spared none of their illusions. In an almost programmatic way, Kalligas confronted most of the issues that plagued his countrymen a quarter century after Greek independence. It is a novel of ideas, therefore, designed to provoke from its readers reactions to contemporary problems but not to advocate specific measures. Its goal is art, not propaganda or thesis.

Thanos Vlekas, among other things, is about brigandage and provides a disturbing look at a national disgrace for which the Greek state of the time was roundly criticized by foreign governments. Kalligas asserts that, despite official condemnation, the government viewed brigandage as a necessary evil for foreign policy objectives. "If the province did not want brigands," a captain whose mission is to crush the outlaws believes, "brigands would not exist; they exist, therefore, because they are wanted."

But Kalligas, a polymath representative of his era, was certainly familiar with the folk adage that expresses the ambivalence of the modern Greek soul that "God loves the householder, but He also loves the brigand," and he obviously felt an attraction to the men his conscious mind rejected as unworthy of the Greece he loved, men like the piratical Zarpas and (initially) the brigand-manipulator Tassos Vlekas, whom he drew so clearly and humorously.

Expansion beyond national borders after the Revolution depended upon the ability to mobilize the brigands operating in the Ottoman provinces outside of Greece. How else to liberate the unredeemed lands (and fulfill the dictates of the Megale Idea that envisioned a reconstituted Byzantine Empire) still under Turkish control? For some politicians, the eradication of brigandage was undesirable, not only because the brigands maintained a warlike and manly spirit but also because they collaborated with deputies and other members of the government by holding foreign tourists and dignitaries hostage for ransom. In this they were only continuing a tradition held in great esteem by the folk. Activities that under foreign domination had been justified as heroic led, once the state was established, to the corruption of its bureaucratic machinery. Edmund About said as much in *Le Roi de Montagnes,* but that a Greek would agree with this assessment and substantiate it at virtually the same time with an intramural witness was viewed as a betrayal.

The problem of brigandage, therefore, though denounced as shameful by its society, was rooted deep in the psyche of the people themselves, as can be seen in the differing meanings of *klephtis* and *listis,* the connotations of the first being patriotic, of the second, criminal. Kalligas, fully aware of this cultural ambiguity, structured *Thanos Vlekas* to deal with the national issue most pressing during his time and placed the source of Greece's dilemma precisely in those virtues, heroism and resistance to authority, that were responsible for the attainment of freedom and independent statehood. He accomplished this by comparing and contrasting the eponymous hero, a young sharecropper who hopes to improve himself and his land, with his brigand brother, Tassos, in whom "ambition was foremost and was joined to bravery." Their widowed mother prefers the brigand, Tassos, to the "frugal ant" and considers Thanos "incapable of bearing arms." He will certainly never have the ultimate accolade of a hero of that time, a heroic song written about him.

Kalligas's assertions that, despite official condemnation, the government viewed brigandage as a necessary evil for foreign policy objectives could not be viewed as anything but betrayal. But it makes sense. The expansion of Greece beyond the constricting borders established by the guarantor powers after the Revolution depended upon the mobilization of brigands operating in provinces still under Ottoman control. For some politicians, as one of the characters states, the total eradication of brigandage was not desirable because the "Revolution and independence are owed to these so-called klephts." But another character remarks that he would rather "flee to safety from the hands of such 'saviors.'"

The problem of brigandage was a national and social issue, fraught with danger and emotion, that neither historians nor journalists could handle at the time. It was left, consequently, to a jurist who could treat the subjects only in the form of fiction, focusing on them so directly that he anticipated by virtually a century the rest of his culture. In fact, only recently have academic historians undertaken to study banditry and irredentism in Greece from 1821 to 1912 and been allowed access to the archives to study the problems Kalligas identified.

But *Thanos Vlekas* has other interests besides brigandage and the Megale Idea. It also deals with another failure of the new Greek state. Not only was the state unable to provide law and security to border provinces, not an optimistic sign for its promised national expansion into land it did not possess, but it was also unable to administer and dispose properly of lands to which it had full title. The novel concludes with the issue of the apportionment of "national lands," the thousands of hectares taken from the Muslim landowners after liberation. The Greek state, lacking the "common sense" Kalligas believes the United States—that antipodal nation full of well-nourished "potato eaters"—showed in its Homestead Acts, allows brigands-turned-politicians like Tassos to assume control over villages by replacing their Muslim masters and inheriting the Peloponnesian villagers as "serfs." It is here that Kalligas shows the evil that "national heroes" can wreak on the nation and ideas of social justice.

Treated tangentially are a host of other issues. One is the problem of language, to which Kalligas himself was not immune. Confronted by the polyglossia of his time, like all of his contemporaries, he was unable to choose a consistent level of diction for the novel because it did not exist. But there was a benefit to this, as post-Joycean readers will understand. He was able to exploit the full resources of his language, from ancient and biblical quotations, several in Latin, to folk proverbs and the dialogue of rustics, to legal language at its most uncompromising, to the contemporary purist familiar to the subscribers of *Pandora,* the noted Athenian periodical. His readers, the limited public of his time who had access to *Pandora,* were expected to be comfortable with the full range of his references, linguistic and historical, from Homer to 1855, often peppered with witty wordplay.

Kalligas also confronts the problem of an Orthodox Christianity, exhausted after centuries of Ottoman control, being challenged by a host of foreign missionaries dedicated to converting the Greeks to their form of religion. The break of the Orthodox Church of Greece from the Ecumenical Patriarchate in Constantinople because the head of the Great Church was beholden to the sultan for his enthronement and dependent on the Ottoman state for his functioning is merely alluded to in an exchange of dialogue. As to the missionary presence, Kalligas himself was to take a leading role as the defense lawyer of the American missionary, the Reverend Jonas King. His treatment of an orthodoxy embattled by the "Lutherokalvinoi" in *Thanos Vlekas* is mercifully brief, since a fuller plot involvement would have attenuated an already programmatic plot.

Finally, Kalligas treats the endemic inefficiency of the Greek state, a charge that few contemporaries disputed, in dramatic terms, without compromise and with much humor for the first, and perhaps only, time in that era. The conflict between the need to make productive and efficient the one state the Greeks, as Greeks, controlled, and the demands for an expanded Greece that redeemed all the Greeks still under Ottoman rule is played out in many guises in the novel, from the justification of brigandage to the episode of the "muck eater," which illustrated the government's administrative

ineffectuality. By far the most significant issue is that of the disposition of the national lands, that is, the process by which lands taken
from or abandoned by Turkish owners were to be apportioned equi-
tably. In the concluding chapters, Kalligas shows his narrative skills
by bringing to fruition the conflicts for which he had earlier prepared.

The villagers of Trivae—impoverished and ignored by their
representatives, attended to only for their votes—have always
been at the mercy of the powerful. That a revolution against the
Ottomans had occurred means very little to them. The arrival of
what seems to be a magnanimous and altruistic man buoys their
hopes that they finally have a protector, but Tassos, the brother
of the noble Thanos, is their last, and most ruthless, exploiter,
and his brutal henchman will have so persecuted the Trivaeans
that they would be provoked to murder. It is a Greek, therefore,
wrapped in the banner of patriotism and with many important
contacts in the capital city, who utterly victimizes them.

Kalligas never wrote fiction again. In fact, when the publisher Bart
asked to reprint *Thanos Vlekas,* Kalligas is said to have responded
that he had never written a novel. Thereafter, he devoted his time
and considerable energies in service to the government and the law,
to historical research, and, toward the end of his life, to his gover-
norship of the National Bank of Greece.

Chapter 1

Taxation, or "the tenths," in Greece was usually farmed out to speculators who were given extraordinary powers. When the grain was ripe, the farmer asked the tax collector for permission to harvest it, but two-thirds of the grain was not gathered until it was overripe because the tax collector had to arrange for inspectors to keep track of what was cut. For the tax man to secure his tenth, the grain had to be taken to authorized threshing floors, even though the straw on which the grain would be threshed may have been needed as fodder for cattle at the very spot from which it was taken and had to be returned, sometimes at great distances (George Finlay, "The Actual Condition of the Greek State," *Blackwood's* 55 [June 1844]: p. 793).

This mode of taxation, typical during Ottoman times, was continued reluctantly by the first Greek governments because of the expenses of the War of Independence. Later, the government tried to collect taxes in cash, since the loans from the Rothschild bank had to be paid in cash, but peasants in some regions revolted, refusing to harvest unless in-kind tax payment was restored. Grain was always ready when it was demanded, but government officials could demand cash when the money was not available, and the peasants would be charged exorbitant interest by the moneylenders, who were often allied with government officials

(George Finlay, *History of Greece,* ed. Henry Fanshawe Tozer, vol. 5, *Greece under Othoman and Venetian Domination,* vols. 6 and 7, *The Greek Revolution* [Oxford, 1876], pp. vii fn, 122–23; see also Tozer's biographical note).

Embedded in the discussion between Hephaestidis and PapaJonas is one of the rancorous issues of Greece's early years, that of language. Kalligas makes a point of Hephaestidis's not bothering to learn German while in Vienna but that he dedicated himself narrowly to the conflicts over which of the levels of the Greek language to use. By foolishly attacking the government representative for espousing the Korais compromise, Hephaestidis hoped to prove that sound classical scholarship could defeat nationalistic claims that the language had not changed appreciably in the passage of millennia.

Chapter 2

PapaJonas believes that Greece's problems can be attributed to the break of the Greek Church from the Ecumenical Patriarchate at the Great Church, the "good mother" who nourished the Greeks' "racial past." The "earthly powers," besides the guarantor nations of France, England, and Russia, include the Austro-Hungarian Empire. If the Greeks were to unite, however, "us[ing] . . . reason and walk[ing] along the straight path," they would fulfill the longings expressed by the Megale Idea, which had not been fully articulated at that time, "and that brotherly embrace much longed for in Saint Sophia on Easter Day will also be achieved."

The reasons for the break on 23 July 1833 were in large part political. On that day, the Greek government issued the new ecclesiastical constitution, largely the work of the regent, Georg von Maurer, a German Protestant, and Theoklitos Pharmakidis, a

Greek Orthodox priest influenced by German Protestant thought. As Philip Sherrard outlines the reasons, "the Patriarch of Constantinople . . . had to do what he could to prevent any revolt on the part of the Greeks because such a revolt would lead the Turks to take reprisals against the Sultan's Christian subjects for whose good order he was responsible—or even to take reprisals against the Patriarch himself, as they did in the case of Grigorios V," who was hanged and his body mutilated. The Greek government, on the other hand, needed to consolidate a national state, a consolidation impossible "so long as the jurisdictional authority over the Greek Church resided in a Patriarch who, in so many ways, was the instrument of the Porte and compelled to serve its interests" (Philip Sherrard, "Church, State, and the Greek War of Independence," in *Struggle for Greek Independence: Essays to Mark the 150th Anniversary of the Greek War of Independence,* ed. Richard Clogg [Hamden, Conn.: Anchor Press, 1973], pp. 182–90).

It was not until 1850 that the patriarch recognized the new status of the Church of Greece, which is governed by a synod.

Chapter 4

The definitions of *klephts* and *armatoloi* are puzzling, for surely the readers of the time would have been expected to know the difference. The *armatoloi* were Christian irregulars whom the Ottoman authorities employed as a means of control, as much over them as over the other threats to good order in the mountainous areas. The use of the term *listis* to distinguish the bandit or brigand from the *klephtis,* who should be respected for his activities during the Revolution, is, according to John S. Koliopoulos, more common after the 1830s (John S. Koliopoulos, "Brigandage and Irredentism in Nineteenth-Century Greece," *European History Quarterly* 19 [April 1989]: p. 193–228; and *Lestes, he kentrike Hellada sta mesa tou 19ou aiona* [in Greek] [Athens: Hermes Press, 1979]).

Chapter 8

In terms highly reminiscent of this chapter, Kalligas addresses prison reform in "Concerning Prisons" (*Pandora* 16, no. 39 [15 September 1866]: pp. 289–98), writing that "the legislator [who] presumes to lead mankind back to the original savagery of every society . . . could not do better" than to maintain "the penal sanctions he has devised." Reviewing Western attitudes toward punishment from ancient times, in which rigor is unrelieved by mercy or attempts to reform, he contrasts the effects of Christian teaching and practice in Byzantium and the West. He cites the efforts of John Howard in England to bring about a review of prison practices. Howard's testimony before Parliament in 1774 resulted in the Prison Act of 1778, and his research into penal practices in Holland, France, Germany, and Switzerland and his book *The State of the Prisons in England and Wales, with Preliminary Observations, and an Account of some Foreign Prisons* (1777) made a great impact, especially among English reformers. Kalligas felt that the Quaker attitudes as expressed in Pennsylvania toward isolation could be carried too far, threatening the psychic well-being of the inmate, as attested to by Tocqueville. He preferred the mixed system as practiced on the Continent, since it employed individual cells and work in common during the day.

Since the "higher class" had the leisure, Kalligas believed, it was up to it to heed Christ's advice about the lost sheep, to cease being indifferent to the fate of prisoners. An example to the

Greeks should have been the British-run jails of the Ionian republic, which Kalligas toured with the new king, George. But after
the republic was absorbed into the kingdom of Greece, Kalligas
was to see these jails deteriorate to little better than the Greek jails
he so harshly condemned.

Chapter 10

The unnamed American missionary is probably modeled on the
Reverend Jonas King (1792–1869), who had arrived in Syros in
1828 to help run the missionary press. After the liberation of
Athens, King bought a 72,000-square-foot lot that straddled Athi-
nas Street in the market area but was forbidden to develop, divide,
sell, or otherwise use it by government decree. He was charged with
slandering the Orthodox Church by preaching what amounted to
the principles of the Congregational Church, of which he was a
member: that baptism (in the words of the accusation) was merely
symbolic, that those who consumed a little bread and wine were
"foolish to think that they shall be saved by this communion," that
"the most holy Mother of God is not ever-virgin," that "they who
venerate her, as well as other divine icons, are idolaters," that "the
sacred [Ecumenical] Councils, and the things ordained by them in
matters of religion and delivered by Tradition to the later Orthodox Christians" were unacceptable, that "the Fathers and the saints
of the Orthodox Eastern Church of Christ were deceivers, and
thereby brought in diverse heresies," that "holy baptism [was]
merely an external sign for Christians," and that "those who
observe Lent are foolish." In his capacity as constitutional lawyer,
Kalligas defended King but lost, though his arguments were later
used at a second trial, in which the missionary was triumphant. The
hyper-Orthodox monk could be any one of a score of clerics.

Chapter 13

The following section on the apportionment of national lands is translated directly from chapter 13 of *Thanos Vlekas* and in the Greek edition appeared between the sentence that ends "in extraordinary cases" and the one that begins "But nothing occurred in time." The section, which is omitted in this translation, is full of puns.

This was reaffirmed by the Second Astros National Assembly in Article 35. This Assembly in its 132nd ballot determined the types of property to be sold, and that by auction, while the Third Assembly at Epidaurus ratified this ballot as salvational [εθνοσωτήριον] by acts of and including the codex of decisions under Number 10. With another vote, Number 14, while groping through the findings and discovering that national properties had been lost, or rather could no longer be found, it gave the necessary emetic to those devouring crevasses [καταφαγόντας βαράθρους]. Those who reported on these matters to the Assembly showed that the auctioneers, despite functioning in the blaze of noon, had worked in the dark, because they had not burned enough of the midnight oil. They had signed themselves as extreme patriots. (See the report in the Mamoukas collection, vol. 5, p. 77.) Because the first dosage of emetic did not suffice, the Assembly resumed its work in Hermione and from there moved to the more ventilated Troezen, ordering a second ballot for the 24th. But this too passed through with no purgation. In the new constitution voted in at this time, Article 61 allowed the lawful sale of only those lands subject to deterioration. The Fourth Assembly of the Greeks at Argos did not appear inferior to those before it. It established two committees, which as usual did nothing (Ballot, 29 July 1829 and 13 November 1830) and allowed the acquisition of properties by soldiers and sailors and for the benefit of the local communities, but these decisions by the Assembly were eventually buried in the archives as well.

George Finlay expresses attitudes similar to those of Kalligas on the task before King Othon on his arrival in Greece, even using the phrase to which Kalligas was so partial, "common sense."

"The greater part of Greece was uninhabited," Finlay writes. "The progress of many British colonies, and of the United States of America, testify that land capable of cultivation forms the surest foundation for national prosperity. To insure a rapid increase of population where there is an abundant supply of waste land, nothing is required but domestic virtue and public order. And in a free country, the rapid increase of a population enjoying the privilege of self-government in local affairs and of stern justice in the central administration is the surest means of extending a nation's power. The dreamer, therefore, who allowed visions of the increase of the Greek race, and of its peaceful conquests over uncultivated lands far beyond the limits of the new Kingdom, to pass through his mind as King Othon rode forward to mount his throne might have seen what was soon to happen, had the members of the regency possessed a little common sense. The rapid growth of population in the Greek kingdom would have solved the Eastern Question. The example of a well-governed Christian population, the aspect of its moral improvements, material prosperity, and instant overflow into European Turkey, would have relieved European cabinets from many political embarrassments, by producing the euthanasia of the Ottoman Empire" (Finlay, *History of Greece,* p. 109).

Notes of credit were given to all veterans of the revolutionary struggle (*falangitis*) as long as they were in the regular army. On the basis of Article 3 of the 1–13 January 1838 law, "Concerning the Grant of National Lands to the Veterans," soldiers and sailors, of whatever rank, who had fought in the Revolution were able to purchase whatever national real estate was available by auction "as long as they had not received wages, pension, or [other] supplies from the Treasury." By the 18–30 September 1835 law, "Concerning the Formation of a Greek Phalanx," various ranks were considered positions of honor. Phalangists were deemed the lower ranks, corporal to lieutenant, but all were considered phalangists thereafter.

Chapter 15

In Liddell-Scott, as well as Demetrakos, the following definitions are given for the word *trivae,* or *trivi:* "a rubbing, a wearing away, a wasting"; "a routine"; "an object of care." *Trivos* is defined as "a worn or beaten track." *Trivomenos laos* is defined as "an oppressed people"; *trivon* as "a worn garment" or "a threadbare cloak."

A *kaca-basi* is an Ottoman land baron. During Ottoman times, Christian and Jewish financiers and tax collectors collaborated with the Muslim civil-military governors, while a class of Greek property managers, tax collectors, administrators, merchants, and usurers served as liaison agents between the ruling Muslims and the peasantry. "They managed the transfer of agricultural surpluses from the Christian cultivators to Turkish landowners and officials, and in so doing won for themselves local power and modest wealth. . . . Their relative affluence and connections with the Moslem governors also gained them prominence in Christian regional administration, especially in the Peloponnesos. Known as *kotsambasides* (from the Turkish *koca bashis*) or *archons* (also *demogerontes*) they won ascendancy by delicate political maneuvering on the treacherous frontier where Moslem and rayah affairs converged" (William W. McGrew, *Land and Revolution in Modern Greece, 1800–1881: The Transition in the Tenure and Exploitation of Land from Ottoman Rule to Independence* [Kent, Ohio: Kent State University Press, 1985], pp. 37–38).

A *paredros* (Πάρεδρος) is an ancient and rather obscure administrative title, which in terms of this novel can be understood as an elder or a leader. Liddell-Scott defines a *paredros* as "someone who sits besides or near"; "an assessor or coadjutor"; "a counselor"; "a lieutenant of a military commander." In modern Greek terms, the *paredros* was a magistrate salaried by the state or an aide to a mayor or a municipal adjunct. What makes things difficult, of course, is that Doudoumis has been described by Kalligas as being barely literate.

Thanos Vlekas

The Cabin of Thanos

On summer mornings, George Hephaestidis, master of the Greek school, and Father Jonas, the parish priest, would often set out from Lamia to visit Thanos Vlekas, a farmer highly respected by all who knew him but especially by these two venerable men. With the aid of his elderly mother, this young sharecropper had managed to establish a small herd of dairy goats from his surplus, while adhering to agreements with landowners whose fields he tilled. Now, he expected the harvest to reward his many efforts.

But today Thanos was worried and somber. Some time before, he'd cut his wheat, piling the stacks high near the threshing floors, but the tax collectors who would calculate the tithes seemed to be elsewhere. The harvest had been bountiful. After he'd paid the landowners their share and set aside funds for his own needs and seed for the next season, Thanos reckoned to have enough wheat to market.

He had considered purchasing oxen of his own so that he would not have to wait for his neighbors to plow their own fields, thus risking the loss of the opportune moment, and had already bought a plow from last year's profit. But since he would need to maintain the oxen for most of the year when they would not be useful, he decided two years before to buy goats, which would produce cheese.

Having taken the first step now, he hoped to achieve his goal and was impatient for the tax collectors. Like a frugal ant, Thanos gradually augmented his capital through austerity and toil in his farming efforts. The fatal epidemic of brigandage was cresting at this moment, though, and, roused from its lethargy, the government had dispatched a captain of the gendarmerie to stamp out this scourge by vigorous pursuit.

Thanos looked forward to the visit of the teacher and the priest so that he could learn the whereabouts of the tax collectors and how the new captain planned to restore order and security. Because the early walkers were among those the brigands themselves respected, they did not worry about the danger they ran in visiting Thanos.

But his mother had her own reasons for looking forward to the visit of the two elders. Besides Thanos, Barbara had another son, her firstborn, Tassos, who, despite long service in the military, had never been promoted beyond lieutenant because of his disorderly life and was virtually always on the inactive reserve, as at present. Tassos was her favorite, though, because he followed the manly profession of his father, who in the Revolution had fallen on the field of battle. Indignant at not being promoted on the strength of his father's service, Tassos occasionally took part in brigand raids himself and maintained contact with the bands until offered amnesty and a promotion. These never came about. As a matter of fact, his mother, recalling that her husband had rendered similar services to the Ottoman authorities, shared his indignation at not being properly rewarded, and loved Tassos the more. Aware that he was setting out with brigand bands again, Barbara said nothing to Thanos, feeling sorry for him, since he was scorned by his brother for a slavish and fatiguing life.

The arrival of the captain and the increase in armed forces alarmed her, but she hoped to learn more during her private conversation with the priest. Often while at her morning's work, she would pause at the door, glancing toward the city from which the two elders would appear but saying nothing to the brooding Thanos.

Finally Thanos saw them coming and told his mother to begin brewing coffee for their reception.

Hephaestidis and PapaJonas were contemporaries and ardent lovers of ancient letters, a perpetual subject of conversation with them. In fact, at the turn the century, Hephaestidis had studied in Bucharest under Lambros Photiadis, whom he lauded while criticizing all other scholars, especially his own contemporaries. He considered Neophytos Doukas, who happened to hold similar views of the ancients, a plagiarist and claimed that all the commentaries of Thucydides attributed by Poppos to Doukas were really by Photiadis, that bright beacon of Hellenism, a man so humble that he was reluctant to publish his work. Many a mackerel, he intoned, had soared with wings that Photiadis gave him, and he derided the "pygmies" of the modern era who weren't even worthy to be followers. "A fool," he'd mutter indignantly when one of them was praised, "with the mind of a scatterbrain."

Whither the Bacchae of that time, the composers of iambs, of wings, of axes, of altars, of eggs, of reeds, and of the like liturgical elements by which he especially admired his teacher? He had the same judgment for all the erudite who left the kingdom of Greece in droves with their innovations to educate society, considering them little better than foolish children.

During the years he spent in Vienna before the Revolution, he deigned to adopt only European dress but learned no German, since he believed the language was not worth his effort. Though considerably his inferior in ancient learning, PapaJonas shared his opinions about Greek education and cherished memories of the time he'd spent in Selyvries of Constantinople, which was frequented by scholars attached to the Patriarchate, where many and various topics were discussed. He greatly admired Hephaestidis and enjoyed talking to him, paying special attention to his innocent ramblings.

This morning the teacher began to deride modern education, even before a topic for discussion had been agreed upon.

"I'm in a splendid mood today, friend Jonas," he said as they paced toward Thanos's cabin. "There's a young scholar from Athens out inspecting the provincial schools. I met him at the nomarch's house. This 'Arabian Flutist' babbled about pedagogical methods and grammar and composition and well-rounded education. Every word turned my stomach, but I listened dutifully until my turn came.

"'You in Athens are always chattering about method,' I began, 'and intriguing and agitating yourselves about jargon, but you confound the modern language with the ancient and lose your grip on the old while trying to create a new form. I'm an old man and have grown tired of arguing about language and dialects, whether the modern tongue is an embellishment of a decadent language or a new corruption, a monstrosity, an abortion, a griffin, neither ancient nor modern but an amalgam of the two, or even an entirely new plant springing up among the ruins, taking root and prospering, producing luxuriant blossoms and lush growths. In my opinion, we have only one duty: to understand the ancients. Until we achieve this, we'll never make progress. As an example, would you care to explain the proverbial line Οὐ σύγ᾽ ἂν ἐξ οἴκου σῷ ἐπιστάτῃ οὐδ᾽ ἅλα δοίης from Homer for me?'

"Wanting to show off, the sage of Athens smiled at how easy a challenge I'd set him and, not seeing the trap, interpreted it as 'Certainly you would not give salt from your own residence to your *overseer.*'

"The others smiled when our friend slipped, but not I. 'What's an overseer?' I gloated.

"'Is that why you're laughing? Or do you find it strange that the word has survived to our days?'

"'Not as strange as it sounds. What's strange,' I said, 'is that Antinous had overseers, some apparently for the vineyards and some for the fields. But why, when they had access to the salt themselves and were nourished by it, did they need Antinous to give it to them? *Epistates,* my friend, is someone who petitions for aid or for a favor, and Odysseus at the time was pretending to be a beggar. *Now* do you see where this confusion leads? To Babylon! According to you, then, τύμβος σᾶς ἀλόχου . . . σέβαζ ἐμπόρων means "merchants and grocers wish to worship" and ἐπὶ χθονὶ πουλυβυτείρη can mean "that land where much butter is churned.'"

"Seeing his mistake, the sage tried to patch things up: '*Epistates,*' he said, 'can be found among the ancients with the contemporary meaning—'

"He had not tried to interpret the word; and I am a witty man but prickly as a gadfly. 'Depends on the circumstances,' I cut him short. You see, Father Jonas, the kind of people in charge today?"

"But dear friend . . ." That the young scholar had been taught a lesson gratified the priest, but he wondered about the consequences. "He's a government official. Won't he submit a report about your school?"

Hephaestidis, his sense of literary honor superior to all other sentiments, dismissed this. "Do you mean that I should be worried about being toasted with the bitter drink of my dismissal? He's capable of that, certainly, but what does Hippocleidis care?"

Chatting in this manner, they approached. Thanos welcomed them, kissing the priest's right hand and receiving his blessing, then returning Hephaestidis's greeting.

The view of Lamia was obscured by a hill, but Thanos's cabin was built on a rise itself and from it one could see the stretch of plain below as far away as Thermopylae and from the peaks of Oithis to the heights of Othrys, between which the Malaic Gulf shimmered like a lake at sunrise. Next to the log cabin, whose roof was mud and straw, there was a well and a shady poplar whose whitened leaves rustled gently in the morning breeze. Behind the cabin, near a shelter for the goats, Thanos planned to build the stable for his oxen. The cabin's roof projected far enough to offer shade to whoever sat at the door.

It was here that Barbara waited for the two elders. After the customary greetings, she entered the cabin with the priest to inquire about Tassos.

"We'll let Kamino make her confession," Hephaestidis said, "though that's not the reason we made the trip." He called her Kamino either because she was always at the fire or because she was constantly whispering to the priest, which interrupted the teacher's ceaseless chatter and deprived him of an audience. "Give me a light for my pipe."

Political Thoughts of Hephaestidis and PapaJonas

Hephaestidis sat under the eaves in an armchair and unscrewed the tip of his walking stick, transforming it into a pipe.

"Child," he said as he took the bowl of water Thanos offered him, "you don't seem as happy as you ought to be. Since the haystacks are higher than they were last year, the wheat must be more abundant."

"My complaints aren't about God, Teacher, only about men. The wheat's been cut for fifteen days now, but the tax collectors haven't appeared yet. A thousand things can happen: the weather's changeable, the province is full of brigands. I can't rest until the wheat's been threshed and in Lamia."

"You're a fine young man. God will make everything right for you. The tax collectors are afraid of the brigands. Once the new captain starts his vigorous pursuit, they'll venture out of Lamia and get to you first because you're nearest."

"I hope to God that's true. But the captain frightens me. He's a cruel man, they say. Suppose he suspects me of giving food to the brigands and throws me into jail before I winnow? Who'll do my work then?"

"Why should he suspect you? You have no enemies, and everyone knows you're a good farmer and an honest man."

These comments did not reassure Thanos, who saw things as they were, not as they should be.

But another sort of discussion was going on in the cabin.

"What news have you of Tassos?"

"He's become a brigand, your Tassos," the priest said, "and God pity both of you."

"Why?"

"The new captain's a Satan, pure and simple. Once he hears that a brigand has relatives, he forces them to reveal his whereabouts. Everyone in Lamia is terrified."

"*Aiyee,* my son, if he gets you, you won't have a second chance. Then you'll have a klephtic song written about you."

"If you can, send word to Tassos to leave and not make his identity known. For the good of Thanos." Having said this, the priest left the cabin and sat next to Hephaestidis, unhappy that his advice to Barbara would be wasted effort.

In a little while, she brought coffee and milk out for Hephaestidis, who during his stay in Vienna had learned to drink these mixed. "Today, Teacher, you'll find your coffee as you like it."

"I hope so," Hephaestidis replied, bringing out sugar and rolls for himself and the priest from his pack, "but, as Astydamas said, 'You're praising yourself, woman.'"

"Since you've started on ancient Greek, Teacher," Barbara said, turning toward the cabin, "I'll go back to my chores."

After Hephaestidis was satisfied, he puffed on his pipe and waved away a cloud of smoke, while PapaJonas limited himself to sipping his coffee black.

"Friend, Jonas," Hephaestidis said, returning to their favorite topic, "there aren't many lands as pleasant as this valley of the rapid and inexhaustible Spercheus. Yet, all of Greece is like this, a prosperous land boasting a temperate climate. And we can see the kind of men who inhabited the land by one of their epigrams: 'O Stranger, go tell the Spartans that we lie here having fulfilled their command.' But see how the laws and institutions of Lycurgus's time differ from our own. Because of the former, many willingly submitted themselves to death, while the current system exhausts or provokes the citizens to murder.

"What else are today's laws and system of government but a maze of public authorities multiplied deliberately to feed the swarm of insatiable machinators who are nourished by the sweat of the people whom they impoverish and drive to brigandage and crime? Before you is a vivid example. This honorable, hardworking farmer has brought forth as much harvest as he could wish from the fruitful land. Yet, despite the many bureaus and civil servants, the government has turned him and his like over to tax farmers who extract from them as much as possible, as painfully as possible. He risks losing all his property because of rainstorms and other natural calamities, while being suspected of supplying brigands from whose depredations he cannot be protected. Do you see the vicious circle? Brigands are products of a weak government. Because the arm of the law can't reach the brigand, it strikes the law-abiding and unprotected citizen instead. I punish you, in other words, because I'm not strong enough to defend you. Am I wrong to ask this question repeatedly then?

"Greece will not prosper until she is governed according to the traditional ways. Every province should have its own leaders, selected to oversee and maintain law and order, and they should assemble annually to deliberate about the common good, in Pylae if you wish. Then you'll see that the citizens will elect men distinguished for their virtue. As Homer sings, 'So that you may become, excellent in words and deeds.' They would be urged to do so out of self-interest. Today, however, the government assigns anyone who happens along in order to save money or to be rid of him. One of the leaders wants to be the general and expects everyone to bear arms so that, in a crisis, Greece would be mobilized against the enemy. 'Shield pressed on shield, helmet on helmet, man on man.'"

PapaJonas considered Hephaestidis the better classical scholar and viewed him as a more perceptive interpreter of the ancient way of thinking; he disagreed with his political theories, though, for the teacher went to extremes, not only in his emphasis on linguistic archaism but in nationalism as well. He tried to modify these ideas somewhat by allowing that society was sick and needed a skillful physician.

"Friend, Hephaestidis, you've said some wise things, but it seems to me that you're judging man only by man's measure."

"Of course," he replied. "I'm a man, and everything about man interests me."

"But remember," the priest continued, "that our Lord 'hid these things from the wise and prudent and revealed them to children.' Listen, then, to the words of an unwise man. Society, whether embellished in the Attic or the Spartan mode, will always be a lifeless and commonplace statue if not animated by religion and Christian morality. Here I've placed my finger on the sore spot. The Church is held in contempt, bishoprics are vacant, the child has been separated from its Constantinopolitan mother, and no one cares about the orphan, whose property is consumed daily.

"Yet, during centuries of bondage our good mother had sheltered us under her wings and nourished us with the pure milk of truth. Within her Ark she's saved our racial past, but we've forgotten our traditions, as though we were made of oak or stone, because we no longer read our history. Ungrateful toward the mother, we've become unjust and insensitive to our brothers, from whom the earthly powers have wanted to separate us, but all they've managed to carve out for Greece have been these unstable borders. If we use our reason and walk along the straight path, these things would pass, too, and that brotherly embrace much longed for in Saint Sophia on Easter Day will also be achieved. But we are very distant from God's will. Since we've abandoned His house, there is no mercy, and our crimes are punished by plagues and diseases and famines and murders and robberies. 'Jerusalem has sinned, and for this a commotion has come upon her.'"

While he was classifying the sufferings of society and the means of healing these, Hephaestidis was saying that "we have knowledge of arbitrary acts of men." A young shepherd whom they had not seen approaching because of their heated discussion suddenly appeared before them.

Hephaestidis interrupted the priest as soon as he saw this sturdy and robust youth. "Look at that shepherd, who though he drinks whey yet has a sturdy leg."

"Indeed," PapaJonas replied with a smile, "but I doubt that he got this way by drinking whey. However, let's leave for the city before it gets too hot and let these good people go about their work."

The shepherd knew that they were speaking about him but, not understanding, barely returned their perfunctory greeting as he entered the cabin. The two elders said good-bye to Thanos and his mother and began to walk toward Lamia, continuing their discussion quietly, unaware that the situation after their departure would change suddenly. The shepherd had come as a bearer of evil tidings.

He waited for the elders to gain some distance. "Tassos has been shot in the leg."

"Oh, God," Barbara screamed. "He's ambushed the captain!"

"Yes, he and his men had set a trap outside Lamia. I don't know if it was the captain himself or another officer. Gunfire was exchanged. Two gendarmes fell. Tassos was lunging at them with his sword when he fell, wounded."

"What a hero!"

"Two of his men dragged him by the leg into a gully and from there carried him to our sheepfold. The others scattered."

"And his wound?"

"The bullet's still in his leg. He needs a surgeon, but we can't keep him with us because the news will get around. He's in the brush covered with foliage and can't be seen. I'm here to tell you to come get him."

"May God take days from me and give you years. Safeguard my Tassos until I come to take him to a doctor. The next time, he won't hit the captain in the leg but in the head. Live, Tassos, and everyone will know what sort of lad you are."

Thanos listened quietly, upset at his brother's misfortune. He loved Tassos and was as sorry for the dangers to which he was exposed as to hear the words of their mother, who was the only person who could have counseled him to change his way of life and to use his bravery to serve the laws and the common good. If he dared express his opinions, though, Thanos would have heard his mother's imprecations, for she had written him off as an unworthy child and a betrayer of the family name.

She wanted to go at once, but the shepherd resisted. "You'll expose us! Come tonight and I'll assign two lads to carry him. I'll stop by to get you. Just decide where you'll take him."

It is unnecessary here to repeat the abuse Barbara heaped on the government, but especially the captain. The enemies of Tassos, for her, were the enemies of God and men. "Why don't I have another stalwart to avenge my Tassos at once?" she complained. "Every day this captain enjoys daylight and shade I feel the burning flames of hell."

Thanos's gentleness sometimes made her even more feverish, but he was silent now and, by skillfully uttering some words about saving Tassos, managed to turn her attention to a search for a practical solution and to moderate her emotions.

"Where will we hide Tassos? Who'll accept him?"

Barbara sat moaning on the ground, pale, gesturing, uttering her maledictions. After long thought, she rose up and shouted, as though suddenly inspired. "Who'll save him? We must leave! Leave Greece! We'll go out, to the Turkish lands!"

Thanos said nothing but eventually acknowledged that this was the safest course. There would be time for Tassos to heal and return when things had quieted down. But as long as there were no suspicions about him, Thanos wanted to stay where he was and do his work. He hoped to send his wheat to Lamia after the tax collectors had left and, if necessary, hide out for a little while.

"Maybe this is better," he thought. "Since Tassos won't mend his ways, maybe it's better for him to be out of the country."

Mother and son waited for nightfall with their own thoughts. As the shadows lengthened, the shepherd, true to his word, reappeared at the cabin, and they left to get Tassos.

The Captain

The difficulty of securing the borders, since they were not estab-lished along high and inaccessible mountain ranges, was the main reason among the many that the province of Phthiotis was scourged by brigandage. The means of pursuit were inadequate as well, for the armed force comprised irregulars, local volunteers who were related to brigands and themselves occasional outlaws. They were in no hurry to pursue their kin or friends seriously, managing usually to arrive after the brigands had left a place, and preferred to desert rather than submit to discipline.

But when the evil became intolerable, special measures were necessary, and these varied with the ability and character of the officer assigned to the pursuit. Some used political craft by recruiting the bravest men into the army and thus undermin-ing the brigand groups, occasionally managing to isolate and to capture or kill the chieftains themselves. Most of the leaders escaped, however, and found refuge among the Ottomans beyond the mountains. But these pursuits merely put a temporary end to the evil. Because there wasn't much gunplay or excessive oppression of civilians, moreover, everyone was pleased with the measures taken and lauded the wisdom and skill of the officer involved, forgetting that the remaining heads of the Hydra had not been severed.

Rare were the officers who declared relentless war against men like Skiron and Pityokamptes, the brigands of Theseus's time, since by tracking them to the forests and ravines of the mountains, they might compel them to mass together and to wage a bloody battle.

But the newly assigned captain used neither tactic, devising instead a system that aroused general panic. Brigands would not exist, he reasoned, if the province did not want them. They existed, therefore, because they were wanted. The root of the evil was a perverse and corrupt will, and whoever wanted to heal this pandemic needed to be relentless in his therapy. People, in his view, were like sacks of superfluous and harmful fluids that could be emptied only by vigorous compression. He suspected everyone and was seldom wrong. He blamed the government and the laws, which hindered him from examining the soundness of the members of every class, but especially of those in high social positions.

Even in his appearance there was something terrible and sinister. His eyes glowed like burning coals under dark, bushy eyebrows, and the wrinkles of his swarthy and humorless face revealed a rawness of spirit and an implacability toward human grief. He was rather short, with broad and hunched shoulders and powerful hands, and he limped, because his legs were of uneven length. His men believed that he was scaly and shaggy as well, claiming that he had a tail, but one tends to agree with the physiologists and deny man that unnecessary extension of the spine.

Though he spoke little, every word he uttered was threatening and blasphemous. Most people thought there was something satanic about him, as though he had been born of Stygos and Typhon. He inspired among his gendarmes the same terror as the head of Medusa on the shield of Athena.

Following his principles and disposition, he proceeded to hunt down brigands systematically. Once he learned of a brigand, he seized his parents, kinsmen, and friends, who, being handier, were subjected to cross-examinations and tortures until they revealed the brigand's location and offered suggestions for tracking him down. Some were whipped, some hanged by their feet, some had large stones set on their chests. Among other devices, he denied his victims sleep for days, commanding his soldiers to alternate in goading them awake, and made use of the rack and red-hot irons. When some annoying legalist accused him of breaking the law, he claimed to be exercising his power where the law was inadequate. "It's even in Holy Writ," he'd say. "'Fathers shall not die for their children.' It doesn't say: 'They must not be tortured.' Besides, no one's died yet."

The whole province, therefore, was in a panic which, even as Thanos and his mother paced behind the shepherd to find Tassos, was on the increase. The shepherd repeated whatever he had heard that day and assured them that many had already crossed over the borders secretly. He had every intention of doing so himself.

These narratives inflamed the fury of Barbara, who wished the worst on the captain's head. Finally, they arrived at Tassos's hideout and found him lying under brush. His mother, hysterical, threw herself on him. "The Catalans have wounded you, my child."

"I'm burning up. Give me some cold water."

"Better get ready to leave," the shepherd warned. "We don't have much time. Here come the two lads. Let's go while it's still dark."

The two helpers set Tassos, feverish and almost delirious, on a stretcher and set off, his arms wrapped around their necks.

"We're off to Turkish lands," Barbara said, following Thanos.

"I'll catch up to you tomorrow," the shepherd added.

They paused to rest for some time at another sheepfold, but Tassos, having breathed fresh air, felt better and asked them to continue.

The shepherd of this flock was a distant relative of the first and seemed to be as willing to help out, providing two young helpers whom he told how far to carry Tassos and where to hide him so that the following night they could continue their trek and reach the border.

Thanos, seeing that his brother had a good escort and that he should be safely beyond the borders the following day, told his mother that he'd send her whatever she needed and turned toward home.

As the captain continued his searches and inquiries within Lamia, he learned that Lieutenant Tassos Vlekas, having deserted months before, had joined with other brigands and had, in fact, formed his own band. Who the party responsible for the death of the two gendarmes in the pitched battle was, he did not know yet, but he learned that the Tassos in question had a mother and brother living on the outskirts of Lamia. He immediately dispatched three mounted police to learn from them, employing the customary methods, where and with whom Tassos could be found.

When they reached Thanos's cabin after midnight, the police found no one inside. On starting a fire, they noticed traces of recent human presence, which led them to conclude that the residents had recently left the cabin either on business or after secret notification but that they would return the following day.

Since there was no place for them to hitch their horses near the cabin, they walked them to the threshing floor and tied them between the haystacks so that they could feed. In this way, the gendarmes reasoned, Thanos and his mother would return to the cabin without seeing evidence of their presence, even though they might suspect that they had been visited.

The night was pleasant, a gentle breeze having dispersed the heat of the day, and the stars shone in the firmament. They drew cold water from the well and sprawled on the stacks, smoking and telling stories about the captain, the fear and irrationality of the rustics, and how comic they were at the moment the tortures began.

"Did you see the way Stathis's rib cage rattled and danced, like he was stepping on hot coals. Claimed to know nothing at first, but after he'd been tied with the straps he sang all night. 'This one's like a lemon,' Capt'n said. 'Dry on the outside. Give it a good squeeze, though, and you got all the juice you want.'"

"They're all alike," the other gendarme agreed. "Grab one brigand and you got them all. But if they don't get scared and see the knife close to the bone, the dogs play dumb so that you wouldn't give two plugged nickels for them. If they think they've found some-one to buy their pig in a poke, though, they've got another think com-ing. 'Do this one by the book,' Capt'n says, 'see if we can cut through the tongue-tie.' That's when the jumping and the yodeling begins."

They were tired of talking and got drowsy, deciding that two would sleep for an hour while the third stood guard. Things did not work out that way, though, and after a short while the guard, too, fell asleep.

Their deep slumber lasted a long time, but a great noise woke them and they were barely able to breathe because of thick smoke clouds torn apart by tongues of fire. They leaped over the flames, rushing to untie their animals, but the horses were galloping around furiously, neither approaching the conflagration nor head-ing toward the town. Finally, they caught and calmed them, reining them in and tying them separately so that they would no longer buck when terrified.

They returned to the blaze, enthralled by its splendor, appar-ently started when a lit cigarette had fallen in the haystack. The property belonged to the brother of a brigand, though, and they felt no sorrow for its destruction, which they had not caused deliber-ately. For this reason, they did not try to save what they could.

"You see, we almost got burned," one of them said, "and he won't feel obligated to us for saving him the effort of threshing."

"No one's grateful," said the other. "That's why I think we should take our pay in kind."

"How?"

"We've been waiting for nothing all this time. Who knows when these people are coming? I saw some goats, though. Maybe we should go to work on the most tender. As Capt'n says, like a charm."

"Perfect," the other two exclaimed and immediately set to work. In a twinkling they'd slaughtered, skinned, and skewered the youngest kid; then, gathering brushwood for a fire, they set the spit on piles of stones and, holding each other by the hand, they danced and sang.

By now, Thanos was on his way back to the cabin, relieved that his brother had fled but also shaken by the stories he had heard from the shepherd's men. He hoped the captain would not learn that it was Tassos who had killed the gendarmes. As he neared, he heard a racket approaching and hid in the brush.

A troop of gendarmes and irregulars passed by, quarreling among themselves as to whether the captain did right by treating people, whether innocent or guilty, in such a hard way. By and large, they approved of his actions, while the sergeant, as the wisest, explained to the others in his own words the captain's maxim, altering it somewhat, that "One pole strikes another."

This discussion, most of which Thanos overheard, increased his disquiet.

After they had passed, he turned toward home, hurrying so that he would arrive before dawn, but he saw a puzzling glow in the direction of his cabin. It became more pronounced as he neared. Clouds of smoke revealed that it was from a large blaze. What, he wondered, could be burning outside Lamia?

From the top of a nearby hillock, he was astonished to view a sea of flames, in the midst of which was the dark spot of his cabin. He ran as fast as he could toward the inferno, then stopped when he saw, like specters in the dazzling glow of the fire, the three gendarmes, holding hands and dancing in a circle. He stood, motionless as a pillar of salt. The tongues of fire, as though out of the crater of a volcano, roared upward, blocking out the stars with a thick cloud of smoke, scattering sparks everywhere and bathing the surroundings in a brilliant glow. A thick ribbon of smoke extended as far as the horizon.

Speechless and with arms raised to the heavens, Thanos stood before the appalling spectacle. All his property and hopes, all the plans he had nourished in his heart for so long, had been destroyed in one moment. The gendarmes, he knew, were waiting to torture him. Yesterday, he was happy; now he was impoverished and hunted, with no place to turn.

As horrible as it was, Thanos broke away from the sight only with effort, for the blaze was greater than the dawning day, and, if he had not heard the sound of horses galloping toward the cabin, he would have been consumed in it himself. It was a mounted unit, dispatched from Lamia to determine the cause of the forest fire. He withdrew as danger and disaster pressed everywhere around him.

He rushed on, often turning his head, unable to consider his next step. But he could not remain where he was, and his only recourse, as the hunted brother of Tassos, was to cross the border himself, looking for a new place to earn his living.

The Refugees

Passing through brush that covered a gap in the rock face, Tassos and Barbara entered a lair where she bathed his wound and attended to him with maternal care. The cold compresses had done him much good, and the night, during which they had crossed the border, had been less painful for him. They had evaded the Greek and Ottoman guards with little difficulty, because they were considerably spaced out.

On the plain of Thessaly they encountered scores of shepherds with their flocks, as well as others who had migrated out of fear. It was a mass flight, and the migrants, because the Ottoman authorities put up no obstacles and seemed to ignore them, no longer feared pursuit. At the first village, Barbara stopped at some ruins and sent a helper to find someone to heal the wound. It was here that much to her joy she heard some of the migrants singing this song:

> There's keening on Oithis's peaks
>   and in Lamia's Vale
> For Tassos, son of bravery,
>   has suffered a great wound.
>
> Right chieftain he,
>   hunting the captain down,
> lunged at him with a sword,
>   despising his own death.

The blood that drenched
   the grass was rich,
Maidens had gathered it
   with blooms of love.

Aiyee, Captain, if Tassos chances
   on you once more,
The mountains won't hide you,
   nor will the woods.

"Tassos," the old lady exclaimed, "you have a song," and she kissed him with joy, repeating the final couplet, which she especially liked.

Ghikas Tramersis, the shepherd who first cared for Tassos, arrived sometime that morning, having migrated with his flock, and paid his respects, happy to see Tassos much improved. He mentioned that at Domokos, known in ancient times as Thaumacia, there lived a rich and compassionate Thessalian named Nikos Ayfantis, who was sure to help them out. Tramersis had had many dealings with him and wished to introduce Tassos personally. He left at once to make arrangements.

Nikos Ayfantis, a caring and generous man, was everything the shepherd said he was. Graying and stout, he was the idol of his servants, for his aquiline features radiated friendliness and humor. His extensive holdings, with numerous flocks and beehives, stretched along the border where he could be useful to anyone who sought his aid, brigand or not, so that while living in the midst of lawlessness, he enjoyed complete security and the protection of those who were harmful to others.

He and Kioura, his wife, had only one daughter, his much beloved Ephrosyne, and when not otherwise occupied, he was always near her, seeking to please her in every way. At sixteen, Ephrosyne was a tall blonde, lithe and blue eyed, her sensitivity somewhat obscured by a youthful vivacity. She returned her father's love and, like her mother, devoted herself to handiwork, especially the embroidery of various fabrics, a skill with which she had great success. During the spring months she cultivated silkworms and, along with girls her age, daughters of nearby farmers usually, she harvested the cocoons and spun the silk, from which she wove and embroidered, resorting to dyers only when she needed to tint the silk. She wove linen and wool as well and in general was very industrious. Her father loved to watch her work, teasing her and informing her of whatever he knew and was currently learning, for he kept no secrets from her.

The shepherd called on him and was immediately shown in. Ayfantis, sending for a doctor, ordered his servants to take Tassos into a small house near his own residence and to provide him with every care. The following day, Barbara went to thank her benefactor and to wish every good thing in life for his daughter: a man as handsome as the dawn and as brave as her Tassos. Her ways, her gestures, the expressions she used when she spoke about "her Tassos," and her venom against the captain delighted father and daughter.

Thanos, traveling with the shepherds, arrived a few days later, distraught and inconsolable. With the help of the shepherds, he had saved a few goats and the plow, but he'd escaped just in time, for the magistrate arrived at his cabin just after he left and, writing out a warrant for his arrest, began confiscation proceedings.

Led by Ghikas Tramersis, Thanos found his mother and a much-improved Tassos. Barbara did not commiserate with Thanos for his loss, while Tassos, acknowledging that his brother was incapable of bearing arms, promised to provide him with sheep as soon as his health improved. But Thanos, who believed that he had suffered enough because of him, replied that he was not interested in owning a herd his brother would provide.

Using the mediation of Tramersis, Thanos asked for work on Ayfantis's estate, for he could not sit idle. Ayfantis accepted him gladly and, noticing that he worked with skill and care, looked kindly on him and gave him various assignments.

"I used to think you in Greece were good only for brigandage," he said to Thanos, "but now I see that you make good farmers, too."

Later Ayfantis learned about the lad's travails, not from Thanos, who never talked about himself, but from Ghikas Tramersis, and these stories he related to Ephrosyne, who seeing him come into their house on business came to share her father's affection for him.

Thanos was a good-looking man of about twenty-four years of age. He was well developed and comely, with gentle and modest features, with well-drawn characteristics, generally, which reflected his moral sweetness, self-respect, and sense of propriety. In everything he was superior to the people of his rank in life and loved cleanliness so much that one would not consider him a farmer. In fact, his mother claimed that he had tricked her, for she thought that she'd borne a soldier but that he had betrayed his destiny. Unlike the rest of his class, who resembled ancient Scythians, he had not shaved the black hair on his head to the point of baldness but had it cut moderately, while his dark eyes exhibited thought and firmness.

All these qualities made Ayfantis and Ephrosyne pay close and friendly attention to him. Ephrosyne asked him to bring her wildflowers so that she could embroider them on shawls, and he brought violets, anemones, chervil, broom, wild thyme, daisies, crocuses, lilies, carnations, and dittany.

On Sundays, he wandered along mountain slopes with his goats to find even rarer species. As a New Year's present and to repay him for his efforts, Ephrosyne embroidered a belt for him, while he selected the most beautiful butterflies, mounted them on paper, and gave them to her to include in her floral embroideries.

When time for silk cultivation came, Thanos took care to bring mulberry leaves, clean them, and set them on bushes to dry. Because of his care, the year was a productive one, for which Ephrosyne felt obligated. The two of them were busy, she directing and leading, and he, new at the work, learning and carefully executing.

"I hope you won't leave us to return to Greece," Ephrosyne said. "If you stay here, we'll spin twice as much silk, now that you'll know how."

"What can I do in Greece?" Thanos replied. "I'm much happier here. Where will I find bosses who think so well of me?"

"And we're Greeks, too."

"I don't know the rest of Greece, but there are no Greeks of your sort in Phthiotis, and there are no Greek women like yourself there."

"Don't they cultivate silkworms?"

"We're all wild and armed there. A few foreigners, refined people, have taken up residence in Lamia now, but they're lost, like field mice in town. I'm afraid that instead of civilizing us we'll probably make them wild."

"Things must be different in Athens, don't you think?"

"I don't know. I imagine Athens must be a wonderful place."

"Yes, we hear a lot about Athens here from those who've seen the city. After the cocoons are formed, I'd very much like to go, to see how fabric is embroidered there." She considered embroidery the major feminine accomplishment, not doubting that Athenian ladies produced marvels of this art.

On his part, Ayfantis rewarded Thanos's willingness by giving him greater responsibility and complete trust, so that the young man was persuaded to sell his own flock and take up residence near his employer. But Ephrosyne warned her father that when the season came Thanos would work exclusively for her, since she would permit no one else to care for her silkworms.

In time, Tassos was completely healed and visited his benefactor in military garb, accompanied by some of his subordinates to give thanks and to show off his power.

Tassos resembled Thanos considerably, except that he was darker and leaner. No mark of savagery or wildness betrayed a brigand's temperament, and anyone studying his character would see that there was nothing in him that was depraved, evil, or brutal, except ambition joined to courage. No education, however, had refined these qualities. On the contrary, in a society where brigandage was considered heroic, there was no denying him his aspirations. He was not without intelligence, either, and he had many plans to rise in stature, but the struggle was not easy.

By and large, the human character is not a simple thing, neither black nor white, but complex and full of contradictions. If he had a coat of arms it might say: "Either a Caesar or a Nobody." For the time being, he was a nobody. For this he was inclined to be gloomy and silent, like "a furrow," as Aeschylus said, "from which an abundance of good counsel springs."

Once his health improved, he considered forming a band to attack Phthiotis, an idea that rather appealed to his mother, too. But the general migration of shepherds had removed the usual supports of the brigands. The captain of the Ottoman border guards, the *derven aga*, had noticed that Tassos distinguished himself among the others for his courage and enjoyed the respect of his peers. It would be to his interest, he reckoned, to hire Tassos to subdue the other bands. He did so and, as Kapetan, Tassos formed a *boulouki* with seven or eight men, received remuneration, the so-called *loufe*, from the *derven aga*, and waited for a more propitious time to fulfill his goals.

As in other regions, the Ottoman authorities in Thessaly employed Greeks to maintain law and order and as a tactic to crush brigandage entirely. Those who bear arms as a profession along border areas are called either *armatoloi* or klephts, the former serving legitimate authority, the latter having resumed their ways as brigands. In Thessaly, however, both are termed klephts, the former "tame" to distinguish them from the "wild."

For the time being, Tassos was "tame," an *armatolos* favored by the *derven aga* and arrayed in his splendid uniform with gilded vest and ornamented *tsaprayia,* bands of silver and enamel work crossed over his chest. The majority of Greek refugee bands remained klephts, however, and their activities provoked a great outcry against the *derven aga,* especially during the spring when brigandage was on the rise.

The klephts were active in Greek territory as well, for which the Greek government made strong representations to the Ottoman authorities. The Ottoman government finally decided to take measures and urged the pasha of Larissa to deal with the problem.

Having received no gifts for some time, the pasha of Larissa was unhappy with the *derven aga* and pleased for this opportunity to avenge himself. The news that another *derven aga* had been appointed took everyone by surprise, and all those in the service of the previous *derven aga* waited for the arrival of the new official to be accepted or dismissed. Among these was Tassos.

The New *Derven Aga*

The new *derven aga* was an Albanian. The pasha thought it best to employ men of this race because, being holdouts against Byzantine authority at the time of the Ottoman conquest, they were hostile to Greeks and, besides being craftier and more warlike, were not easily tricked by them, since they knew their language. Though these were compelling enough qualities, the pasha nevertheless accepted the new *derven aga*'s customary gifts for the appointment, seeing no reason not to benefit from the circumstances.

The regular salary was not enough to compensate the *derven aga*, but he knew that buying his position was in his interest and did not delude himself as to the exchange. There were two ways he could profit from the transaction: he could offer the brigands immunity, demanding the greater share of their booty, or he could frighten the richest Christians by accusing them of supporting brigandage until they understood that it would be wise for them to allow the burdensome bulk of their fortune to diminish. The latter course was better for his purposes, since the pasha demanded vigorous pursuit and needed results to show to his court. It was this course he followed.

The previous *derven aga* appeared to support this plan somewhat, while considering how to undermine it. In order to seem indispensable, as having great experience of the area and its residents, and to show that the pasha had made a great mistake in appointing someone else, he incited all the bands whose chieftains he knew. He also contacted Tassos, as a man able to act more effectively than the rest.

Tassos, though he greatly wished to participate, pretended otherwise, saying that he lacked accurate information, knowledge of the terrain, and a network of relationships for support and assistance that would enable him to learn the whereabouts of his pursuers and to procure provisions. This was his claim, despite the fact that during his residence there he had tirelessly searched out the best locations and had become godfather to the children of many shepherds and local farmers. The old *derven aga* knew these were pretexts to enable Tassos to attain better terms.

In addition to the patronage and assistance he'd been promised, Tassos was offered food and payment by the archon of Portaria if he agreed not to invade the district of the Twenty-Four Villages. Tassos accepted this offer, asking in addition that the notable take his mother to the island of Skiathos, where he had a friend. When Barbara learned of the agreement and its favorable terms, she leaped for joy that her Tassos was to be famous once more. "Spoken like a Christian," she crowed, "and like a saint renowned."

Thus Tassos embarked once more on brigandage, forming a band of about twenty select and fearless stalwarts, some from Greece and the rest, chosen for their knowledge of the terrain, from Myrmidon. His second in command, the robust Skias, an agile and daring young savage, was in fact from Myrmidon. Once he'd chosen his lair, Tassos began to gather information from all areas, wishing to begin a series of astonishing acts.

As soon as the new *derven aga* was established, brigandage became more prevalent and panic spread, especially in the Ottoman lands, because these areas, according to the theory, had to take the brunt of the incursions before an outcry against the pasha would reach Constantinople.

Among those fearing the current climate was Hussein Bey of Pharsala who, during the summer, resided on his farm. Seeing that the bands were numerous and strong, and having no confidence in his few servants, he decided to leave with his family before dawn for the city until security was restored.

Three armed servants walked ahead. He held his son on his lap and was followed by his wife, Fatmé, holding their infant. They were followed by three other wives and two servants on mules. Bringing up the rear were three more armed retainers on foot. In this order, the convoy proceeded slowly until they stopped where a dry torrent had cut through the road.

The advance guard had already reached the other side and Hussein Bey's family was within the gap when a great voice bellowed, "Don't move," and ten or so scruffy brigands, lowering weapons to their chests, appeared before the travelers as though they had leaped from the earth. Thunderstruck, the retainers responded to the brigands' nods and threw down their weapons. Hussein Bey, pale and mute, pulled at his beard.

"We're good people," Skias shouted. "Don't be afraid. We need money to live, too."

Tassos said nothing, not wishing to reveal that he was the leader.

"I've no money with me, lads," the bey said, "but take what I have."

"You've piastres with you, but your florins are in town. We don't want much. Send us a thousand and leave us Fatmé as security."

Hussein was silent and thoughtful for some time. If they'd asked for one of the other three women by whom he'd had no children, or only daughters, and who meant nothing to him now, he would not have been unhappy, but Fatmé, mother of his two sons, Fatmé, daughter of the pasha of Larissa, to leave Fatmé in the hands of infidel brigands was for him the worst possible fate. He considered offering a choice of the three other women as security, or even all three, but he knew the brigands would suspect that they were of little value and demand a higher ransom for Fatmé.

"We don't have time to waste," Skias said to her. "My lady, get away from that dragon of yours and dismount. If the bey loves his beauty, he'll send us the thousand. If he doesn't, then I'll become your bey."

"Don't take my Fatmé," the bey pleaded, seeing that things were getting out of hand. "Here. . . . I'll give you my son as security. And by the Koran, I'll send you the thousand florins. Even more. . . ."

His pleas were wasted, as were his promises to bring more florins. Skias was ready to agree to the bey's offer, demanding double the initial amount or even more, but he saw a negative sign from Tassos and lowered Fatmé from her mule. "Nothing will happen to Fatmé," he said, turning to the bey. "She'll be returned to you the diamond she is. Send the thousand florins to us over there, at the Three Trees. We'll wait until dinnertime. If we don't get them, Fatmé will be baptized in Larissa. You'll be invited to her wedding and given *koufeta* to eat, too."

The unhappy Fatmé, fear and anguish hidden by her veil, uttered no sound. After the servants had been disarmed, Skias undid his weapons belt, handing the other end to a fellow brigand; then, setting Fatmé on his mount, he carried her off in a twinkling of an eye.

The bearer of the ransom arrived before midday at the Three Trees, under whose shade a brigand sat, observing whoever approached, alert for any sign of betrayal. The thousand florins were counted out and Fatmé, brought out by two brigands from the cave in which she'd been left undisturbed, assured the agent of her good treatment. They withdrew and Fatmé left after them on a mule, heading toward home.

This event resounded throughout Thessaly. The previous *derven aga*, full of spite, visited Hussein Bey, pretending to console him, while his furious replacement, having put a price on Tassos's head, sent word to the pasha, swearing to deliver the brigand, dead or alive, before the new month. At the same time, after a vigorous pursuit of the brigands, the new *derven aga* launched a campaign against the law-abiding citizens, the affluent ones in particular, and Ayfantis was among the first.

Besides being one of the wealthiest, the accusations ran, Ayfantis had had many dealings with brigands and always provided them support; he'd given aid to Tassos when wounded and maintained the brother of this destructive brigand chief in his service. One of Ayfantis's neighbors, a Christian himself, made these accusations because Ayfantis had instituted proceedings against him in Larissa for encroaching on his land. He hoped by defaming his adversary to have Ayfantis jailed for giving aid to the violators of the pasha's daughter, whose displeasure he wished to have thrown in his favor on the scales of justice.

But Ayfantis had many friends and was informed in time. Without delay, he dispatched Kioura and Ephrosyne to Volos, from where they were to travel to the island of Skopelos, where he had relatives. He sent Thanos, who was also wanted, to Skopelos as well, but by another route, while he himself hid out, planning at the first opportunity to enter the Greek kingdom.

The soldiers of the *derven aga*, finding no one at the Ayfantis residence, took over the entire estate and sent scouts everywhere to capture him.

Being little known and not an object of the hunt anyway, Thanos took few precautions. He had almost reached Volos, from where he would sail with his mistresses to Skopelos, without encountering any pursuers, though they were rushing off in all directions looking for brigands, when two soldiers suddenly ran toward him and, uttering threats, commanded him to stop.

These two looked at each other, puzzled. They had served with Tassos under the previous *derven aga* and saw that this person, though heavier, resembled Tassos greatly. But Tassos would never have traveled unarmed outside of Volos.

"Aren't you Thanos, the foreman over at Ayfantis's place? Tassos's brother?" one of them asked.

He said he was.

"Stay here till we get back," the other ordered and, keeping an eye fixed on Thanos, went a few paces with his friend. He had a plan. Thanos's head, especially if unaccompanied by the body, would look a lot like that of his brother. And they'd be given the bounty.

"Yes, but what if we're caught?"

"How?"

"Here's how. Tomorrow we hear that Tassos has pulled another robbery. What happens to us then?"

They continued to discuss the pros and cons in Turkish as more soldiers and travelers began to appear. They decided to leave with Thanos, but too many people had seen them. Their trick would be discovered. Better to give Thanos over to the *kaim makam* of Volos, who would certainly reward them.

This they did, and the *kaim makam,* until he decided what to do, ordered Thanos thrown in jail.

The *kaim makam,* an indolent voluptuary, avoided complications as much as possible and occupied himself with his duties only when the spirit seized him, which was when his stomach was not full or when he had surfeited himself of his usual share of relaxation, which exceeded the ordinary measure. According to him, concerns were the enemies of the good life, and he devised a way to protect himself from their insidious ambushes, being counseled in everything by an imam he considered respectable and trustworthy. After morning prayers, he and the imam would visit a coffeehouse near the sea, where they took their coffees and puffed away on their water pipes. When the *kaim makam* attained that degree of well-being the Ottomans call kef—not an everyday event, certainly—he would ask questions of the imam and accept his opinions without question. This was most natural, for how was it possible for the *kaim makam* to set out the problem if he had not found the right spiritual moment?

They had arrested Thanos, the soldiers told the *kaim makam*, describing to him the brothers' similarities, saying that he was on the outskirts of Volos, spying, of course, and suggesting that his head, exposed to public view, would inspire fear among the populace and please the pasha. They waited, hoping for their reward, but the *kaim makam* delayed his decision until he had consulted the imam.

In those days, the *kaim makam* had another tedious matter to deal with. The captain of a Greek merchant ship, along with his crew, was being held in prison for barratry, and the *kaim makam* was being pestered by the Ottoman merchant, who'd been defrauded, and by the Greek consul, who demanded that the accused be handed over to him for extradition to Greece for trial. The Ottoman merchant, however, insisted that his damages be paid before they were all extradited.

This Ottoman, Abdullah, was worthy of compassion. Having loaded wheat on the *Clytemnestra* for sale in Syros, he had sailed along with the cargo for greater security, a precaution that did not suffice, because once the ship entered the Pagassaic Gulf, the captain managed to shift the cargo near the masts in such a way that every gust of wind shook and moved the ship about as though in a storm. Terrified and seasick, Abdullah rushed to his cabin, at which point Zarpas, the captain, no longer observed, unloaded the cargo onto skiffs off the coast of Euboia and sold it. Afterward, he drilled the ship full of holes and sank it.

Zarpas saved Abdullah, not out of altruism but to use him as a trustworthy witness before the board of inquiry at Volos for the accident at sea, hoping to receive compensation from his insurance company at Syros. But Abdullah was inconsolable: not having insured his cargo, he had lost almost his entire fortune. As the testimony was taken, however, he had occasion to learn that there had been no storm and that his cargo had not been lost but sold instead at Oreon. He demanded that Zarpas and his crew be held, and this the *kaim makam* ordered, with the imam's concurrence, despite the objections of the Greek consul, who promised that Abdullah would find total vindication in Greece. Abdullah, however, no longer trusted the gifts of the Greeks. The consul threatened and lodged a protest, but the *kaim makam*, eager to be free of him, disregarded the consul's threats. He planned to be advised by the imam the following day. Until that time, however, he was able to rest easy.

Thanos, in jail with the sailors of the *Clytemnestra* and Zarpas, could not explain to them why he was in prison beyond his being Tassos's brother.

Exhausted by his trip, his sleep was profound but full of dreams. First he saw an enormous fire, in the midst of which a joyful PapaJonas stretched out his hands, blessing. Then PapaJonas and the blaze, grotesquely magnified, advanced toward him so that it looked as though he would be engulfed. Then he was sailing with Ephrosyne, but a powerful storm shattered their ship and threw them overboard. He saw Ephrosyne briefly underwater, being drawn into the deep, and dived after but was unable to reach her. The water choked him when he tried to shout her name. Out of the dream's vividness he rose, terrified, convincing himself finally that it was an illusion before sleeping the sleep of the blameless once more, ignorant that on the following day his fate would be decided.

The next morning, the *kaim makam*, after quickly sipping his coffee with pleasure, puffed on his narghile and began to speak to the imam, who sat nearby, asking him how he should free himself from the verbal badgerings of the stupid consul and the tearful pleas of the ill-used Abdullah.

The imam blew on his bubbling water pipe, pondering this; then, as though sucking out wise decisions, he uttered the following: "Do you see that prison galley there now ready to set sail? Why not ship all these rascals to Constantinople and let the divan decide what's to be done with them? As the prophet says, 'Though something be no larger than a mustard seed and be it hidden within a rock, whether in heaven or on earth, Allah will bring it to light.' When the evil these men have done is brought forth to the divan, let the consul show himself then."

"*Aferim*, Imam. Bravo," the *kaim makam* exclaimed. "To be free the sooner, I'll give the command at once."

He clapped his hands to summon the bailiff and ordered that his command be executed immediately, before the consul had had a chance to pay him a visit.

He remained where he was until the prisoners were boarded and the ship had weighed anchor. Overjoyed by his success, he neglected to ask the imam's advice about Thanos and, assured by the events, returned to his home.

»»» 6 «««
The Crossing

The bailiff did not fully understand his master's order, and when the imam decided the following morning that the brother of the brigand chief—doubtless a brigand himself—should be decapitated, Thanos was no longer in prison, having boarded the galley with the sailors of the *Clytemnestra*. But the *kaim makam*, having been spared the worry, was not especially upset.

Hardly any light from the hatchway reached Thanos and the other chained prisoners in the ship's cramped and suffocating pump room. He was inconsolable, upset for allowing himself to fall into the soldiers' hands. He did not know why he had been loaded onto the galley and was sailing to Constantinople, nor were his fellow cellmates in a mood to console him, since they had worries enough of their own, especially Zarpas. The expectation of a heavy fine did not dismay him, but he foresaw that his profits from the stolen grain would be confiscated and that his fraudulent shipwreck would be exposed to the insurance company, which naturally had the right to deny his claim for recompense.

Zarpas, however, was not one to give himself over easily to despair, and, no matter how complicated and insoluble things appeared, the strength of his character and mind managed to contrive subterfuges. Apparently he was planning something that he judged proper to announce only to the ears of the sailors seated near him. The plan seemed pleasing, too, for he often stopped talking to tell the others a joke.

"Courage, lads," he quipped, "we'll get to see the Queen City and the beautiful eyes of the Psomathian women without paying a fare."

"I don't believe they plan for us to go to Psomathia," said one of the sailors not sitting near enough to Zarpas to share in the confidential news. "More likely it's some black pit in the docks waiting for us, and everyone, blind or not, will see the same things there."

"Do you think we'll be there forever? We petition His Highness the Ambassador and then see if the Turk's ears don't flop out from under his fez. Did you notice how scared of the consul the *kaimakamis* was? That's why he let us go, unless God took half his mind. I didn't see Abdullah the clown coming along. Did you?"

"That's right," another sailor remarked. "He's not here. I was the last one on deck at the time we set sail and he hadn't shown up."

"By the time he screws up his courage to cross the sea again after that last storm, when it looked like he was spewing serpents, we'll have been washed clean by the embassy and be warm and dry in Syros. Then let him cross the sea and go through the hoops again to figure out what he has coming. That blockhead! We should have let him drown. But then he was yelling, '*Aman*, save me and I'll give you anything you want.' But somebody turned him around and I know who. It's that smart guy Chronis. Wanted his share. If he's got it in him, let him move that rusty bucket of a ship of his and do what he can. One mountain can never meet up with another, but one of these days Zarpas and Chronis will meet."

"Can I petition the ambassador, too?" Thanos asked, impressed with Zarpas's confidence in the official's assistance.

"Sure, as long as you're not a *rayah*."

"No, I'm a citizen of the Greek kingdom, but I'm wanted by the law."

"All the better. In that case, you're in luck, because the ambassador is obliged to arrange for you to be remanded to the Greek courts. You're their bread and butter."

"But suppose they gobble me up?"

"Don't worry about that, m'lad. The Greek courts know which side their bread's buttered on. Look, I've been up before them twice. First time for piracy—I came out smelling like a rose—the second time for barratry. They claimed I faked jettisoning the cargo, found me guilty, and treated me to a six-year stretch. Two months later I gave a pal of mine half of what was left over from the so-called jettison and received complete pardon. I wasn't crazy enough to dump the cargo to the bottom of the sea to feed the fish, you understand. What say to that, Tom? If they lead us to the kangaroo court, will we have a good tailwind or not?"

"Whatever fate has written and the straw-headed jury decides, that's what'll happen."

"Listen to me, lads. If anyone has a dream tonight, let us in on it so we can learn what's going to happen. In the meantime, Alexy, sing us a song so we don't get sad."

While Alexios was deciding what to sing, Thanos recalled his dreams but said nothing to the men because they had other things on their minds. Soon Alexios began to sing:

> At the window, the famous Galaziani sat,
> blonde, blue eyed, and bejeweled.
>
> Good captain of the tall masts and many sails,
> tell me, from where do you hail?
>
> From the farthest reaches of the globe, the depths of
> America, paved with gold.
>
> Pearls and florins, diamonds and rubies
> Casks of them everywhere, by Saint Marina.
>
> So, I've come this way to find a treasure,
> and found the best, your dulcet eyes.

Good captain, worthy skipper, where'er you went,
does no one tell lies?

Open the door, my blue-eyed girl, I'll bring my stores,
and if I'm worthy and you want me, I'll be yours.

"Dogs of the devil," the galley's skipper muttered when he heard the prisoners singing below in the hold. "These Greeks sing even in hell, do they?"

As long as they were sailing through the narrows with a tailwind and without incident the ship made good time, but when it turned the tip of Euboia and entered the open sea, the winds picked up and the waves crested with whitecaps.

Lightning bolts sliced through the thick, black clouds that obscured the horizon. The quick-witted boatswain wanted to strike the sails before even greater gusts engulfed the ship. Night was well advanced and only a few stars were visible, but the winds increased in force and the waves began to crest, warning of a storm. So powerfully did the wind strike the hull that the Ottoman boatswain thought he should strike the topsail and lower the mainsail. The sailors were performing this chore when clouds suddenly covered the sky and the gale broke violently, shaking the wind-battered ship, causing its stays and planks to creak as though they had split, and popping the sails as though they were whipped. The skipper shouted madly at the sailors, who ran about crazily, either misunderstanding the commands or hearing many contradictory ones simultaneously. Not securely bolted, two cannons were ready to break loose on deck.

From the pump below decks came mournful shouts. It was being flooded and the men were unable to stand erect because the ceiling was low, nor could they leave because the plug was securely fastened with a sheet of iron that had only a small peephole for light. Chest deep in water, they held each other lest the surges jam them together. Nevertheless, the sail was smashed and, loosened from the stays, flapped continuously. In despair, the skipper, expecting little more from his incompetent sailors, though there were eleven of them, ordered the master-at-arms to unlock the hatch and bring up three or four captives, seeking their seafaring experience.

As soon as the bars were removed, however, they leaped out of the hold, seized the keys, and pushed the jailer into the pump room. They unlocked their chains in an instant and rushed up to the deck, pitching the skipper overboard at once. Their attack was so sudden and unexpected that the Ottoman sailors were thrown into the waves one after the other without knowing how or by whom.

Zarpas took hold of the wheel, while his sailors, scrambling up the masts, furled all the sails and downed the topsails, leaving only the jib, and immediately began to work the pump, with great joy chanting the traditional "Heave-ho! Heave-ho!" in unison.

The elements raged, the towering waves drenched them with heavy froth, the wind bellowed ceaselessly, and jagged bolts of lightning shattered the black cover of the night, but the steady hands of Zarpas skillfully directed the ship through the storm.

"The Panaghia loves us," he shouted. "I pledge ten florins for her grace at Tinos. You pledge, too, and she'll save us."

With courage and good cheer they struggled all night. After a drenching rain, the violent winds finally lessened, and only the squall remained.

The sailors, while searching through the ship for provisions, came across Thanos, who was sprawled below decks and still bearing his chains. After they freed him and gave him food and drink, they paced up and down, looking at everything. It seemed like a dream to be delivered from so many perils and to become masters of the ship at the same time.

"Long life to the *kaimakamis*," Zarpas said. "You'd think he arranged all this on purpose. Now that we have the ship, let's get to work, lads, and get everything shaped up. We'll hide it behind one of those desert islands."

They started repairing the ship with whatever means they could improvise, patching together any tattered sails that remained.

The clouds had scattered and the coming day promised to be clear. The rosy-fingered dawn quickly forsook the cold conjugal bed of the aged Tython and, drawing her saffron-colored veils, quieted the sea's agitation, whose splashing responded as though in melodic unison to the whispers of the morning breeze.

Zarpas, seated at the wheel, turned his grizzled head. His small, merry eyes glittered, and his dark face, because of the way the lower jaw extended, resembled that of a beast of prey that takes its victim in its claws. The other sailors seated on the deck were occupied in mending the sails, while others, singing, hammered out the stays.

Thanos could not understand why the previous masters of the ship were no longer there, nor did anyone have the time, or the interest, to explain. He sat, therefore, along the gunwales, admiring the majestic view of the dawning day, which he had never experienced while at sea.

The ship, lacking sails and carrying only the jib, and that damaged, too, proceeded slowly. The Sporades Islands could be discerned toward the north, and they sailed toward them, distancing themselves from Andros, toward which the gale had sent them. There, Zarpas planned to hide his spoils in a cavern until matters were arranged.

"Andreas," he shouted. "What do you think? Is that something moving outside the narrows of Euboia?"

Andreas left the sail and stared ahead. "Yes," he said carefully. "A ship, heading toward Skopelos. And it's got a good tailwind."

"We'll stop it. Any of the sails ready?"

"In a thousand tatters, like the Greek state, and one rag doesn't match the other."

"We'll cut the ship off and ask for a loan. Or, if it prefers, it'll advance us the money freely. We've got two cannons, don't forget. Check to see if they're in a condition to inspire respect. Look for weapons and gunpowder below decks, too. And get ready."

Eager to execute the new commands, the sailors took turns going below decks, some bringing up swords, others firearms. At the helm, Zarpas sailed straight ahead to cross the path of the approaching ship that tacked with a tailwind, its sails bellied out, borne along the waves like a swan flapping its wings and descending a rushing river.

It was not possible for Zarpas, without sails, to cross its path, but his crafty brain was not without devices. At some point he considered asking for help and, on the ship's approach, employing the persuasive powers of his cannons to attain his goals. With an unerring glance, he reckoned the distance, intending to place himself halfway to the other ship, whose speed had already brought it nearby.

"It's Chronis," Andreas shouted.

"Chronis, Chronis," everyone echoed.

"Didn't I say we'd meet again? Everyone ready?"

"All ready," they agreed.

"At your posts, then."

When Chronis saw the terrible condition of the ship's rigging, he made for it, assuming it needed help, and slowed down, striking some of his sails. As Chronis neared, Zarpas asked him to heave to because he needed help. Having recognized it as the Ottoman ship that preceded him out of Volos, Chronis had no cause for suspicion and was willing to give aid to those who had undergone the previous night's storm, which he had ridden out by anchoring at Oreon. He heaved to closely and lowered all his sails in order to render the necessary assistance but suddenly recognized Zarpas and his crew, all of them armed and two of them standing near the cannons, firebrands in their hands.

"Don't do anything crazy," Zarpas shouted, "because you're done for."

Terror conquered all and they awaited the outcome motionless.

Zarpas lowered the launch and sailed to Chronis's ship with six of his men. An astonished Thanos followed the action, certain that something terrible was about to occur, but his surprise was inexpressible when he recognized Ephrosyne and her mother on the deck of the other ship. Shaken, he called out her name and paced back and forth so that she could see him, but she was attending to the events and watching the armed men as the launch approached, expecting the worst. The wild-looking sailors nearby gestured for him to shut up. And what could he, unarmed and as such a distance, do alone? Uncertain and devastated, he stood, staring fixedly.

"Didn't expect to welcome me so soon, did you?" Zarpas addressed the captain as his entourage boarded ship. "We've got accounts to settle, you and I, and I've got your share to give you."

"I said nothing. I swear on my children. I never asked you for anything. I want nothing from you."

"Now you've become wise and altruistic. Okay, boys, tie him up and take him below decks."

Chronis had fallen to his knees, pleading, while Zarpas turned his fiery and calculating gaze on those present. Satisfied by the look of terror he inspired, seeing that everyone had grown pale, he turned to the contorted Chronis.

"Very well," he said proudly, "let's see what sort of beast you are. Free him, lads, and I'll go below with him." He paced arrogantly toward the hatch.

In the hold, he took a seat while Chronis stood before him like a suppliant, looking down, his hands folded.

"I want to show you, Chronis, that I'm generous. You betrayed me to Abdullah, but instead of doing me harm you did good. Yesterday's storm was great, you see, and I don't know how it happened, but all those good people got washed overboard. And they didn't have time to tell us what to do with the ship. Whether they meant it or not, the ship's ours, understand?"

"Certainly. Of course."

"So, we have to keep it. You're going to give us sails so we can take it to one of those desert islands. I'll come along with you. But you'll say you found us in a rowboat in danger of drowning. Get it?"

"Of course. Certainly."

"Listen well. No one should learn about this, either from you or from your crew, because Zarpas is generous only once. If you're smart and stop your chatter about Abdullah and the like, I'll reward you. Otherwise. . . . D'you follow me?"

"I'll always mention your good name, and so will my wife and children. I swear on whatever is holy that no one will learn anything. . . . Anything!"

"Let's get to work, then."

And so he went up to the deck and transferred the necessary sails to the launch, ordering it to return with Thanos and directing the ship to sail to the desert island. The wildness of his countenance grew calm and the alacrity of Chronis, who had agreed to all his demands, encouraged everyone, though no one dared ask what was about to happen.

The launch returned shortly, bearing a willing Thanos, who wanted to be near Ephrosyne, for he assumed that she had recognized him and asked that he be brought over. He rushed to board first and went to her, but the suddenness of his appearance shocked her. She fainted into the arms of her mother.

"Let me help that young woman." Thanos hurried his pace.

"She's got her mother, lad," Zarpas stopped him. "You come down here with me." And grabbing him violently, he dragged him, startled, below decks.

Zarpas assumed that Thanos knew precisely what had happened and, because he hadn't had the time to caution him along with the others, he needed to teach him beforehand how to discuss the events.

Thanos's only concern with this lesson was that no harm come to the two women. Promising that the women would behave well, he assured Zarpas about his own dependability and was left free.

Meanwhile, Ephrosyne had recovered and, turning her glance, asked her mother if Thanos were on board or had she been deluded.

"It was Thanos, daughter."

"What's he doing with these evil men?"

"I don't know. But he was below decks with that savage."

"Really? Are they friends? Does he work for him?"

The unhappy Ephrosyne, tricked by appearances, believed that Thanos had become a pirate and a follower of Zarpas and felt giddy. Wild specters chased away her idyllic dreams and the tender feelings she nurtured about Thanos, who suddenly revealed himself to be unworthy of them. It was impossible for her to disguise this pain, since she had never experienced its like.

"Perhaps he avoids me because he's ashamed," she thought, though a joyful Thanos stood before her. Her monosyllabic and continually repeated questions made it appear that she wanted him to leave, but her palpitations signified that she preferred that he stay. To defend oneself before someone benevolently disposed is not difficult, and the natural reaction of Ephrosyne merely increased her affection for him; she wished to explain that it was out of ignorance that she'd been unjust to him. Completely inexperienced in worldly matters, though, she assumed everyone could read what was in her heart, which betrayed her tender feelings toward Thanos, revealed by her fainting. A blush of shame flushed her tender complexion. The struggle of contradictory feelings between which she wavered imaged elegantly in her stance, while her long, dark eyelashes, cast downward, expressed the fine symmetry of her eyes.

Not understanding her agitation, though, and overcome by wonder, Thanos told her as much of what he had undergone as his pledge to Zarpas permitted.

Meanwhile, the sailors unfurled the ship's sails once more, and towing the launch, which would be useful to them as evidence of their having been sunk, sailed with a tailwind toward Skopelos. In a short while, the second ship trimmed its sails and made for the desert islands.

Later in the evening, when Chronis's ship docked in the port of Skopelos, he made an immediate deposition, as requested by Zarpas, that he had encountered him, some of his sailors, and Thanos in a launch, saved from shipwreck during a storm at sea. Zarpas then certified to the sinking of the Ottoman vessel on which, supposedly, they were all passengers sailing on private business to Constantinople.

The very next day, Zarpas undertook to send lumber, ropes, sails, and other necessary naval stores to the desert island, along with a dry dock specialist, to repair and transform the seized vessel so that it would be unrecognizable.

Thanos followed Ephrosyne to a friend's house, and his mistress took up her handiwork once more, sending him daily to the port to ask news from incoming ships of her father, for whom she waited impatiently. In the meantime, though, Ayfantis sent word, promising his family that he would arrive within a few days.

The pursuits against Tassos had increased after his great success, and the passes, held by Albanians eager for bounty, were guarded lest he escape to Greece by way of Othrys. But he had no plans to do this since all of his supporters were in Thessaly. Adhering to his promise not to violate the territory of the Twenty-Four Villages, he followed the base of the mountains to Ossa where, by crossing through the Ottoman lands, he hoped to attack the rear guard of his pursuers for a new and resounding achievement.

Led by Skias, a local with great knowledge of the terrain, the band, evading its pursuers, traveled by night as far as Black Mountain, which overlooks Lake Voivoda. Having succeeded in leaving the region where he was hunted, Tassos was encouraged to mount new operations and found his followers most willing. He descended toward Kastri, therefore, passing the columns of the Didyma, and planned to attack the tower of Hassan Bey, on the shore where the Amyros River empties into the lake.

The reason Hassan Bey had left Larissa, home of many apples, to live by beautiful Lake Voivoda was the superb defensive position of the tower. Situated between the river and the lake, it was surrounded by orchards, encircled by flower beds, and ornamented by fountains, behind which stretched grape arbors and other trees. Nature, in this well-watered paradise, did not withhold her bounty but rewarded the skills of the painstaking cultivator.

Skias, who had worked for Hassan Bey as a field hand some time before but had been dismissed for impudence, told Tassos everything.

The band arrived at the tower around midnight and posted guards outside. Tassos, using a hooked rope ladder he had already made, clambered up to the tower's door, which for security reasons the Ottomans place at the top, and was followed by Skias and five others. While the rest went downstairs to surprise the servants, he and Skias strode toward the master bedroom, which was adjacent.

Wakened by the creaking of the door hinges, Hassan Bey, in bed with the most beloved of his wives, raised his hand above his head to the wall where he had fixed his weapons. But Skias and Tassos fell on him, seizing both arms.

The terrified woman hid under the covers. Hassan Bey struggled from the bed and stamped his feet, hoping to summon his servants to his aid.

"You're struggling for nothing," Skias said. "Open your strongbox and don't give us a song and dance."

Hassan Bey threw himself on the floor, writhing.

"I understand. You're afraid for the lady. Relax. Lock her up and take the key. It's the strongbox that's on our minds," Skias added and, with Tassos, hustled Hassan Bey out of the bedroom.

Resistance would be fruitless, since two of the five servants had been injured in the struggle and the rest were bound.

"I'll give you whatever you want," Hassan Bey said when he saw what had happened. "Don't hurt anyone." Taking the key, he descended with two bodyguards to the cellar, where he had stored his money and valuables.

"Bravo, now you're a real bey," Skias, who did all the talking, shouted. "You did well to hoard and hatch this treasure all these years so that it would be useful one day. Today's that day."

Though he recognized him, Hassan Bey said nothing, afraid to reveal this by some sign and invite mistreatment.

"You see, we're very careful. What can we do with so much wealth? We just need enough for our dowries. How else can we get ourselves a black-eyed girl?"

Both stuffed their belts with florins and diamond necklaces, earrings, rings, and the like for what they claimed were their weddings. They let their partners take turns loading up, then with great propriety thanked the bey. He offered them coffee, too, but they turned it down, fearing a trick. They saluted him and disappeared, leaving enough hard-to-carry items in his treasure chest to console him, if he subscribed to the philosophy of Aristippos, for what had been taken.

When they learned what had happened, the Albanians were thrown into a rage and furiously began to hunt down the audacious brigands, whose booty had surpassed their expectations.

After this triumph, Tassos and his men were more interested in protecting their wealth than in continuing their exploits. Hunted down and boxed in by those nearby, they headed for Mount Ossa, hoping to reach the sea and cross over to the islands from there, but the Albanians kept pace with them, skillfully following their trail.

To avoid being tracked down, they walked in the water of a torrent, but even this did not help. All their escape routes were barred and, turning toward Mount Ossa, they paused at the height of one of the mountains above Tempe, where the Albanians mounted an attack that was repulsed with three wounded and two dead.

The peak upon which they had fortified themselves was inaccessible. Bare rocks, as though hewn, rose perpendicular from the edge, with only a narrow pathway running along the outside of the boulders so that whoever climbed was exposed to the gunfire of those above. The almost vertical side of the summit facing Tempe, as though separated during a violent earthquake, is not far distant from the corresponding side of Olympus; and in the depths of this dark chasm the Titarestios, as Homer says, "flows from above like oil" into the silvery Peneius. Nothing is visible because a profound darkness covers everything, and only the babbling of the stream can be heard. At the summit, a few pines provide scattered shade. In the distance, the sea is visible, and at the shore lies Karitsa, where Nikos Tzaras, after his first exploits, was married.

The Albanians and Greeks crouched behind boulders, using them as bastions, but the Albanians were confident that the klephts, once they consumed all their food, would be compelled in two days to give up.

Tassos encouraged his men by reminding them of the exploits of the great klephts of the heroic era, saying that after the ancient gods, the peaks of Olympus and Kissavos had been inhabited by them, whom they should not dishonor and that, if worst came to worst, they would save themselves by hacking a path through the enemy with their swords.

During this time, the Albanians prodded the klephts with challenging words.

"Hey, you, Greek dog. D'you want bread? Here's bread for you," they said and threw stones.

"You know, *mourte,* we're not dead meat yet. We're the butchers. If you're up to it, stand up and let's admire you!"

"Ay, Greek dog. Call yourself a stalwart? Why hide behind the boulder, then?"

To pretend to be taking up the dare, Skias raised the tassel of his fez as though he were about to stand up. He leaped over rocks a few feet away and sat behind another boulder so quickly that no enemy bullet was able to strike him, all having aimed where the tassel had been seen.

"You just saw me, *mourte.* Now let us see Your Lordship away from your bulwark."

The Albanian, taking up the dare and not seeing the trick, leaped up and was struck in the forehead by a bullet, falling backward and rolling down the cliff. The klephts laughed, while the Albanians ground their teeth.

"We'll see about this tomorrow, dead meat."

That night the besieged were vigilant lest the Albanians crawl up to them. But they did not dare. The next day all they had was a little dry bread and, lacking water, appeased their thirst by chewing on tree leaves. Tassos went off by himself for a long time to think about their prospects. To try to escape through the enemy ranks was unrealistic because the path was wide enough only for one man at a time, while the besiegers were many and occupied many positions, which the escapees would need to force.

Finally, he got a bright idea. His men were to cut the strongest limbs of the fir trees and hold them, bushy end up. Everyone assumed that he planned to use these as torches to attack the enemy, but the contrivance was even more ingenious. Daybreak found him studying the less precipitous part of the cliff that faced Tempe. "Whoever wants to save himself," he said, pressing a great limb to his chest, "should follow me."

And he leaped into the abyss, retarding his fall with the limb held upward, its leafy part rubbing against the boulders and the occasional bush. Overcome by terror and giddiness, the others looked down into the depths, which was darker than night and whose resonance was as profound as that of Tartarus, then at each other, groaning in fear, assuming Tassos had deliberately jumped to a certain death, waiting silently, not breathing, attentive to the slightest noise, awaiting the result of his daring operation.

After a while, without being able to distinguish it very well, they heard the voice of Tassos calling up to them from what seemed to be the bowels of the earth. They stared at each other, thunderstruck.

Finally, the less bold following the more, they all jumped, the later arrivals greeted by the early ones. Only Skias, who had jumped with excessive daring and velocity, landed almost unconscious, having received many bruises on his shoulders and head. Fortunately, because there were no rocks nearby, only earth, his wounds were not serious.

They slaked their thirst in the river, because they could do little for their equally great hunger, and set out immediately toward the outlet of Tempe, not especially worried, since the Albanians had suspected nothing of what had occurred.

The Albanians, hearing no voices or response to their challenges, assumed that the klephts were maintaining silence out of some crafty design but continued to lie in wait, expecting them to surrender.

During the night, chancing an approach, they advanced slowly but found no one at the top. There were many conjectures about what had happened, but none made any sense. At one moment, perhaps because a stone rolled by chance, they all turned tail, thinking that the klephts lay in wait behind a boulder. The following morning, though, hearing and seeing no one, they returned to the peak and inspected everything, dispatching scouts in all directions to follow their tracks. Because they were certain no one could be alive down there, no scout was sent to the chasm.

When the escapees passed through Tempe, they encountered shepherds, to whom they gave generous gifts, and, offered lambs, they feasted, seated on stones, singing and dancing all day.

At Platamon the following day they found a small ship that took them, joyfully counting their spoils, to Skiathos.

But Tassos did not forget the *derven aga*. He gave a florin to a shepherd who promised to deliver a letter to the Albanians, to whom he wrote through the *derven aga* that the official could now rest easy, without the expense of the promised bounty, and that he hoped they would meet one day on a friendly basis. If this were acceptable, he wanted to invite him to dinner outside of Hypate in two or three months' time.

The *derven aga* could not believe that Tassos had escaped until everyone confirmed it. He offered many reasons to the pasha for not having executed his promise before the new month and punished the Albanian sergeants, stripping them of their rank for incompetence.

Nothing would happen, Tassos knew. Once they found refuge in Skiathos, he would pay someone off and be protected before the courts were notified that he was on the island. And what, according to the poet, is not possible because of the accursed hunger for gold?

Barbara's joy was inexpressible when, virtually faint, she hugged her hero to her bosom, "This is the way one gets money," she said when she saw his wealth. "Not with goats and oxen, as Thanos believes. Now, my son, they should make you at least a major."

New Ordeals of Thanos

Although Ephrosyne had already received news of her father's escape from the Ottoman authorities, she could not rest until he was near her. When by good fortune he arrived in Skopelos without harm, the brightness returned to her beautiful face. New adventures occurred, though, rekindling the affection she felt for Thanos, which though latent was unexpectedly revealed in critical moments.

The Greek consul in Volos, promising a strict inquiry by the Greek judicial system, had repeatedly requested the handing over of Zarpas and his men and had notified the Greek government, primarily on the basis of Chronis's deposition, to summon the courts, even before the *kaimakamis* had consulted his wise oracle. Thus, the magistrates were aware of what was happening and had instructed their subordinates what to do in case Zarpas submitted himself to their authority.

That was when the news that someone named Zarpas, claiming to have been shipwrecked while on a personal business trip to Constantinople, had arrived in Skopelos. The island's magistrate requested more information from his counterpart at Chalkis and was ordered to arrest Zarpas and those with him and to transfer them securely to Chalkis. The magistrate, having no other work at the time and wishing to show effectiveness in order to be recommended for promotion, executed this order at once. Finding the roster of sailors incomplete, he inquired of Zarpas, who assured

him that the others had drowned. Thanos being one of the res-
cued, the magistrate deemed it proper to include him among
the crew.

Zarpas protested that Thanos had been an ordinary passenger
on the trip, not especially concerned for his welfare but upset that
someone unknown, possibly with a character not stable enough to
keep quiet about the concluding sequence of events, be mixed up
in the case. But the magistrate refused to listen to Zarpas's arguments that Thanos not be included in the roundup, considering
the entire matter suspect. Thus, he dispatched them all to Chalkis.

Ephrosyne, unable to disguise her sorrow, tried to help Thanos
by using her family's connections, speaking often to her very sup-
portive father, but no intercession could sway the magistrate's
strong will. Her moist eyes showed that she shared the burden of
Thanos's ordeal, and her father's attempts to entertain her by
proposing walks and other recreations failed.

Ayfantis attributed his daughter's affection to the fine qualities
of the unjustly tormented Thanos and respected the sensitivity of
her spirit even more. To soothe her, he insisted that nothing bad
could happen to Thanos, who was manifestly innocent and had
absolutely no previous involvement with Zarpas. In keeping with
the wishes of Thanos, Ephrosyne said nothing about the events
of the trip, not daring to reveal them to her father, but worried
nonetheless since she could not know their consequences or even
if they were already ascertained. Finally, her father promised to
get information from Chalkis by way of his friends in Skopelos,
through whom he had introduced Thanos.

When he arrived in Chalkis, Thanos did not need the inter-
cessions of Ayfantis to be exempt from accusations of barratry,
since he had an even stronger defense that was provided by Zarpas
and his collaborators. Zarpas had been granted a loan on the shipwrecked vessel from a merchant in Syros who was a member of

an insurance society. In this capacity, of course, it would have been in the merchant's interest if his firm did not pay its insurance obligations, but as a lender himself he had an even stronger interest in the loan's being repaid. In this circumstance, he and Zarpas were on the same side.

In those days, apparently, insurance societies paid no special attention to the difference between fraudulent and nonfraudulent shipwrecks, since the economic interests of the members were confounded with those of merchant captains. Following the bankruptcy, these same insurance societies quickly reconstituted themselves into new corporate entities and resumed their ephemeral existence, while the creditors were harmed only in their capacity as shareholders of the society: in other words, as little as possible, compared to the profits of the captains. The shareholders of societies that did not lend money to shippers, therefore, unaware of what was occurring, were entirely, as the poet says, "sheep who bore fleeces but not for themselves."

This is what happened in the present case, for the merchant who had lent Zarpas money made every effort to have him declared innocent. The inquiry was conducted quickly and directly, a rapidity attributable less to the effectiveness of the examining magistrate than to his idiosyncrasies.

In this southern clime, where everything ages rapidly and every decade, in a manner of speaking, constitutes one of Hesiod's generations, he must be accounted one of the so-called ancient judges. This magistrate was a judge of the primeval era of Kapodistrias the Governor when, as gossip goes, the minister of justice recommended by encyclical that the judiciary always be guided by Artemopoulos and Clemency, and our magistrate responded that he had managed to obtain a copy of Artemopoulos and had been studying it carefully, but as for Clemency, despite his searches, he was unable to locate the book and begged the minister to send him a copy. Since then, apparently, he had not been able to find it.

The regency was not the first to introduce the practice of using men of other professions as judges and in other services, which was like ordaining priests of Themis to teach the art of Terpsichore or Euterpe, or turning the trident of Poseidon over to the children of Asklepios, and so on. Our own magistrate had served in Wallachia as a tailor in the court of the prince, which meant that he functioned as his confidential adviser as well. He divided his investigations into two classes: the pressing and the not pressing. The pressing cases were recommended to him by certain powerful personages; as for the others, he did not care a straw.

His life was a very orderly one. First thing in the morning he went marketing for choice foods, then occupied himself with judicial proceedings until midday, when he dined. Afterward, he slept, then returned to the courtroom, but for a briefer time than in the morning, because he needed to fit in his evening stroll and supper.

The Zarpas inquiry, because it came strongly recommended, was among the pressing cases and thus proceeded rapidly. In his testimony, Chronis asserted the opposite of what he had earlier told the consul and which, since it did not comprise part of the inquiry, was not even taken into consideration. As was natural, Abdullah, knowing that the sea desired victims, did not dare sail to Chalkis, and his accusations were dismissed as the expressions of self-interest because he would wish to exempt his grain from the common fate of the shipwreck. Not one word was mentioned about the events during the passage. Besides this, Zarpas had various letters from admirals and governments certifying that he was among the heroes of the Revolution, letters that because of their constant use during similar inquiries to which he had been summoned had become soiled and frayed, though they had not lost a mite of their strength as the most powerful detergent of the bearer's dirt. The case was decided in his favor, and the guard, in order to earn his tip, rushed to make it known and to release the accused.

Priding himself as being above the slander to which he had been subjected, Zarpas said good-bye to those still in jail, blessed his luck, and promised many of them the help of his strong recommendation, since it was already seen as capable of many things. His sailors, possessing an equally high opinion of themselves, came after him. Last came Thanos, humble and ashamed to be found among such company.

But the guard pulled him aside. The charge of barratry had been dismissed, but there was still the matter of the warrant from the magistrate at Lamia for collaborating with brigands. He had, therefore, to undergo a new inquiry. The examiner would send this off as soon as he found time to dispatch it.

Until now, the time Thanos had spent in jail, though unpleasant and unhappy, was mitigated somewhat by the rapid progress of the inquiry and the daily information Zarpas provided as to the phase it was in. But alone now and without a protector, he felt all the evils of imprisonment, accused of collaboration in a nonexistent robbery.

The jail was a frigid Tartarus. The medieval builders of the fort of Chalkis had left bare the ground-level area between the two thick walls, roofing it over for use as a storehouse. Into this dungeon, the sun's rays never penetrated, and only one aperture, through the triple arches of the fort's columns by which one enters Chalkis, carried light into it.

Everyone, whether convicted or merely accused, was thrown into this Erebus and many days elapsed before a prisoner was accustomed to the gloom and could see where he was. All day, massing back and forth like herds of wild animals, the convicts—brigands, arsonists, rapists, barrators, forgers, thieves of all sorts—bragged about their exploits, while those awaiting trial were busy conferring and plotting to attain their release.

The worst criminals held the highest rank and treated insultingly those accused or convicted of lesser crimes, while the more accomplished taught the less devious suspects the art of tricking the judicial inquiry. Those with means were able to bribe the guards and maintain contact with collaborators outside the jail, keeping careful track of the inquiry and working effectively against it.

Among the first and most basic lessons the accused learned was the alibi, for which communications were skillfully devised, which rendered the questioning of the accused unnecessary and pointless. It was here, through mutual education, that prisoners exchanged instructions in the science of crime.

The tenure of criminals in this bedlam was neither long nor uninterrupted, for periodic pardons returned the criminals, by now well schooled, back to the society they had mortally injured. Some often passed from society to prison and from prison, by way of pardon, back to society, so that these various stages became little more than a change of address, or as the passage of hours in a year. But second-time offenders were not denied pardon either, and the dungeon was periodically emptied out as though by pump, because all the accused were treated the same.

Since no religious services were celebrated there and no concern was shown for spiritual renewal, the place was more like a zoo than a jail.

The terrible filth especially tormented Thanos, who loved cleanliness. The majority did not change clothes from the time they were jailed until their release, so that they were richer than the fisherman of Homer, who "caught what they could take in hand and ignored what they could not." There were neither mattresses nor rush mats. Except for those who had some resources, everyone slept on the ground, feet unwashed and stomachs empty.

As anyone passing through the arcades and hearing the roars would have acknowledged, the stench surpassed that of the Augean Stables. Thanos, searching for somewhat cleaner neighbors, found a niche between two suspects, a bookkeeper accused of having gobbled up an entire account, ledgers and all, since these had disappeared during a nighttime burglary, and a customs official accused of smuggling. Both men busily discussed their problems all night, drafting responses and writing letters.

Near them, however, were convicts, brigands, and murderers who thought of themselves as lords of the place and hosts of the accused. It was they who determined when meals and bedtimes occurred, and they who apportioned the food. They cursed and blasphemed at will and, despite their chains, smoked, sang, and danced whenever they wanted.

They did not threaten the bookkeeper and customs official because they expected benefits and sometimes money from them, but they had contempt for Thanos, called him a wild goat, and ridiculed him as a gloomy and antisocial person.

The two accused professionals did not stay long. Whatever came to the criminals by way of pardon came to them by way of decree. Most prisoners were released, or their inquiry was temporarily halted, even though they made every effort for this release not to occur, since it might place an impediment to their future progress.

The examination of the two professionals was evidently of the pressing variety. Their places were taken by two forgers, who were released by decree and bequeathed their nests to an embezzler and a bankrupt, and so on until two men were committed for trial who could not pass through the narrows. These two were small-time thieves who had made off with four or five silver dessert spoons. The lighter the stolen goods, however, the heavier the penalty. Said spoons belonged to a powerful personage. When, in the course of regular questioning, they revealed nothing, beatings were administered using special and more efficient procedures that enabled the thieves to confess their acts.

There was humor in that one of the most infamous criminals, Sparos the murderer, received a pardon but was overcome by nostalgia and returned, injured, to his beloved home in due course. He was greeted with open arms and festivities by a phalanx of stalwarts. Violent and splenetic, he entertained the dregs of society with his cynical jibes, and they gathered around him guffawing and encouraging his scurrilous language.

Thanos, having learned nothing about his case and not being summoned before a board of inquiry, went deeper into despair and, avoiding the barbarous obscenities around him, withdrew into the deepest recesses of the dungeon.

Two months passed. Having attended to all the pressing cases, the examining magistrate began to take up the nonpressing ones and finally remembered Thanos. He was led before the magistrate, who sat holding his tobacco pouch and adjusting the handle with his fingers. A black cap covered his bald head, and he seemed to be in deep thought, but his physiognomy was so common that there were many moments when in fact he thought of nothing. Seated nearby, his secretary shuffled papers, preparing to transcribe the proceedings.

The examiner began with the usual biographical questions: name, residence, age, religion, parents, and so on, which Thanos had already answered exhaustively during the first inquiry. These needed to be asked once more, though.

"Another headache now." The examiner frowned. "Why did you leave Lamia secretly?"

Thanos explained again, mentioning Hephaestidis and PapaJonas as character witnesses.

Each question needed to be written out by the scribe and was followed by the response, ponderously dictated by the examiner, who often stopped to ask, "Now what did I just say?" or "Where are we?" and the like. At this point, the door opened slightly and the head of a toothless old lady appeared through the gap. Dinner was ready, she whispered.

"My, my, how time flies!" The examiner stood up. "The work never ends, and we can't even keep track of mealtimes. It's a donkey's life. And we barely scrape by on our salary. Tomorrow, my lad . . . we'll see each other again tomorrow. Roasted turtledoves are waiting for me, and I'm afraid they'll be dry. Very dry." And saying this, he left quickly.

During the days that followed, Thanos did not once see the dove-devouring magistrate. To make things worse, there was another unpleasant episode.

For some time it had been known that the provincial secretary, in charge during the nomarch's absence and in collusion with the prison warden, had been pocketing five of the thirty-five lepta budgeted for the maintenance of prisoners, so that everyone's portion was decreased and the quality of food consequently adulterated, making the bread hard to digest and dirty, more appropriate for animals than for human beings. The secretary had a lot of power, of course, and no one dared complain openly. Besides, some of the civil servants of the nomarchy were circulating a rumor that secretly undermined the position of their superior.

After a great outcry from the press, a general administrative inquiry was ordered and all prison employees were questioned, almost all of whom maintained that the food was not all that bad. Thanos was among the few prisoners who told the truth about the adulteration of food. The secretary, furious, demanded that the examining magistrate, whose life was rendered intolerable by dry turtledoves, provide Thanos a lesson in austerity and black broth and recommended that his stay in prison be extended indefinitely.

Even with goodwill on the examiner's part, the inquiry would have dragged on, since witnesses had to be questioned, especially the gendarmes who had set the haystacks ablaze and who, stationed elsewhere, were not easily available. Besides, the examiner cared little about the case and had received his orders from the governing secretary. Thanos was, in a manner of speaking, buried in jail, forgotten.

Brooding and embittered, Thanos felt condemned to the deepest chamber of hell. The memory of Ephrosyne consoled him, pulling him back from the terrors of despair. He often saw her in his dreams, occupied in her handiwork, or in travail, or in danger of fire, or under attack by brigands, and he tried to assure himself that these visions were illusory.

"What have I done to be persecuted so relentlessly? Am I not innocent? They burned down my haystacks and destroyed everything I had. How am I to blame? That Tassos is a brigand? Did they ask if I could stop him? But the fire is not enough. It's me they want, me they hunt down, because I escaped the captain and his tortures. I'd have been happier away from this if a new whirlwind hadn't blown up while I was in exile and flung me from one precipice to another. But whom have I cheated, harmed, or injured? I'm being punished because I am weak, alone, insignificant, and unknown. Can an innocent man not be heard without the support of the powerful, without gifts and other tricks? Justice must be deaf and blind, because injustice has a hundred hands and feet and can reach everywhere. Must I, God forbid, actually do something criminal to get out of here?" And deep sighs interrupted his thoughts.

As the prison emptied out, he expected the magistrate to summon him and his depression lifted, but this consolation was quickly extinguished when a flow quickly succeeded the ebb. His aversion to all those around him, including the guards who never spoke to or noticed him, made his solitude complete. There was consolation in being considered a misanthrope, however, for no one approached him and he could be indifferent to their sarcasm.

But time passed slowly, inexorably, dripping bitterness into the depths of his heart, while the monotony of his isolation left him bereft of intellectual occupation and abandoned to the perpetual and unequal struggle of his misfortune, which withered his powers and denied him every aid and recreation. His eyes grew hollow, he became pale, and he often felt giddy or had ecstatic moments of fixed staring, as though observing visions darker than those of the Cimmerian darkness wherein he resided.

He got some relief when tears came, but usually he saw only frightening visions. Demons, not gendarmes, clanked chains and danced in a circle of fire, and he, in the middle, tried to escape and was turned back with satanic jeers, white teeth grinding and eyes glittering white in dark visages. The others, seeing him pace back and forth, took him for mad.

At other times, the angelic voice of Ephrosyne whispered and he strained to hear but could not distinguish a syllable. The shadow of his mother came to him from the other life and he heard her calling him an unworthy child. He would come to, face forward on the ground, eventually understanding that all these were agitations of his fantasy.

As much as he suffered, no one ever heard him blaspheme, and all the injustice he experienced could not undermine the purity of his character, which rendered him, of course, worthy of ridicule.

The people to whom the friends of Ayfantis wrote had no connection whatsoever with the judicial authorities and only through third parties was it learned that Thanos was being subjected to yet another inquiry. But Ayfantis did not remain on Skopelos for long, as we'll see immediately.

»»» 9 «««

Ayfantis in Athens

Ayfantis could not rest easy as long as his daughter was gloomy and dispirited. Even the impassive Kioura, who concerned herself with little beyond household duties and precisely performed religious obligations, was not indifferent to Ephrosyne's low spirits. Though she attributed them to homesickness, which she also felt, she assumed that she was consoling Ephrosyne when she assured her that they would soon be returning home.

But Ayfantis knew his daughter's heart much better, for she never hid anything from him, because only he was always willing to listen to her and to divine her thoughts, even when unspoken, and was attuned to her sentiments. But even he attributed her melancholy to the indignation she felt at the injustice shown to Thanos.

Returning home was impossible as long as the security of the borders was assigned to the current *derven aga*. Since their stay in Skopelos had become intolerable to all three, however, and hopes for a rapid return to Thessaly did not exist, they decided to cross over first to Syros, where Ayfantis had some business interests, and from there to Athens, where arrangements might be made for their return home. Besides, since she had once expressed an interest in visiting the capital, Ayfantis hoped the trip would improve Ephrosyne's mood. Another reason for going to Athens, though, was that her father might be able to gain Thanos's freedom from there.

Among the first people Ayfantis saw in Syros was a happy and boastful Zarpas. His many-pleated britches were of the earthen hue of a Karamanian sheep's tail, and his huge silk handkerchief, one corner jammed into his multicolored belt, the other held in his hand, revealed that business for him was coming along nicely.

Ayfantis approached him to learn news of Thanos, but Zarpas was unwilling to speak about "that lad," as he referred to him, and immediately turned the conversation toward himself, blaming slanderers, who had reached the level of impudence to accuse him of barratry, as though his character was not known to everyone.

"Thank God the directors of the insurance society recompensed me at once. Now, I'm off to Skopelos to build a new ship. But first I've got to make a pilgrimage to the Panaghia at Tinos. Sir, if you want something of me, Zarpas is at your command."

"Thank you. I'd very much like to know how we can get Thanos released."

"That lad? Among those poor in spirit, he is. Expects Divine Justice to come, take him by the hand, and lead him out. Things like that happened a long time ago."

"Yes, I understand. To whom should I direct him, though?"

"That I don't know. If you want, I can introduce you to my agent and he'll take care of the business for you, no matter which jail your man is in. Just so he's alive. The dead he can't resurrect. As long as you pay commissions, legal fees, and all expenses, ordinary and special, he'll do your bidding. With these he can even marry off a bishop."

Zarpas's introduction, it turned out, was unnecessary because Ayfantis had had dealings with the merchant in question. He set out for Athens, then, taking the necessary steps, expecting to take action there.

Ephrosyne was not morose during the trip, for her hopes had taken wing. On the ride from Piraeus they approached the celebrated capital by way of Odos Ermou, encountering a large mob in the square of Athens that brought them to a halt. Noisy people

of every social class surrounded the carriage, complaining and gesturing. "A terrible situation," they shouted. "We can't take it any
more. We must protest! We must be heard!" Others, saying nothing, pointed to a crowded balcony.

Finally, silence won out and a speaker, not visible from the carriage, was heard saying, in fragments and with interruptions, "Why
are you upset? Why this indignation? Do you suppose the government, today as yesterday and the day before, is not tireless on
your behalf? Why else does the government exist if not to care
for your welfare, your security? That's why you have ministers,
governors, captains, magistrates. . . ."

"Yes," a voice rang out, "and crooked police."

Laughter broke out from one end of the crowd to the other.

"You say that the police chief and the constables stole. Yes.
That's the reason they've been dismissed. Immediately. From this
moment on. The crook is no longer police chief. His policemen
are no longer policemen."

"But they'll be reinstated tomorrow," someone shouted.

"We have laws. We have courts of law, police courts, courts of
misdemeanor, criminal courts. They'll try him. They'll punish
him according to his misdeeds. He'll be imprisoned, isolated,
chained. . . ."

"Yes," another shouted, "but in a short while he'll be pardoned, too."

"What ails you, John?" another added. "What's always ailed me."

"No, no. No pardon. Whoever heard of a police chief being
pardoned? Never! The wolf was exposed in the fold, wearing the
shepherd's cloak. What should the head shepherd do? If he for-
gives him, he'll jump in secretly once more and devour all the
sheep. The wolf doesn't change his ways. Don't be upset for nothing. Just as the good father, because he loves his children, cares
for and worries about them, so does the government care for and

worry about you. We neither rest during the day nor sleep at night, so that you can enjoy the good things of life and lay your heads on the bed of roses of carefree security for all the labors you've undertaken. What other payment do we want but to see the increase in your happiness, the way a gardener enjoys seeing his trees in flower? Yes, go back to your work in peace and sleep at night in comfort and ease, because the guards are sleepless and the wolf has been unmasked. You see, the government brings good out of evil. The police chief stole: he committed a crime. Behold, he can no longer steal. Instead, he's become an example to others who act in the same way."

"Yes, yes, examples of robbery," the mob shouted.

"Examples of the law's strictness. If you have my word, you have all."

"We want action. We've had our fill of words."

"Give us time. If you see no action, you're still the masters. You have the right to bind and to loose. You, the simple citizens, who always were and always will be lovers of law and order, worthy descendants of Themistocles and Pericles, are sovereign."

These words gradually soothed the agitation, and, buzzing as many tribes of bees, the noisy Athenian rabble broke up into groups of discussants about what had been said, dispersing in a short while.

The carriage once more began to make its way slowly through the thinning mob, searching for an inn, while Ayfantis considered what had happened and said, "I understand. No matter where you go, everything's the same."

He met many from his province and through them found a place to stay. Among these were men he'd hosted and cared for when they'd fled from revolts or brigandage and now lived, honorably and with distinction, in the capital. While visiting one of them he unexpectedly met Tassos, about whom he had heard nothing until then.

Many changes had occurred in a short span of time. According to the most recent change in the ever-changing ministry, many of the previously wanted men, by a series of events that led to the same political result, or, according to the current lexicon, belonged to the same "system," received amnesties, pardons, and even honors. Among these was Tassos, who, besides being amnestied, was given a promotion to lieutenant as well. The captain, previously assigned to combat brigandage, had been recalled, placed on reserve status, and in effect pushed aside, while border security was once more the task of the regular army, to which Tassos was attached. He was given permission to stay in the capital, though, where he hoped to arrange his captaincy, a rank he had been promised by the minister in charge.

Tassos's mother was also in Athens. One day while she sat on her porch the morose captain, scowling as usual, walked past the house. The servant girl pointed him out to her, saying that he was the notorious captain, a descendant of those who had crucified Christ. Barbara rushed to drop a clay flowerpot on his head and would have done so if the servant had not managed to grab her hands. The captain, gloomy and preoccupied as always, noticed nothing.

Ayfantis could not understand the way one brother, a brigand, went unpunished and was even rewarded, while the other, who suffered from brigandage and lost his possessions, was hunted down as a brigand and could not even go to trial.

After they had greeted and embraced each other, Ayfantis asked Tassos to explain. "Why should Thanos be persecuted because of you, even though the government, acknowledging that you've been persecuted unjustly, recompenses you with promotions and awards."

"What promotions and awards? I'm barely a lieutenant, and everyone in the Revolution was given this distinction. If the sacrifices of my father, who died during the national struggle, were taken into account, I'd be something grander today."

"Yes, but you're no longer in dire straits, while Thanos . . ."

"He's in trouble because he was in Skiathos when the decrees for amnesty were given out. It didn't occur to me to have his name included."

"But I still don't understand. There's a ministry of justice, I hear."

"The minister does not interfere into judicial proceedings."

"But why did he interfere for you and not for Thanos, who did nothing wrong?"

"That's precisely the problem. If Thanos had borne arms, he'd have been amnestied. How can he expect amnesty when he's done nothing wrong?"

"I think I follow you. The ministry . . . torments the innocent . . . so that no one will think that Justice sleeps."

"Yes, well, I suppose a foreigner has a hard time understanding how things work in Greece. The Bavarians drew up our laws and we function because we've grown accustomed to them. The fact is that I have no connections with the minister of justice. I asked the minister of military affairs and he said he'd talk to him, but he's one of those intellectuals who look for needles in haystacks."

"Isn't there another way?"

"I wrote to a friend in Chalkis, and even promised to pay him off, but haven't received a reply yet. Perhaps next week. . . ."

"Even though he's your brother and it's not my place to speak to you about him, I love him as my own child and am willing to make every sacrifice in his behalf."

Ayfantis narrated all that had befallen him, in part on Tassos's account, but did not wish to let him understand that he attributed the cause of his troubles to him. He had come to Athens to arrange his return to Thessaly, he said, expecting to use the Ottoman ambassador as mediator with the Turkish authorities.

"I may be able to do you a little favor and to erase a small part of my great obligation to you. A close friend of mine has many contacts with the ambassador and might speak to him. If you wish, we'll go to his residence tomorrow."

This friend of Tassos, Leon Iapetos, was a remarkable man. He had gentrified his surname, Kapotas—his father was a cloak maker in Patras who hoped his son would devote himself to the craft inherited from his grandfather, but capricious nature did not pass on this skill to the fourth generation. As a child, Leon's intelligence charmed his mother but saddened the father, who saw that the boy was endowed with a gift that was not only unnecessary to the cloak maker's craft but even harmful to it. Succumbing to his wife's entreaties, Kapotas allowed Leon to attend school but never praised his progress or encouraged him to take pains in his studies. After attending Greek school, the young man wanted to go to the Gymnasion in Athens, but his father gave his approval only after the intervention of another member of the guild, who planned to establish himself in the capital and was willing to undertake the care of the young man as long as he promised to work in his shop. Since he saw no way to prevent it, Kapotas finally submitted, expecting nothing good from the assent.

Once the bright Leon arrived in Athens, he shook off every commitment and devoted himself to the embellishment and display of his inclination. So as not to betray his background, he changed his surname at once, wore the most fashionable clothes, learned music and dance, and generally familiarized himself with the accomplishments of a higher social class, which the advance in Athenian luxury performed in a great leap and separated the recently emerging generation from the older as though they were two different races.

It was impossible to believe that Leon Iapetos, the ornament of every dance, the loquacious heartbreaker, the skillful equestrian, the discriminating judge in the audience of Italian operas, the first to applaud those who excelled and the first to hoot the failures, the daily companion of leading ladies and other show people, that this Leon Iapetos was the son of a shabbily dressed Sotirios Kapotas, who was chained at his labors from morning to night, ceaselessly sewing in his Patras workshop. Nothing displeased Leon so much as when, in the company of one of his patrician friends, someone who recognized him said suddenly, "Hey, aren't you the son of my good friend, Sotiris Kapotas?"

Better for him if his father had had no friends at all.

The business of Kapotas did not suffice for expenses, but even if it had, the father certainly had no interest in granting him the use of his small business profits. The mother always sent a little something, and this secretly, but she had little at her disposal. Luck, however, helped the freely spending youth so that he did not need the deprivations of the maternal grants. His dancing and riding skills appealed greatly to an ambassador, a lover of beauty who wished to make his acquaintance and who received him with many attentions, and introduced him to the minister, as one capable of bringing honor to the service by his seemly ways. It was because of the exhortations of this art-loving ambassador that the notorious encyclical, instigated by the Holy Synod that called for the listing of all those civil servants who danced well, was rescinded.

The ambassador made many other demands concerning the useful reforms of various branches of service, but the minister skillfully avoided these by offering various pretexts as not wishing to betray the traditional mores of graft and depravity. To do a favor to the ambassador who recommended Iapetos, the minister immediately hired him as an ordinary office worker in the ministry.

The fact was that Iapetos did not perform any discernible work in the ministry, though he spent a few hours in the offices daily,

Thanos Vlekas

gathering and passing on the news, but actually acting as inter-mediary between minister and ambassador with whom he had, as the French say, *les petite entrés*. This immeasurably increased his importance, and anyone with significant business that required individual attention had recourse to Iapetos, the skillful initiate. He had entry, therefore, to the homes of all the ambassadors, and all paid attention to him.

At that time, Tassos had two beautiful and powerful steeds and because of them had become acquainted and formed a bond with the horse-loving Iapetos. They often rode together, training them, clambering over fortifications and vaulting over trenches.

On the day he had met Ayfantis, Tassos rode with Iapetos and suggested that he make the acquaintance of a beautiful girl from Thessaly newly arrived in Athens and mentioned the reason he wished to introduce him into their home. Iapetos willingly promised his mediation and they agreed to the visit.

The following day, the two friends went to the home of Ayfantis, whom they found playing checkers with his daughter. Though Ephrosyne, according to the custom of their country, should have retired into the women's quarter, she remained because she was in a foreign land where women spoke openly and because Ayfantis wanted his daughter near him, hearing and learning everything.

As Ayfantis received the visitors, Ephrosyne's cheeks, under the sharp glance of Iapetos, were suffused by a becoming and delicate blush. A black kerchief, whose two ends were tied in back, covered her head, while her mane of blonde hair burst out in locks from her temples and flowed down her back. The fairness of her complexion, the comeliness of her vivid features, and the sheen of her hair gave her an ethereal look. Though she gazed downward, little seemed to evade her attention, and she extended her hand to the table to move a piece, revealing long and well-shaped fingers.

Her natural and unaffected beauty struck even the fashionable and affected Iapetos. His mincing stride, his honeyed voice, the fragrance of his perfume revealed that he knew and could employ the amiable charms of every craft.

The *foustanella* was the rage at the time, and Iapetos surpassed all in the wearing of it. His blouse was of the finest embroidered linen, while the tassel of his fez dangled gracefully over his right shoulder. But there was nothing noble in his features, and his small, darting eyes and constant smile revealed a careful man who wished to win everyone's goodwill by his affability and smooth ways. His manner was lively and full of pleasantries, inasmuch as he always spoke lightly of serious matters and seriously of trifles. Sometimes he tapped the *foustanella* with his slender riding crop, sometimes he held the gold handle at his lips while humming a tune, but he kept his bright yellow gloves on to hide his swarthy hands.

"Mr. Ayfantis, you are a persecuted man and a refugee in hospitable Athens." As a masterful and communicative man, he began to speak first.

"There are many witnesses to your benefactions here. Especially my friend, Tassos." The modest blush of Ephrosyne he attributed to the charms of his foppish bearing, and as a clever tactician he decided not to extend her agitation, judging it wiser to remove the fiery rays of his stare so that he could study her movements later.

"My contacts are not great, certainly, but perhaps the little acquaintance I have with the Ottoman ambassador, who visited me just yesterday in my absence, might aid in your return. Through his auspices we might be able to use other ambassadors friendly toward me. It would be a good idea for you to meet them. But I won't keep secret from you the fact that in the recesses of my heart I hope we'll fail, so that Athens would not lose what she has so recently gained. To be frank, therefore, I must say that I'm not a sincere ally of yours."

It was impossible, Ayfantis said as he invited them to take seats, that those who knew how much they suffered away from home not to wish himself, his wife, and his daughter to return.

Iapetos inclined his head toward Ephrosyne, giving her his respects, before directing his comments to her.

"And do you think that I'd be given amnesty when they learned that I conspired to help your lady daughter leave? I'd have to return to Thessaly with you."

"We certainly wouldn't have the means to help you return to Athens," Ayfantis replied, "but don't fear to be condemned for your philanthropic act."

"As though you yourself weren't condemned because of your philanthropy. But I believe that once you get to know Athens, you won't want to leave so soon."

"We like Athens, but as foreigners we . . ."

"And what of that? Foreigners especially frequent our celebrated city. Visitors come from every corner of the earth. My Parisian friend, Count Savau, left the other day. The amusing Lord Beckson is planning to stay all winter, while Prince Fouffof of Moscow, whose acquaintance I made just a few days ago, confessed that he's been charmed by the beauties here."

"These friends of yours are tourists and like to see different sights, while we . . ."

"You'll find here whatever you desire. It is Paris in miniature. We have balls, theater, carriage races. Our shops are full of all sorts of luxuries. In a few days, as a matter of fact, there will be horse races at which the royal couple will preside, awarding prizes to the best riders. I'd like to arrange for you to have proper seating for this spectacle."

"Thank you. I'm curious to see your horses and equestrian skills. I suppose that it will resemble the Turkish *tzirit*."

"We're able to offer other sights, too, as long as they amuse your lady daughter."

"You hope by entertainments to help us forget our deserted home, but our nostalgia won't permit us to enjoy ourselves. Be careful, too, that we don't stay the spring, when it would be impossible for us to find the cool greenery and the nightingales' song of Thessaly."

"Well, I can't be that cruel. I only meant that you shouldn't leave right away."

"Get our release and we'll stay as long as you wish. You think, then, that we'll be able to get the ambassador's support?"

"This evening I am dining with him at the residence of a certain lady, and I hope to prepare him and to ask leave to present you. He is of such a simple character that I have no doubt about his willingness, except that he would be doing a terrible disservice to his own government by providing his best subjects to Greece."

"Believe me, we'd be most grateful to you."

"You love your homeland very much. If I were appointed secretary to the embassy in London or Paris or Constantinople, I believe I'd never want to be recalled."

"Why didn't you say 'ambassador'?" Tassos asked. "Out of modesty, certainly."

"I don't wish to be greedy by leaping over the rights of the revolutionary heroes and their descendants."

"Much good those rights did us, especially my brother, Thanos."

"Is he still in jail in Chalkis?"

Ephrosyne was unable to disguise the careful attention she was paying to the conversation. The watchful eye of Iapetos spied this out.

"And who would you expect to free him?"

"You, like a good brother."

"I'm working on that."

"Without success, since your horses preoccupy you."

"That's why I request your assistance."

"Yes," Ayfantis responded, "I entreat you as well, because I love him as a son, I assure you."

"Then the concern becomes mine. I'll write to the appropriate office today." Iapetos, pretending not to have noticed Ephrosyne's happy smile, continued. "He must be worthy of love, since you think so highly of him."

"I assure you that I would like to see Thanos freed as much as I wish my own problems resolved. He and Ephrosyne collaborated in all her work."

She blushed, inclining her head to hide her feelings but exposing them even more.

"He has good supporters and will suffer nothing. Whoever is loved this much is a happy man, if indeed he knows it." And bending over to offer his salutations, he looked at Ephrosyne. "I hope to bring good news in a short while for you and your beloved Thanos."

The two friends departed. Though her father was unable to fathom them, the sharp-witted Iapetos was not fooled as to Ephrosyne's feelings, but he pitied her for loving a man, in his opinion, hardly worthy of it. Once she learned what comprised grace and fashion and found a person who embodied these qualities, to the degree to which Iapetos possessed them, certainly, he would be able to displace her love, he believed, though he was· mistaken. "Ethiopians and Eskimos love their own," he said to himself, "but only because they don't know the Iapetoses of this world."

Ephrosyne thought otherwise. The manners of Iapetos, his dissolute glance, his foppish dress, his conceited chatter, his voluptuous croon aroused her slight and secret smile.

"Well," her father asked, "what did you think of him?"

"A real wagtail."

"He promised things beyond his power, I suspect."

Iapetos, nevertheless, began to proclaim the news of the fair Ephrosyne all over town, arousing the curiosity of many who envied him when they learned the truth. His visits, using his mission as a pretext, became more frequent, and he took Ayfantis to the home of the Ottoman ambassador, who promised to write to Larissa and to intervene on his behalf.

The more amiable Iapetos was toward Ephrosyne, however, the more he repelled her. The full exercise of his charms went to waste. Neither his tenderness nor his magnificence, neither his arousal of animosity nor his pretended indifference helped him attain his goal. His passionate behavior did not evade the notice of Ayfantis, who advised his daughter to encourage his zeal toward them, to receive him with grace, but Ephrosyne was unable to pretend and, compelled to be present during his visits, was often unable to disguise her ironic smile.

As obstinate as the defense was and so stubborn was the attack that his favorable reception in their home encouraged Iapetos to believe that Ayfantis was not against his suit. His effort was worthwhile because the father's fortune was not contemptible. Since it was hard for him to believe that a feminine heart could be invulnerable to his charms, he attributed Ephrosyne's coolness to her rustic and uncultivated traditional ways.

According to her upbringing, he thought, it was wrong to reveal that she was attracted to someone. But nature was stronger than nurture, which can only regulate behavior. It was impossible for her not to feel pleasure in the passion she inspired.

He used the parish priest, since he was more respectable, as mediator, but the response was neither positive nor negative. Before present conditions had been resolved so that he would know where he'd be established, Ayfantis could not make a decision about his only daughter, with whom he expected to live out the rest of his life.

But he did learn two bits of good news: the Albanian *derven aga* had been dismissed and would be replaced by his predecessor, while the trial of Thanos had been placed on the docket and the jury would be summoned shortly. The first news would bring him, he hoped, closer to his goal.

They soon had direct confirmation that the Albanians had departed. Ayfantis's adversary had succeeded in winning his legal case against him, but this was a matter of indifference to Ayfantis. He wrote to the new *derven aga* and, after his reply, considered returning to Thessaly.

Iapetos often remarked how much he longed to live the agricultural life in Thessaly, under the shade of trees, taking pleasure in watching oxen pull the plow.

"You mustn't wear gloves, then." Ephrosyne immediately rued her joke, not wishing to show friendliness toward him.

"I would certainly dress as a farmer then, and the clothes, I believe, would look good on me."

Iapetos understood, when Ephrosyne grew silent, that if he did not make the first move himself to wear farmer's apparel, Ayfantis and his daughter would not help him, so he began to consider matters more seriously before the prize left Athens.

»»» 10 «««
The Trial of Thanos

Although Thanos was not released, despite many recommendations, he was at least summoned before a jury for collaborating with brigands. Criminal proceedings had to be convoked for this, however, and trials were held only once or twice a year. Since a council had not met for some time, by good fortune this was due to occur soon, and Chalkis was designated as the venue.

Hephaestidis, currently in Lamia and unemployed because the inspector of schools, the "Arabian Flutist," had finally repaid him for his sarcasm, was subpoenaed as a witness. He took advantage of this opportunity to go to Athens, where he planned to publish his *Grammar,* wishing, as he said, "to visit tiresome Thebes and illustrious Athens."

When he stood before the presiding board to provide evidence for Thanos, Hephaestidis expressed indignation at the good farmer's travails, lauding his virtues, diligence, modesty. By great effort and austerity these qualities had enabled him to attain prosperity, from which, in one instant, he had been deprived by the good gendarmes, servants of law and guardians of public order.

The contrast of the amnesty for Tassos, who was in fact guilty, and the remorseless persecution of Thanos, who was blamed for his brother's act, moved the jurors. The presiding officer often interrupted Hephaestidis as he sneered at the laws and authorities but was unable to put an end to the raging torrent of words.

"Yes," he said to the president, "you're right, and the Hebrews freed Barabbas, though the Old Testament says, 'a great weight, and small abomination to the Lord.'"

Despite this, the prosecutor continued to press for conviction. He was, in fact, one of those who hungered and thirsted for justice, but while he struggled to draw within his web small insects caught in the invisible and fragile filiforms, terrible beasts had already torn them to shreds. He needed, therefore, to magnify and transform houseflies into elephants. He began by describing a society inundated by the weight of crimes toward which the jury was able only to extend helping hands.

"The lack of punishment," he banged his hand on the table, half of which was covered by his enormous belly, "the lack of punishment has increased the evil to the point where everyone wonders if laws exist today or if they sleep. Releasing a guilty man not only violates your oath, but acts as a goad to the criminally inclined to attack the innocent, against the industrious citizens, against each and every one of them. That's why collaborating with brigands is more destructive than brigandage itself." He stopped after this startling statement, happy at the effect the tricks of the craft had on their faces.

"Yes, it's worse because without collaborators, brigandage would not exist. If the collaborators did not offer the brigand the opportunity, if they did not signal to him that pursuers were on their way, if they did not provide him with a way of escape, a means of hiding his booty, never—for justice's sake—by the protecting laws, would there be brigandage!"

A great uproar followed when the prosecutors began to discuss the deposition of Hephaestidis. Was it possible that a learned man, a student of grammar and the sciences, who went once a week to Thanos's cabin to drink cow's milk, would not know what was happening in all that time in that very cabin?

"Certainly," Hephaestidis jumped up, "and once a month you drink the colacretan's milk and that's why . . ."

Fortunately, the judge, not understanding that this was the sort of milk he himself drank, cut him off as a disturber, because Hephaestidis wanted to add, "and that's why you have such a great belly."

"Of course, the interpreter of Xenophon's *Economics* and Theokritos's *Bucolics* might be tricked by illusion that inside that very cabin only cheese and butter were churned, because those were the only things he tasted."

"Oh, tasteless . . ."

The judge once more called for order, but Hephaestidis replied that it was impossible, because he would burst.

"Then I order you to leave the courtroom."

After Hephaestidis withdrew, the attorney concluded his summations quietly, with many innuendoes, after which the defense attorney rose up to praise the virtuous schoolmaster, who had become the main subject of discussion, as though he was the one on trial.

"Who is to blame if society is scourged by brigandage? Hephaestidis, who believes in the innocence of a good farmer? Or those who lavish amnesty and pardons on professional bandits who are worthy of the gallows and who employ the rigor of the laws against those who from the sweat of their brow earn their daily bread? Hephaestidis, who teaches us the wisdom of our ancestors? Or those who nurture wolves and punish sheep? Doesn't it seem strange to you that an innocent is used as scapegoat to disguise the ignominy of having rascals go unpunished?"

The judge rebuked the attorney for his digression and put an end to the discussion. In a short while, the jury returned with the verdict, declaring Thanos innocent.

Hephaestidis jumped up and embraced Thanos in the courtroom, declaiming the line from Euripides, "I saved you, as all Greeks know."

Poor Thanos was so downhearted that he found it hard to believe his trials were at an end. His face was gray and his eyes, because of his long stay in the dark, were closed, avoiding the light of day. He had the general appearance of someone emerging from the dungeon of Trophonios.

Hephaestidis took him to his lodgings, taking care of him as a father would, reviling attorneys, the government, and laws throughout the day. "O, Demosthenes, the beasts of Athena are no longer three, the owl, the dragon, and the mob. They are countless: ministries, attorneys, captains, inspectors of schools. . . ."

But before leaving for Athens they waited a few days for a convoy to be formed, large enough that would not risk running into brigands. Among their many fellow travelers were two peculiar personages, of opposing positions, an American missionary and a Father Lavrentios, a monk notorious for his hatred of other creeds.

They set out on horseback one morning for Chalkis, unacquainted with one another. The American immediately approached Hephaestidis as more learned than the others and, in the everyday language, asked, "You're a teacher of Greek?"

"That I am."

"You were, it appears, dismissed."

"Yes, I was *reviewed*."

"And found wanting?"

"No, found surpassing."

"How?"

"I found fault with ignorance. And who, pray, are you?"

"An American minister."

"Why abandon the well-governed homeland of Washington and Franklin for the torments of a Greece plagued by terrible institutions?"

"We Americans are all philhellenes, and I was sent to proclaim the word of Truth and contribute to the spread of education in the land of renowned men, whom we admire and wish to emulate as beacons of political wisdom and virtue."

"But how do you expect to teach us when you are not knowledgeable in Greek?"

"We don't propose to teach the ancient language, but the word of Truth."

"You propose, in other words, to interpret Holy Writ into the wretched mixed and barbaric language, hiring some vulgar semi-literate who'll exploit this miserable rabble."

The American, startled by these comments, responded softly to make the conversation less confrontational.

But Father Lavrentios had been keeping a careful eye on the missionary and, having heard a lively conversation and the voice of Hephaestidis growing louder, spurred his horse past the others and approached the schoolmaster.

"My dear man," the missionary said, "forgive this remark, but we foreigners, wishing to learn the everyday language of the Greeks, are greatly puzzled. No grammar exists and you educated men don't agree among yourselves."

"Use the ancient form then," Hephaestidis replied, not noticing the monk nearby.

"But the ancient is neither spoken nor written today."

"Whatever is not ancient is incorrect."

"You're among those involved in trying to waken the sleepers, it appears. Your objectives are noble, but allow me the freedom to doubt whether that is feasible."

"Doubt all you want."

"I doubt because we Americans don't aspire to absolute perfection, which is above the powers of man and is an attribute of God. We're satisfied with the naturally possible and the relative good. We make steady progress because we take no steps in vain."

Father Lavrentios inclined his head, whispering, "Don't answer this accursed man. He's a Lutherocalvinist."

Hephaestidis turned and cast a pitying glance at the monk. "I agree when you say that the perfect is unattainable, but how can you pass over it in silence when we know it and it's in our midst?"

"Perfection is never found in the midst of things or in the marketplace."

"Why not? We have the ancient poets, historians, rhetoricians. We won't err if we follow them."

"I don't think you can follow them. And if an exceptional mortal manages to attain their level, he merely proves the rule."

"About that you're right. Besides Lambros Photiadis, I know of no superior Greek. The rest have abandoned the true path."

"You see, in striving for the impossible, they failed. We in America . . ."

"Horrors, horrors, " Father Lavrentios interrupted, raising his voice somewhat, "a poisonous serpent, born of vipers."

The American looked at the monk but, not understanding what he was saying, continued: "Here's how we view these things in America. The best is what pleases the majority of people. Two are better than one. Common sense, therefore, is what the majority accepts and that's what we embrace."

"How can this be? The majority is ill informed, feebleminded. How can the mass regulate language properly? Whatever is declined in the genitive case the masses decline in the accusative or the dative. Does this make sense? This applies to everything, too. When you are sick, you go to an accomplished physician, not to the mass."

"You see," the monk addressed Hephaestidis, "he doesn't accept the holy tradition of the one catholic, apostolic, and ecumenical church."

"You're right, but I didn't explain myself fully. The wiser teach the mass of people, providing proof with syllogisms and clarity—

what we call 'evidence.' Common sense accepts whatever is made clear; when it rejects something, it does so because it isn't clear. Every perfect mechanism has its counterbalance, its 'regulator.'"

"Here we go again," Hephaestidis shouted. "When Galileo taught that the earth revolved around the sun, who was right, he or common sense, that mob of illiterates and superstitious . . ."

"Blaspheme not," the monk interrupted. "When Joshua said, 'I set the sun against Gaboun and the moon against the chasm of Ailon . . .'"

"Look, in this day and age there are still those who maintain that it's the sun that moves. Common sense is the child of folly and will never deny its mother."

Those in the back of the convoy, hearing the lively discussion and knowing that it would be interesting, because of who the participants were, spurred their horses and approached.

Only Thanos exhibited no curiosity, delighting in nature, which he'd done without for such a long time. The sun's rays reanimated him, and the view of the clear sky, the blue sea, the hills, the greenery, and the trees filled him with wonder, as a blind man who suddenly regains his sight. Every time he reached a height where the horizon stretched out before him, he gazed at it in ecstasy.

Among the travelers was a Xenophon Pteridis, a young man who had pursued many studies in the universities of Europe but had not specialized and could not be classified in any discipline. For this reason he was inaccurately considered a philosopher. This Pteridis was indolent and took no interest in the conversation either, disdaining all those who had not done university studies. But an acquaintance of his in the convoy called him over to listen to the diverting discussion. He approached mechanically to please him, though more intrigued by the birds that flew in the sky.

The missionary was overjoyed to see that he had drawn everyone's interest and that his teachings would benefit all, but the monk was upset and cast baleful glances around him at the throng, whose intellects he suspected were not adequately inoculated against the snake's poisonous bite.

Using as a pretext his fear that he had not sufficiently explained himself, the American repeated the subject of the discussion, his ideas concerning common sense and clarity, so that it would be known by all. He also raised his voice and distinctly stressed virtually every word. "Your comment," he continued, "about Galileo does not undermine the foundation on which the philosophy of my fellow Americans is built."

"Get thee behind me," the monk sighed, "unclean spirit."

"Galileo was right, but so was common sense, because Galileo hadn't provided the common people with sufficient evidence. Clarity, therefore, was not total. For this reason, your distinguished neighbor, who perhaps is not aware of the interpretation by natural law of the Old Testament, which is accepted today in America, is still unconvinced."

The American's reference to him shook the monk as though it were an electric spark. "Why do you listen to this blasphemous infidel? His mouth is an open grave."

Everyone condemned this rude comment and shouted disapproval as one, while one of the travelers, a merchant by profession and a wag, worked his way into the center and addressed himself to the monk.

"Father Lavrentios," he began, "we all have two good ears," he said, "and an average Greek brain, which can clear things up for us. When we are without a mind, then you can shut our ears, but even then we'll free them with our little finger. God pity whoever has a head that attracts lice." And he bared his bald head, saying, "Behold a melon. It has no hair and it fears no louse." General laughter at the monk's expense broke out at the sight of the bald pate. When the noise died down, the American, knowing that he should place little faith in the momentary goodwill of the mob, avoided every expression of triumph and continued as though nothing had occurred. "I'll use an example to explain my idea. The various zones of the earth are subject to different temperatures, but among them there exists an influence that we in America call the Gulf Stream. The 'River of Ocean' we can call it, which equalizes all the temperatures. Common sense or general opinion can understand this. The Gulf Stream, you see, is warm during the winter and flows from Florida to the northern regions of Europe, passing on moderate temperatures that are pleasing to men."

By using an image to explain his theory, the American believed he was achieving two objectives at once, rendering it comprehensible and passing on knowledge concerning physical matters. But the opposite occurred because no one understood what the Gulf Stream was, since they were hearing about it for the first time.

"Behold," the monk said, "he wishes to turn us all toward the Perverted One. Lord, save thy servants."

Another traveler understood it otherwise. "I once heard a ventriloquist, but I don't recall his being an American. If you want, let's ask him to show us his tricks."

"Well," said the merchant, "I'd like to be in America right now. They dig into the earth, it's said, and find gold. The inhabitants had hidden it when Alexander the Great was setting out on his military campaigns."

"What's that you're saying?" another asked. "How long ago did Columbus discover America? I've heard that my granddaddy sailed to Minorca with Columbus."

"I get it," the merchant said, "you're promoting the idea that Columbus got the idea of discovering America from your grandfather. Let's ask the American."

On hearing this Greek Babylon even Pteridis laughed, but the missionary did not lose the thread of his lecture, though the questions were trifling. Everyone was paying attention, which pleased him, and he maintained the same seriousness and didactic manner, and these he combined to answer the merchant's query.

"Columbus discovered America about the end of the fifteenth century, but not even two and a half centuries have passed since the Pilgrim fathers, my coreligionists, landed on the wild shores, yet today our civilization surpasses the European, as the steamer speeds past the sailing ship, and not even a century has passed since the American Revolution. The United States already numbers twenty-five million residents. There are grand cities everywhere, with arterial canals and railroads connecting the far reaches of this vigorous body, and since they are not in old Europe, are accountable to whatever is beneficial for human life. We're the first to implement every discovery and to perfect each invention. This progress and glory are exclusively attributable to the right principles, which we've followed by always conforming to experience and being subject to the authority of common sense. We are especially involved in the transmission of knowledge and maintain that, though property is private, knowledge is held in common."

By this time, the convoy had arrived at Dramesi and planned to travel to the seashore by way of the gap, but the moss on the pebbled surface made the going treacherous, so that from this point on they had to devote themselves to finding the safest passage. The lesson was ended, therefore, to the great satisfaction of the monk, who hoped the entire road to Athens would be this way.

"Behold," the American said before turning seaward, "the avenues of Greece. My fellow citizens first build roads, then universities."

"And where," Hephaestidis asked, "are the madhouses of those who know everything?"

"By what route do your students come to the university?"

"Carelessly," Hephaestidis said. "In their bare feet."

"Then, my friend, having acquired shoes, they won't return to their villages, where they might wear them out."

"How does our friend strike you?" a man pulling up near the merchant asked.

"First-class American cloth," he said to the laughter of all those present.

The others followed the missionary, the horses pacing in each other's hoof tracks, carrying their riders as far as Dilessi, a short distance from the village of the Holy Apostles, along the coast under Oropos of ancient fame. There the travelers rested, eating their meal in the four or five newly built huts.

Hephaestidis, knowing that the American would not travel without being well provisioned, sat next to him, taking Thanos along, followed by the merchant, Pteridis, and a few others. The American spread out his rug and lit his stove in order to brew tea, offering some to his companions. Hephaestidis and Pteridis accepted gladly, while the others looked curiously at the contraption.

"What are you doing?" The monk passed by, hoping not to have missed anything. "Viewing the infidel's magic tricks? Don't you know that the fire of Gehenna was prepared for such as he?"

"Our tea would be ready by now if we had a fire like that," Pteridis said.

"Ah, you've supped on the poison of that most profligate, the soul-destroying, Christian-hating Voltaire."

"You've just named one of the minor poisoners. You're offering praise, not sarcasm. More terrible men have appeared after Voltaire. People like Kant, Fichte, Schelling, Engels, and their hordes."

"These are the gates of hell, which will never prevail."

"These are today's prophets, from whose hands the light of knowledge shines."

"From the beaks of ravens cries emerge. Far, far from you, O faithless and adulterous generation. . . ." And speaking thus, the monk left quickly.

"We've come up with the right antidote," the merchant remarked. "These eggs of yours, Pteridis, are so rotten even he can't swallow them." He might have been aware of his pun on the man's name. "Keep them for tomorrow."

Everyone laughed but the missionary, who was preoccupied with his fire. Hephaestidis, knowing that he was easily carried beyond the bounds of good sense, avoided pursuing this discussion before the large crowd.

After tea, which a few besides the three of them tasted but found sour and unpleasant, they rested.

They set out again for Athens the following morning. Pteridis had proved to be the severing knife of the general conversation; the monk avoided his presence, and the missionary did not wish to provide the pretext for a philosophical discussion, which he considered totally out of place and harmful. The merchant cracked a few innocent jokes, and they arrived in Athens before evening and went their separate ways. The monk was the first to disappear.

Hephaestidis accompanied Thanos to his mother's house, but Tassos was not there. He'd been gone for many days on important business.

»»» 11 «««
The Sorrow of Ephrosyne

Unpleasant things were happening in the home of Ayfantis while Thanos was on trial.

If good tidings came to the family from Thessaly, and if Thanos were found innocent, Iapetos knew he would be dismissed as redundant and quickly forgotten. So far, his elegant appearance, charming ways, longing glances, and stifled sighs had accomplished nothing, while his invitations to balls, to the theater, and to other entertainments were rejected one after the other. When the mild approach proved ineffective, the time had come, he knew, for more vigorous measures. He decided to try a daring maneuver.

An audacious failure differs little in its result from one that is indecisive, but in his attempt Iapetos had hope, pale though it was, that he might change matters somewhat. Various thoughts encouraged him. He could not believe that Ephrosyne's coolness to him was not feigned. If she were sincere, one had to admit that the arrows of Cupid were impotent, in his opinion, that charm was no longer invincible, that Tithonios himself had been transformed from the most graceful of men to the most vulgar, and that the Apollo of Praxiteles and the tribal mask of savage Africa differed little from one another. Perish the thought! Ephrosyne's apparent indifference and coolness he attributed to patriarchal mores and her rustic upbringing, which she would have violated by welcoming his attentions while under her father's charge as chattel. She could not

reciprocate, despite her own wishes. If into this beautiful statue he
breathed a spirit, toward whom but her Pygmalion would she open
her arms? And then, what recourse would her father have, who had
no other child? "I'm the one," he'd tell him then.

When he considered the wealth of Ayfantis, which he expected
to receive as dowry, and its probable uses, his imagination soared
even higher. "Then, like Ambassador Tade or Deina, I'd have a
beautiful house, servants, horses, a carriage, a box at the theater.
I'd give dances and dinner parties. I'd tour Europe. What would
the Parisians say when they saw such a handsome man? And in
my gilded uniform! Spending without a care! Through me, Greece
would be glorified. It wouldn't be at all strange if I were appointed
ambassador to Paris or London, if necessary without salary. If
what they say is true, of course, that she has an income surpassing one hundred thousand silver pieces."

The needling of his desires often chased away his sleep and,
leaping out of bed, he paced back and forth in his room or rolled
on the rug, as though floating on the waters of the Paktolos River.
"I want French furniture, English or Persian rugs, oil paintings of
the Italian masters, Japanese or Sèvres vases. My house will be lit
up every evening. Ambassadors will arrive, card games will be
played. The music teacher will sit at the piano to play accompani-
ment for the leading singers of opera. You will be stunned, Ayfantis, when you see this crowd. What other son-in-law can raise you
to such heights? On equal footing with ambassadors! 'It's to you,
Mr. Iapetos,' they'll say, 'that we owe what little entertainment we
have in Athens.' 'How gracious you are to me, O gentlefolk. You
do me the honor to ignore the poverty of my humble home. Any
day now I expect a collection of alabaster and mosaics from Flo-
rence and have ordered a new style of French furniture, which
should be arriving at the same time as the shipment of Burgundy
wine. As you know, our retsina is undrinkable. . . .'"

This was the future his imagination conjured up for him if he succeeded in marrying Ephrosyne. After conceiving many intricate strategies whose execution was problematic, not wanting to resort to violence or abduction because, ignorant of the girl's disposition, he might have found himself at an impasse, he finally discovered what he thought was the most effective plan. Since it did not require the help of another, it was better still, and because time was pressing he began to implement it at once.

Ayfantis and his spouse, he knew, frequently left in the afternoon to visit homes in the neighborhood, while their daughter remained alone, occupied with her handicrafts. When Ephrosyne learned that young Athenian women did not devote themselves to embroidery, as she had supposed, but acquired their adornments from Paris, she had no interest in meeting them and making friends, because ornamenting one's person with one's own work was preferable. Besides this, she was melancholy on Thanos's account and worried about the outcome of his trial.

His conviction threatened a twofold misfortune: he was in jeopardy and might become desperate, in which case they would need to use the repellent Iapetos's mediation. On the other hand, if Thanos was released, she had decided irreversibly to be "at home" to Iapetos no longer, leaving the room whenever he paid his visits and showing complete indifference to his mediation with the Ottoman ambassador on their behalf. After being released, Thanos, she hoped, would accompany them wherever they went. Her father would be unable to deny her this favor, nor would Thanos be able to resist it, since he had become virtually a member of their family and had no means of livelihood in Greece.

Iapetos kept track of the time when Ayfantis and Kioura left the house and, finding the servant girl seated at the front door, sent her after her employers, claiming that Kioura had asked for her. Mindful that she would be leaving Ephrosyne alone in the house, the maid thought it wise to lock the staircase door before hurrying off to her mistress.

Iapetos entered the courtyard and, hanging from the balcony's iron railings, leaped into the kitchen, then headed for Ephrosyne's bedchambers.

Seated and bent over her loom, she did not see him enter and advance toward her on tiptoes, assuming it was the servant she heard. Suddenly, the hated Iapetos appeared before her at the very moment she expected to be free of him forever.

She stared fixedly, trying to assure herself that she was mistaken, but the terrible vision of his effeminate smile, the moist passion of his eyes, and his extended arms seeking her embrace sent her back in her chair with a sharp cry. She fainted, the threaded beam of the loom hanging from her dangling hands. The pallor of her cheeks and lips made her light complexion look even more pale, and her blonde curls tumbled over her right shoulder, toward which her head inclined, so that she looked like a sleeping cherubim or a lily of the valley, stepped on and crushed by a careless passerby.

Iapetos was stunned, and the ardent words he'd hoped would warm the heart of Ephrosyne were extinguished on his lips. Holding her shoulder with one hand lest she fall, he groped with the other for a pitcher on the table to sprinkle her with water. But he could not reach it nor call out to anyone for help, since he knew the door was locked. He spoke her name and began to shake her chair, hoping to bring her to her senses.

His face was drenched with perspiration in his uncertainty. If he left her like this, he might be the cause of a serious accident, but if he stayed until someone—her enraged father, for example— came, his bold plan would have failed disastrously.

While these ideas whirled in his head, the servant returned and, hearing her mistress's name spoken in a man's voice, rushed upstairs and took her hands, freeing Iapetos to grasp the pitcher. She rubbed Ephrosyne's hands while he sprinkled water on her and brought her to her senses.

The servant's reappearance calmed Ephrosyne, who did not see the intruder. After a deep sigh, she covered her face with both hands, overcome by palpitations and tears. Iapetos nodded to the girl not to mention his presence and, softly setting some gold coins on the floor, tiptoed toward the door, knowing that his continued presence would be harmful to Ephrosyne. The servant gestured for him to take back his money, but this he rejected and rushed off without turning, dodging the coins the servant threw out of the window at his head. The tip, of course, was an effort to make it look as though he was there by a previous understanding with her.

Though he had failed, Iapetos did not lose hope, assuming that Ayfantis would question his daughter's innocence. The best way to make Ephrosyne appear suspect was to start a rumor about what had happened so that only marriage to Iapetos could save his daughter's reputation.

Lending credence to the execution of his plan was the consequent illness of Ephrosyne. She knew that her father would not suspect her, but the possibility of a rumor was mortifying. Death was preferable to having her name on the lips of Athenian wags, insulted by this odious man. Who could silence the coffeehouse wits? Who could know what they might suppose?

She wept bitterly in the arms of her father, who tried to console her, but she was shaken by powerful palpitations, followed by a fever. A doctor was summoned.

Two days later Thanos arrived in Athens and immediately headed toward the home of Ayfantis, whom he found gloomy because Ephrosyne, though improved, was still bedridden. The news of Thanos's arrival filled her with joy and gave her new strength, and she struggled to show a more rapid recovery so that she could leave her bedroom.

Iapetos, full of pleasantries and jests, informed everyone about the "diverting" incident, changing things to make himself look better and Ephrosyne worse, and had the audacity, moreover, to present himself at her home and, not seeing her as usual, inquire after her health.

Ayfantis, too mild tempered to treat him as he deserved, received him coldly, replying that his daughter was well, and continued to talk to Thanos. When he saw that no attention was being paid to his excellent person, the brazen Iapetos decided to rejoin the conversation, ignoring the affront and showing interest in the troubles of Thanos, to whom he pretended compassion and gracefully mentioned his own efforts at mediation and support.

The patience of Ayfantis was nearly exhausted and, affording no audience to the babbler, he gave Thanos the opportunity to talk, telling him how sorry they were about his misfortunes and inviting him to dine with them. By suggesting that dinner might be ready, he hoped to remind Iapetos that it was time for him to take his leave.

Retreat was unavoidable when Iapetos saw that his intrigues would not be rewarded. The release of Thanos was a new hurdle, and the obtuse Ayfantis was in no condition to properly evaluate his twofold interest, to disguise Ephrosyne's disgrace and to acquire a son-in-law who would brighten his home. Though his stratagems had not succeeded up to then, as they should have done, Iapetos did not consider his first foray repulsed nor his hopes rendered vain. Ayfantis had not denied him access to his home and it was possible to launch another attack. A truce was necessary for the time being. In order to sweeten the bitterness of his defeat, he gave himself in the interval to other love affairs, more physically tangible ones, while waiting for his second chance, for which execution he would prepare more adequately.

In the meantime, consoled by the presence of Thanos, whom she was eager to see, Ephrosyne recovered. At times, when alone, she recalled what had occurred and shed bitter tears, but Ayfantis, who rarely left home so that she would not be alone, was not fooled.

But Thanos's health had been shaken by his imprisonment. The time he spent in darkness had rendered him unable to bear the brightness of day.

To relieve Ephrosyne's concerns, Ayfantis asked Barbara's permission to care for her son in his home, and Barbara—claiming Thanos's problem was due only to his sulkiness—cheerfully granted this. "That child is all bitterness and trouble" were her words.

But in the meantime, good tidings had come from Thessaly, and Ayfantis made preparations to return to his homeland after Thanos had recovered, taking him along and encouraging his mother to accompany them. She agreed to this.

Hephaestidis Perplexed

Hephaestidis, however, was concerned about other matters.

He burned especially with a desire for revenge against the "Arabian Flutist." Unable to receive any other satisfaction, he wrote a long diatribe against him, paying careful attention to the mistakes and stylistic flaws in the man's writings, which were not numerous, dragging in many matters of a personal nature and ridiculing them. First of all, the most obvious: Where to begin the attack? He started by enumerating his grammatical errors in a stroke-counterstroke, greeting every flat note with a hurrah. Whipping his Marsyas in this manner, he prayed to the gods as well: "Silence, O Zeus, this barbarous voice." He did not limit himself to this opponent, however, but campaigned synecdochically against all modernizers, pointing out their beliefs and contradictions and chanting: "And this, for all evil learned men, except for you, Hephaestidis."

The printer of a newspaper to whom Hephaestidis offered the publication of his treatise gave it a cursory glance and called his attention to the fact that it was a satire and a libel against a not negligible personage.

"Yes," he replied, "this pamphlet I admit has the bite of ginger and the piquancy of mustard, but I can no longer bear the clatter of the Persian tongue and the Asiatic tendencies of our intellectuals."

"What are you saying? You've set before us all the roses and lilies in the anthology of abuse, and you don't seem to care that your dirty linen should not be washed in public."

"But these public servants are really hangmen and executioners of language and of men, as Pindar says: 'Men are selected through trials.'"

"I can see that you're fervent for true education and one of the few wise men of Greece, but . . ."

"But what?"

"We publishers have many expenses. We pay typesetters, inkers, pressmen. Add newsprint, responsible editors, et cetera, et cetera. And instead of recompense, what do we earn? The enmity and hatred of people whose acts we censure."

"I don't catch your drift."

"A spade a spade, then?"

"I'm listening."

"'Cross my palm and we talk' is the publisher's only principle. Without money he doesn't eat or drink and, consequently, doesn't sleep. He's not nourished. When the body suffers it's not possible for its tenant, the mind, not to partake of the pain. Does sleep come upon the hungry fox?"

"Yes, I acknowledge the conjoined nature of body and soul, nature and intellect, of mortal man, because that is precisely what I teach. But when the teacher, who is poorer than a church mouse, is fired what is he expected to give to the printer?"

"My friend, I've never undertaken to solve the problem of how to get money from one who doesn't have it, though by its solution a great relief would descend among men. A professor of economics is more competent to answer this than I."

"Therefore, you're telling me to get lost?"

"God forbid, but let me ask: Do you teach for free?"

"No, because the baker, the butcher, the greengrocer, and all the other rascals give nothing away for free."

"Likewise, I don't print gratis. Behold what is written on my sign: 'The Charge for Every Line Is Fifteen Lepta.' Your pamphlet amounts to about one thousand lines, therefore . . ."

"But don't you print literary articles for your subscribers?"

"Subscribers? Do you know how rare a bird of passage that is? Reproaches, satirical poems, and generally all that the penal code includes among terms of abuse, insults to one's honor, false charges, defamation, these are for the printer the field, the vineyard, and the olive grove."

"These are the manure of Augeus, from which plagues are nourished. Lo, the other beasts of Athena. I understand, I understand. . . ." And he stormed out in a rage.

But as he continued down the narrow street, his first rush was calmed and he tucked the manuscript under his arm. "You're finished, Arabian Flutist," he muttered, "you'll get what you deserve. When I get the money to print my pamphlet. . . . And I won't subtract one word, either. I'll even add some, maybe. You'll pay, pig, for the grapes you've gorged on. But how can I earn this money? With my *Grammar!*"

He rushed toward his lodgings, replaced the manuscript under his arm, and returned to the printing shop.

"Sir," he said, "I bring you the distillation of my work for many years, the ripe fruit of my old age, my sixty-year-old *Grammar.*"

"For me to print?"

"Yes, to enlighten those who travel in darkness. Behold the lamp!"

"Is this according to the new system?"

"Well said. It does not use foreign phrases, nor does it ape, err, or barbarize. It is a violet-crowned Athenian maiden."

"The aged Elpiniki, then?"

"It does not stutter. It does not stammer."

"But does it drivel?"

"Sir." Hephaestidis, indignant, was unable to find the proper word, but he was reluctant to use a phrase that might provoke the printer, whom he wished to render amenable.

"Don't be upset. I don't think that you plan to spend two thousand drachmas in order to become a bag maker supplying fishmongers with wrappings for salted cod. My job is to publish printed matter. Respecting your age, though, I'd like to urge you, in your own interest and without regard to my own, not to cut open your purse."

"But I wasn't proposing to spend my own money. I was offering to sell you my manuscript."

"I'm not about to change my mind."

"Consider it, though."

"What's the point? There's a committee that advises the ministry of education on school matters. The schools use whatever this committee approves. They could even sell coal for gold. Otherwise, you're casting pearls before swine."

"My *Grammar* . . . to be judged by the committee for schools, one of whose members is the Arabian Flutist? Then I'm lost!"

"Watch over that Athenian maiden of yours on the bier until she reaches seventy or eighty. If that zombie gets any balder, she won't need a comb."

The bile of Hephaestidis bubbled over, reaching the limit, and he was unable to utter a word. Retrieving the manuscript, he turned his back and repaired to his lodgings where, unable to find an outlet, he leaped about like a mountain goat that encountered impassable rocks everywhere.

"Jackass journalists and slaves! Boorish bondsmen! Creatures of committees! Printers!" he gnashed his teeth, "I'm undone, finished!"

It would not have been difficult for him to get the necessary sum from Thanos's mother, whom he visited and no longer called Kamino but Madame Barbara. He was proud, though, and hated the suppliant's life, considering it undignified to borrow when he could see no way to repay the debt. If he wished, it would have been simpler to borrow from Tassos, who had returned from his trip two days before and at that moment was entering his house with Iapetos. Both were in a more than usual good mood, having just come from a tavern where they'd had a few drinks.

The schoolmaster, roaring with frustration, was pacing nervously in the hall when Iapetos encountered him.

"Look at Hephaestidis," he laughed loudly, flinging himself on a sofa. Tassos had also taken a seat. "Doesn't he look as though he's giving birth to an irregular verb of the aorist second conjugation?"

Hephaestidis shot him a vicious glance and made a fist. "Right now," he said, "I wish all of Greece had one head."

"To chop it off, I suppose, as a mistake."

"What's got you so angry?" Tassos asked.

"Stupidity, abomination, malignancy!"

"A godless disrespect for grammar?" Iapetos suggested.

"The villains. He called her Elpiniki. Accusing this ageless siren of driveling."

"Who's the villain?" Iapetos stifled a laugh.

"The villain! The glutton. Instead of offering, he wanted two thousand drachmas."

"Who and why?"

"The abomination. The peasant! The Boetian boar!"

"For what?"

"To typeset and publish the light."

"Two thousand drachmas, Hephaestidis? It is easier for a camel . . ."

"Yes, a camel and a lousy one at that, but this camel can carry the load of many jackasses."

"Listen, Hephaestidis." Iapetos fought a smile. "There's a way, if you're willing, to earn much more than two thousand drachmas."

"Is it honorable?"

"Most honorable and much easier than a schoolmaster's life. Say the word and it's done."

"Go on."

"I can get the minister to assign you to oversee a 'muck eater.'" He broke out in laughter. "A dredger, in other words. . . ." He could not finish.

"Methinks," Hephaestidis interrupted, "you're a wine-soaked muckraker yourself."

"Don't be angry, Teacher," Tassos said. "It's true, we've had a few drinks, but he said nothing to enrage you."

"Did he not call me a muck eater? That was the voice of alcohol I heard."

"He's not suggesting that you eat muck. The job involves supervision of the machine by which harbors are dredged of silt and mud."

"It hurts my feelings, Teacher," Iapetos said soberly, "that you consider me lacking the proper respect for you. Listen and you'll see that my offer is favorable and, I can even say, most flattering, *éminemment flateuse.*"

"Let's see how you propose to emerge from the mire yourself."

"I'll come out as white as a swan. Listen to the fantastic tale of this mythical beast, named the muck eater or dredger, about which the Father of History knew nothing. This all-devouring beast was born in England out of Hephaestus and Harmonia."

"A most unsuitable marriage," Hephaestidis relented somewhat.

"For this reason it was born a monster."

"Without the grace of the Immortals."

"But Greece, having entered the harmonious chorus of civilized nations, is obliged to be free of mire and, no new Heracles having come forth, the beast was purchased from England for five hundred thousand drachmas. Two Englishmen with credentials in the business of dredging, at a monthly salary of twenty pounds sterling, accompanied the beast to Calabria, where they turned it over to Poseidon. Our government, however, not satisfied with the merely ideal, demands absolute perfection. The British may be masters at fabrication, but the Germans are their superiors at repair. The two British metalworkers, compensated by the government, returned to their country, and the supervision of the beast was undertaken by another child of Hephaestus."

"Another Hephaestidis?" the old man muttered, furious once more. "Why not say it?"

"I assure you, Teacher," Iapetos struggled to suppress his laugh. "I intended nothing of the sort. Listen. The beast was then turned over to another child of Hephaestus, a Bavarian this time. Said Bavarian Archimedes received the pieces of the fragmented beast with a charge to reassemble and, at a monthly salary of six hundred drachmas, exclusive of every other expense and including an assistant's wages, to breathe new life into them. But on route to Athens, he could not to fit together the assorted parts and tried like Procrustes to file them down. He was in no rush, either, since he'd promised to have the beast assembled in Modon within the year. After exhausting all the special credits and funds and accomplishing nothing, though, the Bavarian Archimedes, instead of assembling the muck eater threatened to mire the treasury itself and was dismissed. But the government, having choked on a mosquito and later deciding to swallow the camel driver as well as the camel, acknowledged that the Bavarian was not up to the challenge of the dredger, though he devoured without profit a great deal of money. To compensate the treasury, therefore, he was appointed supervisor for the drilling of an artesian well, a skill of which his countrymen in their water-rich homeland are ignorant, still at the salary of six hundred drachmas, though his pay was garnished in order to indemnify the money futilely expended on the dredging machine. Notice the ingenuity of the plan. Until the

Bavarian Archimedes reaches the center of the earth, or has bored clear through to the other side, the government has been compensated to the last obol; and if the well succeeds, it has achieved both objectives with the same investment."

"The dredger is delayed, then?"

"Behold, Teacher, we have arrived at the crux of the matter. The government sees everything. So that it will not suffer the fate of Pelops, whose shoulder, as you recall, was never found, the dredger must have a foreman, seated at the wheel and guarding the parts of the beast. This is the position I offer you. It is honorable and undemanding. You can, if the spirit moves you, supplement your grammatical text with new forms of the aorist while gainfully employed."

"Vile drunk. You want me to be known as Hephaestidis the Grammarian of Muck Eaters."

"Forgive me, Teacher, but it seems to me to be better than Apollonius the Difficult."

"The American is right," Hephaestidis exclaimed with a shudder. "Common sense does not exist in Greece." He left the hall and the house, not knowing where he was headed. "What can the masses think that is important?"

While wandering outside the city, he met his missionary friend, whom he had not seen since arriving in Athens. Unable to hide his sorrow, he told him something of what had happened. Why not, at a monthly salary of two hundred drachmas, the American suggested, undertake a commentary on Holy Writ or a series of tracts concerning Christ's ethical teachings? This work was more honorable. Hephaestidis, unemployed as he was, asked only that he have full control of the commentary, without anyone's intrusions, corrections, or changes.

A few days later, while seated in a coffeehouse, he read among other things in a newspaper the following: "Concern has been expressed about the muck eater that has devoured millions. N.N. has been appointed supervisor. Worthy. Worthy. Worthy."

"Behold," Hephaestidis said to himself, "what you had almost become: a victim of the villainous muck eater."

The Symposium

The party of Iapetos and Tassos had not taken place without reason. They had been hatching a major plot for quite some time, laying the groundwork carefully and celebrating the good omens of an assured success. The worship of the fatted calf surpassed every other in their hearts, and each set out to find his own Golden Fleece. Iapetos, though for the present observing a serviceable truce, expected eventually to carry off Ephrosyne as plunder.

The presence and care of Thanos in the Ayfantis home displeased him, certainly, but like all the affluent and self-conceited, he deluded himself, dismissing Thanos as a dog in the manger and unworthy of the prize that belonged to the bold, the charming, and the clever. Nevertheless, he did his best to find a way to rid himself of this annoyance, and events seemed to be coming around to this goal.

Tassos, unaware of the secret machinations of his coconspirator's fantasies, was even more positive. After having sailed along many coasts in search of his own Colchis, he had finally found safe harbor, blown in by a propitious wind. Though he lacked education, his mind was keen, and he was a quick study. Arriving in Athens with his Thessalian spoils, he cast a rapacious glance around for loopholes in the law through which he would advance to his goals. It did not take him long to see that these loopholes involved the national lands and the national properties.

The first National Assembly of Greeks, after serious deliberations, decided that the national lands, available after the eviction
of their Ottoman owners, should not be seized once more by new
conquerors. The new constitution, in one of its articles, forbade
the disposal of these lands without the consent of Parliament, per-
mitting this only in extraordinary cases. But nothing occurred in
time; the provisions of the Assembly at Pronoia concerning the
distribution of national lands were not effected before King Othon
arrived from Bavaria, nor were those men successful who, snuff-
ing out the light of the National Assemblies, proffered their little
lamp as the only beacon to the many and to the close friends of
the new leader and the nation. They erred, however, because the
regency found itself in the dark and was compelled to use the
privileged sulfurous tinder to illuminate the Sphinx's new riddle:
land without people for people without land.

The torchbearers of the fog-shrouded Teutonia, and as many
unrecognized prophets from that same land, had come to ply their
trade in darkness. They weighed, calculated, estimated, and bal-
anced all the opinions and maxims, after which they funneled and
filtered and percolated and extracted the most delicate flour,
which is useful for everything. We must not deny the cleverness
of this design when we compare it to the dull simplicity of the
fellow citizens of the missionary who had just hired Hephaestidis
to provide his commentary on Holy Writ. These potato eaters of
the North American antipodes, unable to square the circle, could
merely triple the triad and, being very primitive and childlike,
classified their own lands into three or four categories, appraising
them at so much an acre. The prospective buyer, be he foreigner,
native, aboriginal, or immigrant descendant of Adam, took pos-
session of whatever land suited him and, once he paid the agreed-
upon sum, became master of his holdings. Now these small-minded
squatters have become solid and portly, multiplying like ants

while suffering, unfortunately, from an oversupply of food. We, on the contrary, have retained unspoiled that inseparable co-dweller of the Greek, hunger, and, not tormented by the ailment that ravages the life of the rich, do not need to whet our appetites with the mineral waters of Carlsbad and Wiesbaden.

During a dialogue in *Plutus,* Hunger asks Chremeles "what good thing" he wishes to accomplish and learns that he wants to expel Hunger from Greece. But nothing, Hunger responds, would "do men greater harm" than this.

How can our paternal government have misunderstood the great-great-grandfatherly Aristophanes? First it proclaimed the law of 20 May 1834, by which all the soldiers and sailors, no longer able to serve, and therefore unable to farm, would receive up to 240 *stremmata.* For ten years the government would keep track to see if the land was being cultivated by its holders; otherwise, it would undertake its cultivation itself. In the event that the government itself failed, ownership would be assigned to the municipalities. Only then, after proving themselves good Robinson Crusoes for a decade, would the warriors of Marathon and Salamis become holders of their share. This was succeeded by the law of 26 May 1835, after which all those of Greek blood received two thousand drachmas' credit toward the purchase of land by auction, to be amortized at 6 percent a year for thirty-six years. Thus, two sources of wealth bubbled up with only one drilling, one to the Greek landowners and one to the treasury. The law of 1 January 1838 finally rendered phalanx notes acceptable in all auctions and introduced this new article of commerce into the market, by which means whoever is able to receive the sanction of Jacob's validation may purchase the rights of the firstborn revolutionary warrior and famished Esau for a mess of pottage.

The most intelligent spokesmen had often attempted, through a tornado of reports, to inform the uninformed economic ministers of every clan and hornet's nest, but these, being drowsy, said, "Let's postpone the more important matters for tomorrow."

Tassos, however, immediately grasped the ins and outs of the system. Greatly aided by Iapetos, with whom he had formed a silent and anonymous partnership, he learned about the best available land, located in Trivae, a village in the Peloponnesos.

Tassos supplied himself at once with the requisite phalanx notes, obtaining them at 70 percent below their face value, once more with the agreement that unless converted into cash they would remain with their miserable holders, who were deprived of every means of exchanging them for land.

With a substantial sum of money on his person, he traveled to Trivae and found it better than he expected, with vast stretches of fertile farmland irrigated by abundant wells. The unhappy villagers had spared no effort to become owners of the land they'd farmed since time immemorial and on which they'd always been serfs, repeatedly seeking the support of all the archons of the province, who were quite willing to accept the gifts they brought and who promised infallibly to employ their great and manifold means. What they had set aside for the purchase of the land, however, had been spent on these honorable gift devourers, though nothing had been accomplished. When Tassos arrived, they were despairing, having nothing left to give to those who had gobbled up their credulity as prey.

Tassos moved very carefully to win their trust. He was in their midst by chance, he claimed, brought there by other affairs. His sojourn in Trivae he explained by professing illness and was grateful for the care offered him there. He listened apathetically to the Trivaeans' complaints about their problems and finally expressed amazement that, despite all their efforts, they'd been unable to attain their objective. With Athens he seemed to maintain a daily correspondence and, in the letters of Iapetos, ministers were mentioned as close friends. His sympathy toward the plight of the Trivaeans appeared to increase imperceptibly and, while giving money to the local boys who brought him ancient coins or vases, he revealed himself to be generous and extremely wealthy. In the course of his convalescence, he became godfather to the infants of various villagers, whom he astonished by his gifts.

The idea for the villagers to seek his protection emerged of its own accord and without his provocation. Initially, claiming serious preoccupations and major concerns to which he needed to attend, he sought to avoid the issue, but eventually, giving in to the repeated requests of groups of villagers, he promised to look into the matter for them. For himself, he wanted nothing, however, no gifts, no retainer, no sacrifice at all. He had only one request to make: he must have their obedience and complete trust. If they listened to the gossip and slander of the evil-minded, he'd withdraw at once and no longer pursue the matter.

In a short time, he managed, through the auspices of Iapetos, to begin the proceedings toward the auction, and the villagers, seeing Tassos surmount the previously insurmountable obstacles, were even more devoted to him, considering and venerating him as a savior sent from on high.

On the day before the auction, Tassos assembled all the villagers and explained his plan.

"Matters must be expedited," he said, "so that I can be in Athens before the current ministry collapses. Who knows what may happen? Tomorrow, other ministers, not friends of mine, may be appointed and all my efforts up to this point will have been wasted. If our validation is not approved, we have nothing. I'm not asking you for any money. I don't need any. I've arranged, you see, to get phalanx notes, for which the treasury must be reimbursed. These notes have been ordered in my name. For all these reasons, and to resolve matters quickly, and because the notes have been issued in my name, the land has to be granted to me. This is the reason you must petition the government, according to our plan, saying that you are poor people and without resources, that you fear the village lands may be granted to strangers, to people capable of harming you, that you know me well and have known me for many years, that we have many and various ties, and that you would consider it a great boon if the government approved the land grant in my name, since as a favor I gave in to your tearful pleas, et cetera, et cetera. You must believe that I have absolutely no intention of keeping these lands."

"Yes, yes," they all exclaimed.

"If anyone here has the slightest doubt or would like some reassurance, let him speak up."

Everyone was silent.

"Are you all agreed, then?"

"You have our blessing, O Man of God."

The petition was signed, the auction was concluded, and the following day a doxology was chanted in the church at Trivae, in which the villagers, in tears, embraced each other as during Eastertide and escorted their savior to the edge of the village, where he kissed them all one by one.

"May God repay that man." The village elders, knowing well the evils of serfdom, sighed deeply and raised their hands to the heavens.

Tassos brought his spoils to Athens, planning to legally transfer his property with Iapetos's help. After the legal documents were submitted to the proper authorities, whose decision was expected, the two partners met at the most elegant inn of the capital to feast on the most varied foods and selected wines. Their faces were merry and they joked about everything.

"You wicked intriguer," Iapetos said, "You put the Trivaeans in the sack and tightened the knot so that no one can loosen it."

"Until the approval is on my pillow, I'm saying nothing. A doubting Thomas."

"The petition and sobs of the villagers moved the minister to tears."

"Be joyful, devil, in your satanic works."

"The plan was devised in *your* diabolical brain, though the words were those of the guileless Iapetos. In operettas, you see, music directors are also given credit."

"If we weren't alike, as the adage has it, we wouldn't become in-laws."

"To your health, then in-law."

"To your health."

"And the villagers consider you their messiah. . . ."

"If their blessings are listened to, I'd become a saint for sure."

"It's only paradise you lack, vessel of election. But I'm sad that we must part, you for the upward path, I for the downward. Still, before you leave to taste the sweetness of paradise, you must sip the tartness of this Rhine wine."

"I prefer the Madeira, but as a favor to you . . ."

"Suppose now, my noble lad, that you get the approval. How will you appear before the Trivaeans after all those promises and litanies and doxologies . . ."

"And why should I wear out my days with those beasts of the Lord?"

"To cultivate your lands and receive a large income."

"I don't intend to become a farmer and to ply the plow in the prefecture of Tiryns. I'll send Skias in my stead to let them know what it is I want."

"Skias is a good and worthy man who won't let them forget that they have a master, but you should also send a trustworthy agriculturist. You have your brother for this."

"Yes, yes . . . the idea is interesting. Thanos would direct and oversee the villagers and Skias would apportion the profits: one for me, one for you, and one for me, and one more for me, and so on. Marvelous."

"You want to squeeze them to the last drop. The ewe must be milked as long as she gives milk daily."

"We'll let things ride a bit. There's time for plans, once we get the approval. Then you'll see what we set up, always with your suggestions. But tell me, rascal, how you've been entertaining yourself during these lean times?"

"Moderately well. I started a passionate and most complicated drama, but the first act . . . died unpleasantly on me. Now I'm enjoying myself with episodes and windfalls."

"I don't follow."

"I'm nibbling on salty and tart foods, to whet my appetite, until the main course."

"You've found, then, something like a . . . mouth-watering olive?"

"An olive most succulent."

"The champagne's here."

" Pop it, and hail to the Spiritual Bacchus of Champagne."

"Hail, hail."

"Listen:

> What is champagne but a spirit
> leaping forth out of a wineglass,
> with its bubbles sparkling over,
> draining all your cares away?
> Hurrah, hurrah, hurrah!"

"Brilliant, Iapetos, if these verses arise from your own noodle. . . ."

"If you doubt my versification, then listen some more:

> What is champagne but a stallion
> charging lightly 'cross a field,

> breaking silence with its snorting,
> vaulting, frothing,
> with a spirit daunting?
> Hurrah, hurrah, hurrah!"

It was from this carefree and playful drinking session that the two partners encountered Hephaestidis and told him the story of the dredging machine.

»»» 14 «««

Iapetos Caught in the Act

Thanos soon recovered, thanks to the care of those who loved him. The simple heart of Kioura had much to do with this. It was she who nursed him, coming and going from the invalid's room day and night and caring for him herself according to the doctor's orders. Ayfantis and Ephrosyne saw him often during the day so that time passed imperceptibly.

Being locked up with savages had made him so misanthropic that he thought he would be happy to withdraw to the heart of the most remote wilderness, far from contact with the dregs of society.

Suddenly finding himself among people whose every mood was good and every word pleasant reminded this outcast of the affection that springs eternally within the bosom of a family. In one moment he had acquired father, mother, and sister, all of whom loved him ardently and were dedicated to his therapy. It was not surprising that he would think he dreamed and that his ophthalmia bordered on the illusory. Often he would not respond to Ephrosyne, unaware that he was being addressed, because her melodic voice, so sweet to his ear, washed over and transported him.

But gradually his sight was restored and he saw that his good fortune was real. This insight was not unmixed, though. He wanted to accompany them to Thessaly, interested in Ephrosyne's plans for what they would accomplish there. He'd found refuge among them when persecuted; now free, he did not consider it right to continue being supported as though a ward, without being of some use to his benefactors.

When alone, feeling oppressed, he searched for a way to attain autonomy while still living among them. He would show his gratitude by visiting the family occasionally, he decided, and wanted to mention this to Ephrosyne but did not dare, knowing that he would appear ungrateful and sadden her, though he himself was sad without admitting the reason.

After Thanos arrived, the terrible apparition of Iapetos appeared less often and more palely to Ephrosyne, especially since she was preoccupied with preparations for leaving Athens. It could not be completely effaced, however, and sudden noises startled her when she was alone. Far from Athens, no longer afraid to see Iapetos suddenly materialize before her, she hoped to forget him.

Despite their objections, Thanos left the Ayfantis home when he had fully recovered, no longer wishing to be a burden. He did not refuse outright their suggestion that he follow them—this would have seemed ungrateful—but he neither packed his luggage nor decided on a course of action.

Tassos, by this time, had achieved his goal. The phalanx notes had been approved and their certification was in hand. Accordingly, he dispatched Skias to the estate to take over as his agent and to unfurl the banner of his authority in the village.

Iapetos's suggestion not to depend on the vengeful Skias but to engage Thanos for the agricultural management of the estate made sense and Tassos adopted it. But to convince Thanos to leave Ayfantis and his family, he claimed that the government had finally acknowledged their paternal rights and, in an effort to make up for its previous neglect, awarded Trivae to the two brothers. Because the full value of the estate exceeded the sum of the award, Tassos needed to use the notes to complete the dotation process, and only his name appeared on the documents because Thanos had been absent at the time. As a good brother, though, and not wishing to quibble, he would divide the estate equally and share it in common. There was only one condition, though, a very just and natural one: that Thanos, since he was experienced in these matters, manage the property. Tassos, as a soldier, was required to serve with his unit, hoping to be promoted and to honor the Vlekas name. As far as drawing up documents that demonstrated joint ownership of the estate was concerned, he said nothing, nor did he intend to do so.

So convincing was he that it never occurred to Thanos to suspect anything. Already predisposed to going off on his own, he accepted the proposal gratefully, believing his brother and not considering his statements improbable or unlikely. He went at once to the home of Ayfantis to announce his decision.

Ephrosyne was speechless with dismay at this unexpected desertion, and Ayfantis himself was saddened, though he could offer no argument against Thanos's claiming the paternal share and wishing to run his own affairs. Only the words of Ephrosyne might have prevailed against these claims, but she would have had to admit her feelings and to confess the pain she experienced while Thanos was in prison. Otherwise, Ayfantis had to divine what was hidden in her heart. As long as these words were unspoken, Ayfantis had to consider Ephrosyne's sympathy as a mere token of her feelings. If his experience and observations had been more seasoned, he would have seen that the sympathy of these young people was deeper and would have raised his arms toward Him Who held in His power the hearts of men, then placed his own on the heads of Thanos and Ephrosyne, subjecting them to the divine will and exclaiming: "Thy will be done."

Ayfantis, thinking of Thanos as his own child, was unhappy that his son was leaving and, considering Ephrosyne's affection sisterly, viewed her bitterness as a reaction of a girl whose brother was leaving home. The assurance that they would write to each other and the hope that Thanos would return assuaged this bitterness. Thanos pledged both.

After setting his affairs in order, he would fulfill the sacred obligation to visit his benefactors. He was agitated, which affected his speech perceptibly, and he wished them all the best from the bottom of his heart. He gave his solemn word to see them off, but as the hour of their departure approached, the parting grew more difficult, and he felt as he had when he was thrown in prison. The decision was irrevocable, though, and his sense of honor did not permit a change of mind.

Another sort of diffidence made Ephrosyne hesitate to express her own feelings to Thanos. She did not wish to show her weakness to Thanos and used every means to hide her anguish, pretending to be concerned for him only as a friend, afraid that, far from people he knew, among men unknown to them, he would be subjected to greater dangers. Her father's consoling words that the master of a large estate would be self-sufficient were like fuel thrown on fire. If he needed no one in the future, he did not need friends now, either. How could the large landowner of Trivae be expected to remember Thessaly, those people in Domokos, silk cultivation, and the like? Often, one who wishes to console, because ignorant of another's secrets, reopens rather than soothes a wound.

At any rate, the preparatory phase of Iapetos's plan to distance Thanos was successful. In fact, after Thanos had declared his decision to go to Trivae, the delay of Ayfantis's return benefited Iapetos, allowing him time to execute the rest of his plan. This critical assault would demand all of his tactical craft, since if it failed he could no longer hope for anything. He could not address, directly and frontally, the one person so cruel as to ignore the courteous declaration of his passion. He would conquer the inaccessible and fortified village only by way of tortuous paths, and he arranged his siege thusly.

The only person capable of exercising some authority over Ayfantis, Iapetos reasoned, was the Ottoman ambassador. As a resident of Thessaly, Ayfantis would not be able to leave Athens easily. Iapetos would make himself useful, gaining his good favor and making him his champion before their common interest was revealed. Accordingly, he devoted himself entirely to his attendance on the Ottoman ambassador. By daily visits, he passed on the day's news and whatever he had learned of a confidential nature, though it might have been only from his own office ministry, so that he would be considered an indispensable eavesdropper. Since he would know more than others in the diplomatic community what had been said, done, and proposed, the ambassador could not possibly undervalue the importance of this service by which he would be distinguished. Iapetos, like Argus with his hundred eyes, would be sought after as a font of information, fulfilling Frederick the Great's adage that "an ambassador is a privileged spy." Planning to become so indispensable that the ambassador would come to depend upon him as the nearsighted depend upon their spectacles, Iapetos, by one means or another, would request the ambassador's intercession, manipulating his sense of rivalry, and ask for Ayfantis and Ephrosyne as his reward. Next he would publish a pamphlet in which his love affair with Ephrosyne would be revealed, with details about alleged secret meetings, and circulate many copies near Ayfantis's residence, delivering some to the house itself, so that Ephrosyne's fall would be known to all.

This scandal would compel the ambassador, as guardian of a subject's reputation, to promote the wedding to her lover as the only solution for a young woman slandered by evil and jealous men. How was it possible for a young man, known to the ambassador and admired for his great accomplishments, not to make happy his beloved and, through her, her father, whom she loved above all in the world? Ultimately, Iapetos hoped to break the impasse on the one hand by embarrassing Ayfantis with scandal and defamation and, on the other, by employing the fear, instinctive in Ottoman subjects, at arousing the ambassador's wrath by seeming to ignore his exhortations and thus turning the authorities in Thessaly against him.

Because his efforts for the ambassador were welcome, his success seemed assured and he saw a clear increase in goodwill. But more time and greater service were needed, he believed, before he felt bold enough to request this favor of the ambassador.

Until the second act of his well-made play, Iapetos, unable to bear the mustiness of monotonous inactivity, occupied himself in what he called episodes. Every evening, late, he would visit a lady who had been left alone all night by a husband dominated by a chronic passion for cards. This "juicy olive," as Iapetos referred to her when talking to Tassos, glowed more because of her opulent flesh and the care of her autumnal beauty than because of her tender youth. Not satisfied with the pale radiance of her complexion, she rouged her cheeks and dyed her eyebrows and lashes. With hair as dark as her deep-set eyes, her face was a battlefield between dark and light. Her voice had two tones: abrupt and brazen toward familiars and servants, mild and sweet toward guests. Her face had a teasing look, and she walked with a provocative sway. Her conversation was not without wit, and she learned everything, though not from her spouse, whom she saw only during dinner and then staring mutely ahead as at an oracle. Her children, two angels whom she loved madly, went to bed early. Seated at the divan, she would chew mastic gum noisily and wait for a rational animal with whom to exchange her shallow ideas and to indulge in pleasure, free of her absent husband and the boorish and tiresome chatter of her servants. The witty lady had read the novels of George Sand and recounted charmingly the most enchanting, though questionable, of their episodes.

As it happened, on one of the days that the votaries of chance did not gather in their lair, the good husband came home early, before Iapetos had fluttered off. Since the bedroom had only one door, Iapetos was compelled to dive under the bed. Out of sorts because the card game had been called off, the husband entered, breathing heavily like a drowsy old man, ignoring his wife who lay on the bed, pretending to be asleep. Making for the bed at once, as was his wont, he groped mechanically to untie his shoes. Unfortunately, while creeping, Iapetos had dragged the slippers with him among the many pleats of his *foustanella,* forcing the husband to bend over and, instead of his slippers, encounter the lover cowering in the corner, like a mouse suddenly attacked by a cat.

"So, our couple isn't made up of two only," said the card player, "but of three. Come out, sir, so that I can see what you look like."

Reaching his hand under the bed, he took hold of the thick, greasy hair and, dragging Iapetos out like a sack of hay, attacked him with fist and foot. Before Iapetos could stand and defend himself, a nearby chair smashed over his head and showered him with a rain of wounds. During this time, the chaste Susanna had fainted twice and thrice unnoticed, with no harm to her exuberant health. Her husband would not have stopped his mad pounding of the supine Iapetos if the servants, drawn by the racket, had not rushed in, their intervention putting an end to the beating and bringing the infuriated spouse slowly to his senses.

He wasted little time sending for a public prosecutor, an examining magistrate, and a police officer, then turned to his wife, who still lay in bed and whose complexion had not changed, insensitive to the shock undergone by her spirit.

"Madam," he said, "you haven't been as lonely as you've complained about being. From now on, though, you'll have greater freedom to entertain yourself, because as far as I'm concerned, you are entirely free."

"I'm innocent!" The wretched woman leaped from the bed, hands tearing at her hair and scratching her cheeks, flung herself at her husband's feet, and sobbed. "I'm innocent."

"Yes, yes, just as Beatrice in the opera. We'll see what the prosecutor says."

The prosecutor, police, and constables arrived at the same time and, having written their report, led the exhausted and battered Iapetos away. Until the courts would come to some decision, the husband left home and asked the advice of the best legal minds on how to divorce the wife without returning her dowry. His gambling friends offered many suggestions, hoping to share in his windfall, since their good friend had been losing for some time and, having run through his fortune and assigned a portion of his salary to them, was now playing on credit.

From this incident, the unhappy Iapetos, who had often capered over ditches, fell unexpectedly into the most ordinary of cesspools, from which he would emerge only by passing through magistrate's court. The tragic episode was reaching farcical proportions throughout the city, and those who whispered about the supposed sudden illness of the wretch, who claimed to have fallen on cobblestones at night, began their ridicule. As the time of the inquiry neared, the rumor grew and, when he was dismissed from the civil service, he knew he was completely destroyed. Entrepreneurs and plotters like himself, not mimicking actors in nonspeaking roles, surrounded him, sharing his pain and offering help and alliance against the covetous husband and cruel tyrant of the ever-obedient and all-suffering pure-hearted wife. The support of these dedicated friends was probably harmful to Iapetos, the undisputed protagonist of these exploits, because the trial was quickly committed to open court as a way of making an example of him.

"You didn't ask, sirs," the lawyer for the plaintiff said, "if the culprit had been caught under a mastic bush or a holm oak, since we proved to you that it was under a bed. The situation is not a new one, according to Theophilos the comic, not the jurist:

> As a large ship, its rudder snapped by the cable,
> is persuaded to find
> another port at night. . . ."

The lawyer of Iapetos, brought up in the school of the ten rhetoricians, used the argument of those who wished to avenge the murder of Eratosthenes: that Iapetos was ambushed by the home-hating card player with designs on the dowry. Observe the legal agreement by which he turned over one part of his salary to his gambler friends. Observe the virtuous husband, observe the affectionate father, and to what uses he devotes his salary. Why all these wounds? If my client had been caught red-handed, why was he beaten senseless? The prosecutor, the policeman, all say that they found him mute, comatose. This terrible act was administered at the door. Why then were witnesses summoned to the bedroom and not the front door?

The defendant, dressed in black, wiped tears from her eyes and interrupted her attorney often as he narrated an *Iliad* of wrongs to which her husband had subjected her.

"Don't, for God's sake, sir," she pleaded, biting her lips, "don't say that about my husband, the father of my children . . . the man to whom I've vowed trust and devotion."

"Allow me, please." The attorney, according to prior agreement, rejected her pleas. "It's not you saying these things," he pressed on. "It's your lawyer, who's obligated by law to tell the entire truth."

But none of these devices did any good. The defendants were found guilty and were placed in the same jail, as though living together would be punishment enough.

If these faults had not found grace from the jury, they nevertheless did so from the prison guards. All Iapetos's friends and champions came to pay their respects, bringing entertainment and drinks and transforming the jail into a many-celled museum of every imaginable pleasure not meant for the approval of strict guardians of morals, unless these were courtiers and decorated by Anakyndaraxus Sardanapalus: "Eat, drink, make love: nothing else matters." The insignia of Sardanapalus depicts two hands snapping fingers over a head. Iapetos and his partner in crime certainly deserved the rank of grand brigadier. The great achievement in the life of Sardanapalus was that he was able to terrify the cities of Tarsus and Anchiale on the same day. Perhaps the libertine partners of Iapetos who thought and acted like him hoped to do likewise in Greece.

Iapetos did not limit himself to recreation only while in jail. By permission of his good jailer, he was smuggled some nights out to his friends, where similar orgies, worthy of the pen of a Hogarth, were performed but at greater leisure.

Yet whatever Iapetos had schemed against Ephrosyne came to naught and, as the adage had it, "He lost the sow, the talent, and the jawbone."

The Village Trivae

Trivae, worked from time immemorial by the inhabitants, lies inland about ten hours from the Alphaeus River among hillocks that crown the extensive and irregular plain. Though the earth is fertile and the topsoil deep, the land was barely cultivated, most of it covered by couch grass that is good only for mules and dry in the autumn, with no trace of verdure or vineyards, which could certainly be expected on the sunny slopes. The entire region, full of rolling hills and mounds, was bare of vegetation.

The villagers' huts, humble and wretched, patched together from cast-off material, were hidden in the recesses of two hills, scattered about indiscriminately as though a lack of space and previous disasters had diminished the number and the well-being of the inhabitants.

Plowing was a common effort, and there was no trace of borders or fences. Each person had his own animals, one keeping goats, the other sheep or pigs, the next mules, and only the oxen for plowing were common property. This mixed system, holding communally whatever was harvested from the soil and owning the rest individually, was retained from time past, and the villagers were unaware of any other way of life.

The land had never belonged to them, though in Ottoman times it was owned by a *spachis* who received his tithe. At that time, however, the villagers themselves came up with the taxables and, through their elder, paid an additional head tax to the chief of the district, who passed it on to the pasha.

For many reasons, they did not cultivate more grain than they consumed themselves: no one needed it locally, and marketing it meant transporting it to the sea by pack animals, fording rivers without bridges, negotiating forests and precipices and gorges, and in general suffering everything ignored by the person who travels by carriages. It was not profitable. Their few livestock provided cheese, for which the Trivaeans, as a matter of fact, had some renown; wool, from which they wove their clothes; and cash, provided by those who owned mules by renting them to travelers. Whatever money was earned, especially from these sources, was hidden in the earth so that their Ottoman master would not think they prospered and increase his demands on them. "This the Mede should not keep," as Herodotus writes. Relatively few silver coins, which constituted their dowry, hung from the necks or dangled from the foreheads of their daughters. Their language was the commonly spoken demotic, not the Albanian, so that only by chemical analysis could the Fallmerayer thesis be proved that the blond blood of the ancients flowed through their veins without admixture. After the Revolution and the restoration of order, it seemed that their fortunes would improve because the lord of the manor, the *spachis*, had left and the head tax had been abolished. But then the "double-tenth" was introduced, which was the tax of usufruct, whose collection by the so-called rentiers gobbled up both head *and* shoulders. Before the tax collector could measure and receive his portion, the farmer was forbidden to touch his haystacks or be considered a thief. When the long-awaited tithe collector finally arrived, the villagers learned through a donkey's disaster how distribution was effected. The procrustean collectors counted by full measure and the villagers kept quiet. When the so-called double—really a quadruple—tenth was taken, the villagers, without complaining, were obliged to transport the grain on their own pack animals to the storehouses of the collectors in the capital of the prefecture; they would not be free until the grasping Harpies had sated themselves with the best of their crops.

This was also a major reason for the lack of progress in agriculture. According to the tax system, the land baron, whose estate may take up the entire prefecture, pays no tax at all if he does not farm the land, while he who owns only enough for his burial plot and cultivates that of someone else bears the entire tax burden on his shoulders.

Our economic authorities assure us that in the Greek south it cannot be otherwise. As Shakespeare says, "Thus says Brutus and Brutus is an honorable man." The civil servant is the natural partner and collaborator of every worker, taking a larger share without effort or risk: without effort, first, because he passes on his share to the tax contractor or, in the Doric, the tax confiscator, and second, without running any risk, since when the contract is validated, according to the most recent findings, the cost cannot be lessened even by an act of God.

In this way, the tax collector, if he is a careful student of what is to his own benefit, a *diligens paterfamilias,* will act according to his own interests, which are never identical to those of the taxed; for while the civil servant is the constant collaborator of the farmer, the tax collector appears like a cyclone only at the hour of reckoning. In times of rich harvest, therefore, he expects to be recompensed for the times of poor crops. And, in truth, when the Trivaeans, God willing, fared well, they suffered great misfortunes from the tax collectors, who would not begin the process until promised an adequate recompense. In order to save the crops exposed to the elements, the villagers accepted whatever terms the tax collectors demanded, learning the truth of the adage "nothing to excess," which convinced them that it was wiser not to cultivate more than they themselves could consume.

This, however, was not the only time the villagers fed the vultures. None of the civil servants, soldiers, or gendarmes who passed through Trivae was convinced that the wretched huts sheltered poverty, believing only the voice of their own greedy stomachs. Since they completely lacked arbor or viniculture, the Trivaeans were exempt from the excessive evaluation of their annual revenue, but they were shorn as baldly by the pastoral tax as a seven-times-shorn she-goat, with the threat of being sued for false declaration hanging over their heads. If we add to this the monitors and enforcers of this taxation and the tumult of municipal and parliamentary elections, we would not wonder why the Trivaeans lived like nomads in temporary camps and in patched-up huts, under the same roof with their livestock, despite springs of abundant fresh water, blocked at their source, that only provided puddles in which their hogs rolled.

What made them invulnerable to despair and degradation was not the priest, who mechanically fulfilled religious rituals and was as ignorant as they, who could not inspire them with the holy treasures of the Divine Word by raising their spirits to scorn the transient evils of the present and to ennoble them so that they could anticipate the eternal verities of the future, but the hope of becoming masters of the land that annually decimated their children with endemic fever and that covered the bones of their ancestors, who for centuries had longed for the day of liberation.

Lured by this hope, they invested little of the money they had buried and the dowry coins their daughters had draped around their necks or hung from their heads. And the acquisitive notables of the prefecture, purged of the Turkish name of *kotzambasi* but not his morality, had done nothing to improve the villagers' lot, remembering them only before elections, because they had no gold or silver, merely cheese and wool to give.

Lately, the unexpected arrival of Tassos, who professed to be burdened by illness yet seemed sensitive to their problems, fanned the virtually extinguished flame of their hopes. He appeared as though *ex machina,* initially reluctant to help, then—out of noble sentiment—magnanimously proffered his own money, unlike their notables who demanded payment in advance. Though he appeared in the guise of Tassos, a lieutenant, he was like an angel, according them grace, attributing his benefactions to the troubles they unjustly suffered. He dominated their thoughts and inspired them with faith and security.

Nevertheless, the sale by auction using bonds with Tassos as signatory did not occur without noise or tumult. All those in the prefecture involved in the process knew that Trivae was being auctioned off and, it was claimed, for the benefit of the villagers. Yet this stopped no one from erecting as many obstacles as possible to the procedure and suggesting that there seemed to be many irregularities, while also assuring the villagers of their eagerness to be useful. But the Trivaeans no longer trusted these predators who pretended to have become tame. These altruistic patrons, unable to bend the authorities to their wishes because of the precise commands from Athens through the connivance of Iapetos, made innuendoes about Tassos, warning the Trivaeans of a trick, though even a blind man might have seen the trap when the petition to the government requested Trivae be validated as a benefaction in Tassos's name. Whoever tells many lies is not believed even when he tells the truth, and the villagers ignored them: even if their generous lord were to trick them, they were still fortunate, since he lived in their midst and would lavish his wealth on them.

The auction was concluded, despite the advice and efforts of the provincial powers, proving them unable to do the villagers either harm or good; and so a stranger to the prefecture, not even a Peloponnesian, but a man of surpassing enterprise and great power, though unknown and obscure, was setting himself up in their midst, leading and sustaining the people and undermining the foundation of the long-established class. When to these resentments was added the outrage to local patriotism, an incalculable power emerged that would try to overturn everything and show this insolent fortune hunter "from a distant land," in their own words, "how many pears were in the sack."

At their first opportunity, the local powers showed their displeasure through the military draft. The municipality of which Trivae was a small unit was obligated to provide as many as three conscripts, but all three positions, as though by chance, were to be filled by lot from this poor village. Greek genius by then had already perfected the art of voter fraud, and the ballots containing the names of Trivaeans eligible for military service were, because of size and texture, readily ascertainable by touch.

In general, farmers or shepherds do not willingly give up their plows or crooks to take up weapons, but when the change from rustic freedom to slavish discipline is historically recent, the conscript considers himself lost and diminished among men. If the results of this draft were perceived not as a matter of chance but of injustice and fraud, the sense of bitterness is augmented, and only someone who has ever been unjustly treated can understand how infuriating this can be.

How the three lots fell to them the Trivaeans did not know precisely, but no one could convince them that the draft was fair, since every act up to then revealed a general animosity toward them and pointed to injustice. To make this even more obvious, their nobles told them that they should not despair since they had a great chieftain as their patron.

Downcast, the villagers gathered in the chapel, which was shaped rather like a pigsty, for a gloomy meeting presided over by Doudoumis the *paredros* and PapaVlasis the priest.

"The poor man has a poor fate," Doudoumis said. "They persecute us because we've found a good man to free our land."

"The injustice cries out to the third heaven," old man Lahanopoulos complained. "I've one son and he's to be a soldier! Who'll take care of the livestock? I'm old, my legs are crippled, and I've got two daughters to marry off."

"Don't despair," PapaVlasis consoled. "Justice isn't lost. With God's help we'll find it again. It was He who sent us this holy man to save us from the mouths of the wolves."

"Bah," shouted an old lady with a sharp, brazen voice, "by the time he hears about it in Athens, the regulars would have done in my child."

"Rest easy, Kyr-Asimina," the priest said, "he won't die that easily. As an only child your son is exempt. That's why you should draw up a petition."

"And who'll draw up this . . . partition . . . for me? May the lightning bolt wither them."

"I've neither father nor mother," a young man, recently shorn, cried out. "If I go into the army, who'll take care of my sisters and brothers? The wolves will gobble them up."

"You're all yelling at once, like dogs in a sheepfold!" Doudoumis covered his ears. "Who can hear what you have to say?"

"Of course, you think we shout too much," Asimina noted. "They're not taking *your* boy. D'you hear? He wants us to be quiet while they slaughter us!"

"You do well, Kyr-Asimina, to scream. Scream some more. Then tell us what's come of it."

"Yes, yes, that's what my old mother used to say. Those not in the dance know a lot of tunes."

"And won't you let us tell you what we think?"

"All I know is," old Lahanopoulos shouted, "that I don't have a penny to free my child. All the big shots gobbled everything we'd set aside and now they're taking our sons, too."

"May Charon take them," Asimina crowed. "Didn't I sell my deep pot the last time we gave money to pay off the tax man!"

"Yes," the rest shouted at once, "we've got nothing left. Let's not start all over again. Give money to the mayor, to the eparch, to the secretary, to the bailiff. Give till everyone is full."

As in a choral dialogue, whenever the outcry stilled, Asimina took up the response and, leading the refrain, said: "With their *give, give*, they've wrenched the soul from our lips."

Bewildered, Doudoumis and PapaVlasis looked at each other.

"I know what to do," young Tagaropoulos grunted. "Chop off my thumb. The army won't want me after that."

"What a mess," they shouted with one voice. "Must our children be mutilated to be saved from their grasp?"

The outcry of the men and the wailing of the women were joined by the cries of the infants and the squeals of the children so that the gathering sounded like a flock of seagulls caught in a squall.

At the height of this polyphonic outburst a man—pointed out by Doudoumis—was seen approaching from far off in haste. They all quieted to learn who he was and from whence he came.

"Is he coming to take our boys?" they all groaned. "We won't give them up, won't give them up."

"Hold on. It won't happen so fast." Doudoumis passed through the mob to greet the arrival. "Let's find out."

The traveler neared them, surprised at the uproar. "What's happening?" he asked Doudoumis. "Is Tassos's man coming to transfer the lands?"

At Tassos's name all grew silent, staring at the new arrival.

"Why," Doudoumis asked, "has the auction been approved?"

"Certainly. I'm here for my commission. Tassos is sending Skias so that the transfer can take place. He'll be here tomorrow with the ephor, so prepare yourselves to receive him."

"You see?" PapaVlasis said. "The all-compassionate God has heard our prayers and is sending us a good man to put an end to our sufferings."

"Blessed be God," all chanted.

"You are great, O Lord," Asimina shouted, crossing herself. "Our great-grandchildren will be talking about this miracle."

All the faces were immediately joyful, all adversities forgotten. Even the children responded, leaping for joy and kissing their parents.

Doudoumis gave orders for the stranger's reception and the decision to receive Skias the following day with every pomp was unanimous.

The next day, indeed, the villagers went to meet him as a group, receiving him with cries of joy and cheers. On their return, the scampering children led the procession, the boys doing somersaults, followed by those beating drums and clashing cymbals and blowing bagpipes, in total cacophony, followed a few steps later by Skias, arrogant and lordly, occasionally swinging his riding crop. He had twisted mustaches, and there was something dog-like about his face, while his bloodshot eyes glimmered in the morning's glow. The smirking ephor, whose dress was dull because he was unarmed, accompanied Skias and was obscured by the glittering armaments that surrounded him, borne on the bodies of the four ruthless and tipsy guards. Behind them came the rejoicing village men, chanting. The women, most carrying screeching infants, brought up the rear, accompanied by their daughters, who sang.

Thus they arrived at the church, where Skias and the ephor reclined on rugs and pillows, viewing the villagers arrayed before them as they interminably sang their praises. Remote from the crowd and upset at the villagers for the clumsy arrangements, Doudoumis, tall and slender as a reed, and PapaVlasis, from whose white robes only his ruddy cheeks, guileless eyes, and black beard emerged, served the coffee with a rustic gentility, trying to divine Skias's wishes from his look.

After the guests had drunk their coffee and smoked, the ephor took papers out of his sack and began to speak. Everyone stopped talking.

"From all indications I see the event for which we've gathered here today is a joyous and desirable one, and that you are celebrating it as though it were a feast day."

"Yes," all exclaimed. "It's our salvation."

"Before I draw up my report I'm obligated to put the question to you. I've come today to install the honorable Lieutenant Tassos Vlekas in the village of Trivae. I ask, do you accept him as lord and master of all surrounding lands of your village?"

"Yes, yes."

"From this point on, he and only he is lord of these lands, arable or not, of the units and waters and in general all things that are found within this region. You all agree and give your approval?"

The ephor recited these last words carefully, stressing each one and glancing sardonically at the villagers, who turned to each other, puzzled by the repetition of the questions. Not perceiving anything behind them and, following the voice of the one who responded more promptly, they all answered, "We want him."

"And whoever doesn't like it can lump it," one added and got a big laugh.

"Why so many questions?" another asked the person next to him.

"That's the way things are done by the big shots," was the reply. "Only they know why."

"Then listen to what I write in my report so that all who know their letters can sign it. 'Today. . .'" and he read aloud.

Besides Doudoumis and PapaVlasis, only two or three signed, but the ephor had brought along two witnesses who certified as to the wishes of the illiterates.

Skias was the last to sign, saying, "I may as well mark my 'X,' too."

The ephor gathered the documents to leave. "I hope you enjoy your dealings with Mister Vlekas as you wish."

"May he live, may he live," all exclaimed. "He'll be our master and may the Lord keep him strong."

"Don't leave us, Mister Ephor," Skias said, "before we enjoy our *kokoretsi*."

"Yes," Doudoumis added, "the food will soon be ready."

In a short while the whole roasted lamb was brought on the spit, at the end of which were coiled the roasted innards and organs, while Skias tore apart pieces for the ephor and himself, squirting wine from the leather sack lest he become thirsty, then immediately passed it to the ephor, who in turn passed it on to the henchmen of Skias and the two witnesses seated behind them, dismembering more roasted lamb for them as well.

"We have very cold water, too, " Doudoumis suggested.

"But that's for sheep," Skias replied.

In this manner the gullet was sated and washed, arriving in small increments at the point the German poet brilliantly depicts by saying: "I feel the same cannibalistic pleasure of five hundred hogs," or, according to the contemporary expression, "the force of five hundred hogs."

"Vre, Kaliakouda," Skias said to one of his henchmen, "let's see that bag of guts of yours dance."

Kaliakouda, known as "the Crow," immediately leaped up and, taking the hand nearest him, that of a grizzled old man, began a circle dance which all followed with delight.

The ephor, having completed all the forms of installation and claiming other pressing obligations, said good-bye to the representative of the newly installed Tassos and, again with a smirk, paid his respects to the villagers, whom he left dancing, but still hungry, around the supine and fully sated Skias.

"Go to the good, ephor," the villagers shouted.

"And good riddance," added a jokester and was applauded by all who heard him.

Skias, having drunk much from the wineskin and lulled by the dancing, fell asleep, and the villagers, not wishing to disturb his slumber, went elsewhere, taking along the four henchmen of Skias to continue their circle dance. Happiness, repressed and virtually unknown in Trivae, burst out and overflowed their hearts so that the elders, who had barely sipped wine, were drunk, fired their rifles, and emptied whatever they had stored at home to contribute to the general revelry.

The bright orb of the sun, pacing on its downward journey, gilded the hilltops with diamond and emerald and silvery sparkles with its last rays. The emerging shadows, as accompaniments of the wandering apparitions, silenced the human tumult and lowered the wings of well-being. The villagers' noise gradually stilled until it stopped altogether.

To these events only Skias was insensible, snoring away on his pillow. But his henchmen, Crow, Wildcat, Fist, and Club, carried him by the arms and legs to the cleanest hut, chasing away the protesting and squealing hogs that dwelt there also. In his deep stupor, Skias thought the villagers were speaking to him. "Tomorrow, clowns," he muttered. "Tomorrow . . ."

The Farewell

While these things were occurring in Trivae, the time was coming when Thanos would bid farewell to his good patrons, go to the estate of which he was half owner, and begin his work. The joy he felt in returning once more to the pleasure of his agricultural regimen was marred by another sentiment, unknown until then. As the day of separation neared, he and Ephrosyne became downcast but did not acknowledge the reason for their melancholy to themselves or each other. While they had been talkative before, expressing their changing moods effortlessly in conversation, they were now silent even when alone, gazed at the ground, not at each other, and spoke in monosyllables.

Assuming that their separation would be brief, Ephrosyne could tolerate being away from Thanos, but when his plans changed, she stopped preparing for the trip and made no mention of a timetable. Something, apparently without premeditation or invention on her part, seemed to come up every day that needed attending to. Occasionally, the daily tasks that occupied her back in Thessaly came to mind, but her low spirits, now that she was in Athens, did not allow her to concern herself with them. Thanos had also promised not to leave first, but his decision to establish himself in Trivae was irrevocable. As all human affairs are liable to change, however, this decision, too, could be canceled by something unforeseen, such as some resistance to the installation of Skias. But nothing unexpected occurred to change what had been planned.

Time, whose heavy feet advance steadily and irrevocably, seemed to hurry toward the day of their separation. But nothing disturbed the monotony of that unpleasant prospect, nor could Thanos share in Ephrosyne's joy when she learned what had befallen Iapetos. He barely knew the man and was ignorant of what had occurred between them. But the humiliation of Iapetos would have provided no relief, either, since it did not alter things. If both knew what Iapetos's motives had been, Thanos might have taken another course of action, pleasing to both him and her. The plans of Iapetos had been frustrated, but the intentions of Tassos needed to be uncovered as well: what Trivae represented, how it was acquired and how maintained. At present, though, all these factors were among the unknowns, and the sequence of events followed the path that led from the first cause.

If Ephrosyne, struggling against her desire, had not maintained her self-control, she might have caused her affectionate father to misconstrue the truth of her feelings, and this conflict between her sense of honor and her passion animated the usual serenity of her face, clouding its cheerful character and making it sweeter still.

Nevertheless, her father saw that she was troubled and unhappy, which she would not have been if she'd learned the lessons of experience that time smooths many rough places, joins opposites, and solves many problems. It was on this wise physician of human sorrows that Ayfantis placed his hopes, believing that Ephrosyne's worry would quickly be stilled by news of Thanos's progress. To predispose her for the good auguries of the future, he spoke often in her presence with Thanos about the management of his estate, about agriculture, and about the most proper means for its development.

The situation in Greece would not improve, Ayfantis believed, if the large landowners continued to lack specialized knowledge and sufficient capital to implement methods appropriate to every specialty of their fertile land. Agriculture would not develop as long as the land was owned by those who did not oversee it and was occupied and cultivated by those who did not own it. He compared owners of large villages who lived far from them to those who tilled their own lands. While the former grew poorer daily, and certainly did not improve their holdings, the latter increased their substance daily. But the slow and gradual improvement of small landholdings did not make for the rapid progress of the nation's agriculture. The large landowners needed to outlay money to develop proper techniques of cultivation, while the master of a small corner of land rigidly continued the traditional ways without deviating one iota.

Why every means of encouraging innovations was not employed to draw the capitalists to invest in the land perplexed Ayfantis. Greece possessed abundantly watered earth, rich topsoil suitable for every type of cultivation, a temperate climate not subject to sudden changes, and in most places a sea nearby for shipping the produce, yet everything was as parched as in a desert. Nature had provided everything possible; the rest was up to man. The soil of Greece was not the most fertile in the world, certainly, but Ayfantis, from what he himself had seen, judged that Greek agriculture could at least be as productive as that of Thessaly, which still bore on its neck the yoke of subjugation.

He was neither a specialist nor a student of political economy, but having overseen the management of his own affairs, he had a large landowner's experience, and he loved the subject, so that in talking to his daughter, he digressed and forgot his initial purpose, trying to show her ways by which Thanos could become prosperous.

There can be no agriculture worthy of the name, Ayfantis believed, if ownership of land is not complete, free, and legally secure. If he could imagine that men, with names unknown to him, were proposing that land be owned in common, he would dismiss their ideas as monstrous products of sick imaginations. The earth demands great initial investments. Its sources of water are deep, and to reach them one must drill, but much plowing and weeding is required before the soil yields its abundance. If farmers could not depend on a secure and stable system to enjoy their profit, why would anyone, unless he were an eccentric, decide to farm. He had seen men of this sort spending large sums in Athens for amphorae and the like, which to him were worthless, but they believed that these antiquities belonged to them and were certain they could be passed on to their heirs. "But when I farm land and don't know whose it will be tomorrow," he'd remark, "why shouldn't I plant crops that provide an immediate yield?"

There was no stability and security for the farmer in Greece. The large mass either cultivated the national lands temporarily, or waited until they had fraudulently obtained their plots, which they then allowed to go fallow, or were uncertain that they would retain them, while the large landowners, deep in debt, wandered in a labyrinth of court proceedings or, because of brigandage, dared not inspect their estates, or as employees, because of bad management, covered their losses from the public treasury. The few who possessed a share devoted most of their time and effort to small-scale agriculture. Ayfantis, without the gift of prophecy and feeling only the invalid's pulse, predicted that time would do what law did not: the incompetent landowners would lose all rights to their estates to those who cultivated the land. This change would not occur peacefully or without suffering. Whatever had been written about the cultivation of grape arbors, wine production, silkworms, or agriculture in general was worthy and admirable in his opinion, but what he did not know was who would implement these studies or for whom they were being developed.

Ayfantis also advised Thanos on dealing with the villagers. The estate owner and his villagers could not work together if their interests were opposed. Reconciliation could not be achieved if there were no moral bond between them. When the landowner tried to improve the peasant's lot, recompensing him justly for his labors and increasing his substance, when he came to his aid in times of bad harvest or of disease, when he provided a dowry for his daughter or cared for the orphans of the deceased, the peasant would no longer consider him an oppressor for whom he labored as though under a yoke, but as one sent by divine providence. But in Greece the opposite takes place. The landless peasant considers the estate owner a usurper who has denied him his inalienable rights and the share assigned him from on high. If an adequate stretch of land were granted every peasant for his ownership, agriculture—as though by a magic wand—would immediately advance to the second and third phases of its development, quadrupling the public revenue.

"I don't advocate that all the land be turned over to the peasants," Ayfantis emphasized, "only that a large portion be set aside for the establishment of large holdings. You and Tassos, for example, would do yourselves much good by setting aside part of your holdings for the complete ownership of the peasants. Whatever you give up will be returned to you a hundredfold. You'd gain their goodwill and devotion from the start. By giving them the means of furnishing their homes, you'd help them provide all their necessities, and they wouldn't envy your own prosperity. As they prosper, they marry, have children, and multiply. . . .

"But do you think your fields will remain idle? Far from it! By overseeing, by supplying seeds and making other investments, you'll encourage them to join together willingly to devote much of their time to cultivating the earth, which will provide them, not a loss, but a clear profit. I'm basing myself on what I've seen here in the Greek state and feel sorry for the wretched situation. Because the landowner believes it more advantageous to be free of every risk and care, he not only demands the farmer's labor but expects his initial investment as well. How costly do you think this disastrous indifference is? The farmer can't make substantial investments in seed and other necessities, which means that he tills a small portion of the estate. But if a lean year, or some other misfortune, comes to pass, he'll be ruined and the landowner will not help him, since advance payments run counter to his theory, especially at a time when there's no likely profit. Besides, how do you suppose the farmer feels toward a landowner who never provides, yet always demands, who always receives, who deducts his share in advance and takes the larger share?"

Ayfantis offered these thoughts from his experience, evidence that they agree in large part with Askraios, who himself had not read the latest studies *On the Art of Becoming Wealthy* by the impoverished author So-and-So.

Hesiod instructed the great Perses, his younger brother, to "be generous with grain / so that the Man Who Sleeps in the Daytime won't be getting at your goods." Concerning herders of oxen he suggested "a forty-year-old man, still young enough to follow / the plow" with "a full four-piece loaf to eat," since "such a man will keep his mind on his work / and drive a straight furrow." Disagreeing with Hesiod, who suggested that the "hired man [be put] out of doors" and "a serving-maid with no children [be hired], since one with young to look after is a nuisance," Ayfantis taught the contrary: that female workers be provided dwellings of their own and that humane concern be shown to nursing mothers.

Thanos took these teachings to heart, having received practical experience during the time he'd worked at the Ayfantis estate. If other considerations were not on his mind, he would have pressed for details, but by then Tassos had been posted to his unit, making difficult their communication. Nevertheless, he planned to urge his brother to accept these suggestions and agree to implement them.

These long consultations did not reassure Ephrosyne, because Thanos, if he planned to put into practice all of her father's teachings, would need to live in Trivae many years before becoming prosperous. Since there was little likelihood for change, her sorrow deepened.

Evil presentiments tormented her about the future, and her resistance to them wavered, especially in the struggle between her love for Thanos and the demands of virtue. On the eve of their parting, as much because of the disorder of their moving as of the maid's carelessness, the lamp before the icon of the Virgin Mary, which must never be extinguished, was overturned, spilling the oil. Ephrosyne paled and shed tears as large as pearls from her blue eyes. Unable to sleep, she glanced all night at the icon of the All-Holy Mother of God, imploring forgiveness for her offenses but not daring to ask for relief from her sorrows. She who held in her bosom Him who bore away the sin of the world would, without supplications, help Ephrosyne, when worthy of her grace, attain that for which she longed. Her serenity and her tender look toward the Child, glowing from the light above and promising to shine upon the earth once more in the future, calmed the sufferer and sent her divine solace during the darkest shadows of the lonely night.

The first rays of the brightening day broke into her thoughts, which were succeeded by the bitterness of parting. The household was busy early and many family friends and countrymen of Ayfantis gathered to say good-bye, among whom was Thanos, who stood in a hidden spot in back, silent and abstracted, unseen by all except Ephrosyne who occasionally appeared. Ayfantis finally noticed him as well and called him over for a few more pointers in estate management, supplementing those that he had developed more extensively a few days before. He asked Thanos to correspond often and keep him informed about the progress of his work, promising to share his opinions immediately, happy to pass on to those in Greece the knowledge he'd gathered through long experience. Thanos gladly accepted the offer, especially since he would have news of his benefactors, whom he promised to visit without fail when the affairs of the estate had been settled.

The tide of those coming and going to bid farewell continued until midday, when many, Thanos among them, escorted the travelers to Piraeus. From there they would board a steamship to the island of Syros, from which they would travel home by sailboat. Ephrosyne, seeing nothing, sat mutely on the deck, staring at the coast of Attica as it gradually receded until only an ethereal mist shrouded the mountain ridge. Behind this, the declining sun appeared to be carrying away her hopes and pulling her with them on the silvery wake, churned by the steamer's wheels, of a marbled sea.

After their departure, Thanos, too, left Athens without having received a reply from Tassos, for his stay had become onerous. He attributed his brother's lack of response to the many duties he had now as aide to the chargé d'affaires of the so-called Leader, the director of the border guards. Since there was no doubt in his mind that Tassos would consider this advice sound, he asked his mother to send the response on to him at once and suggested that she remain in Athens until he prepared a suitable place for her in Trivae.

Barbara gave him her blessings, admonishing him not to upset by his clumsiness matters that her Tassos had arranged so nicely.

Thanos in Trivae

The day after the peasants had greeted Skias, their elders, led by Doudoumis and PapaVlasis, paced toward the cabin where Tassos's envoy slept and stood there in a troop waiting to hear from his lips the preludes of the good news of which he was bearer.

His bodyguards emerged and he followed, with a baleful look on his face. Glancing at them savagely and twisting his mustaches, he said, "You came to learn our wishes? Since there are five of us, we must every day have an *oka* of mastic raki and ten *okas* of wine. Every morning there's to be a lamb and a goat hanging by their forelocks outside my door. Is that understood?"

The peasants were mute, their necks bent, afraid to look up.

"That's for every day," Skias continued. "But on feast days, I want appetizers, too, an occasional ewe, a fatted piglet, a calf, and the like. And plenty of cheese and bread. Good-bye."

The mob of peasants, dumbstruck, drew back as he glided through them like a fish, brandishing his whip, followed by the henchmen.

When he had distanced himself and when the peasants found their voices again—indeed, they found them simultaneously in a symphony of guttural sounds—they blamed Doudoumis and PapaVlasis for not bringing up their problems.

"We have to keep track of who's giving what!"

Doudoumis and PapaVlasis quieted them down, recommending patience, though they themselves did not like the looks of things.

Nothing was said for many days because the leaders were afraid to speak out and, since his demands were carried out precisely, there was no need for Skias to say anything, either. But the peasants could not sustain these expenditures for very long. Besides, sowing time was approaching and the peasants had to know who would provide their seed and the obligations of each at harvest time. Add to these the anxiety of the conscripts facing the draft and their neighbors' needling with their "how're you getting on with your patron?" one can understand the village's mood: feverish, but almost comatose, the stage preceding paroxysm.

Skias, however, was executing precisely the instructions of Tassos to guard the village lest someone else take it over, to avoid discussions with the peasants, a stricture that applied to his men as well, and to eat only what was necessary. In Skias's opinion, though, his bill of fare was as frugal as possible. More instructions would follow with Thanos, who was to supervise the farming. But neither Skias nor the peasants knew anything about this.

The importunate demands of the peasants compelled Doudoumis and the priest to go to Skias as suppliants. The elders and both leaders gathered early one morning before the cabin of Skias, who was surprised at the encounter when he emerged.

"What do you want?" His booming voice had the knees of the first two trembling.

"To learn . . . if you're in good health," PapaVlasis stammered, "and to inquire . . . of our good master, Kapetan Tassos."

"You see, we're like fish in water. When I left him, Kapetan Tassos was as fresh as a daisy. Since then, he hasn't had time to wilt."

"Does he write when he'll be coming, so that we'll enjoy his presence?"

"Bah! What work does he have here? To dance himself silly with the old-timers? He's out with his unit."

"And when, pray, are we to separate?" all asked, rather astonished by the puzzled reaction or encouraged by Skias's manner.

"Separate? Whoever heard of such stupidity? To separate from your master! What do you clowns expect from Kapetan Tassos?"

"But wasn't it for us he bought the village? Didn't he promise to give it to us?"

"God on High! Whoever saw such cattle? What do you take Kapetan Tassos for? What's 'power of attorney' mean?"

"We consider him our benefactor, sent by God, to watch over us, someone whom we'll venerate as our master."

Saying this, they all bared their shaved heads and bowed, extending their right hand, palm up.

"So . . . what do you want from me?"

"We'd like to hear the good news, to learn from his magnanimity what's his and what's ours, how we'll manage to sow, what . . ."

"D'you hear that? What nonsense is this? I'll bow before you, Madam, but you've got to give me your husband and take this dummy. What foxy peasants you are!"

"By the Holy Cross, Kapetan Tassos promised us our village. He should tell us what his costs are and we'll take out a mortgage. . . ."

"Leave me alone, all of you. Crafty peasants! Weepy Christers!"

"But we have no seed. If the village isn't in our name no one'll lend us money. We've run out of cash. We've no more wheat. We're out of livestock."

"I'll give you a taste of what you need, you rotten Morean tubs of guts."

Raising the whip, he brought it down on the suppliants who surrounded him. "About face!" he shouted.

The whipping made them all turn and run, but Skias, not satisfied with this and wanting to provide a more thorough lesson, chased them. Being the swiftest runner, he caught up to PapaVlasis and then, one after the other, all of them, measuring the length of his whip across their shoulders.

The cries and moans of those fleeing and being whipped terrified everyone; many, emerging from their huts to see the lamentable sight, rushed back as fast as their feet could carry them. Skias would have chased them, too, profusely beating them regardless of their prudence, if Asimina were not among those in flight. In her rush, she dropped first her right clog, then her left, skipping from one foot to the other in the meantime, inciting the laughter of the Man with the Whip. Coming back to the road, panting and happy about his achievement, he said to his men, "No matter how fast they ran, I managed to put some sense into them. Did you see how they looked, with their 'Lord have mercy on us'? They came to have words with *me?* They can come and keen for us after we kick the bucket. Kapetan Tassos didn't take this village with his little sword to turn over to those rheumy-eyed beggars."

Contemptuous of what he considered crocodile tears, Skias believed that "the fox knows many things, but the hedgehog knows only one big thing." Nevertheless, the whip rent the Temple's curtain and dispersed the haze that had misted the eyes of the Trivaeans; they saw that they were not dealing with a perch but with a scorpion fish. A dirge and lamentation broke out, but no one dared as much as cough and, seeing the Man with the Whip, all of them fled.

His triumph was complete and, as he had hoped, prudence won out completely, for fear and shame abide together.

But the silence that followed was only superficial. Those who had lost every hope and did not dare to groan aloud decided to meet secretly to discuss what to do without exciting the suspicions of Skias. Before daybreak, and by different routes and with ears perked, they gathered behind a small hill where they could not possibly be seen even in midday. For a long time no one dared speak first nor had any suggestion to make.

All in the neighboring villages were pleased at what had happened, which was no longer a secret, and contemptuous and apathetic toward them, since after so many warnings they'd still fallen into such an obvious trap. They had no one on earth to turn to but themselves. Worst of all, they had no legal recourse, since in their petition they had attested to their complete concurrence.

"Many are the whips of the evil man," PapaVlasis said, taking onto himself the role of consoler and wishing to provide an introduction to his exhortation, "but he who trusts in the Lord is encompassed by mercy."

"That's true," a young man more impudent than the others added, "you should talk about whips, since you're the first to have tasted one."

This impertinent observation incited the rest to expressions of indignation and, as usually occurs in times like this, the Trivaeans attributed all their misfortunes to their leaders. PapaVlasis and Doudoumis heard them by the carriage load. "You advised us. You told us to sign. Who knew Kapetan Tassos? It was your children he baptized." And a host of other comments motivated by the turnabout. In vain did PapaVlasis extend his hands invoking God, or the good Doudoumis plead for someone to listen.

"Betrayed!" all shouted. "They've betrayed us!" The uproar would have continued, becoming louder, if an old man had not reminded them that the Man with the Whip would certainly hear them. The name, Skias, stifled the tumult; they glanced toward the village, afraid to see him coming their way. After they'd had time to cool off, they knew that they should disperse quickly, before their meeting had become known, and they all turned to the leaders again, asking what their course of action should be. Many opinions were advanced, but nothing could be done without the cooperation of one of the powerful people in the province. Unlike the priest, who knew how to read, Doudoumis could barely write his name, and these were the beacons of the village. Who would draft a report to the government, setting out the fraud of the crafty usurper who had violated the most sacred pledges? It was impossible that the government, learning of this injustice, would not withdraw its approval and at least deliver them from their oppressor. They had lived under wretched conditions before, but they had never fed strangers all year long who repaid them with beatings. They had always known what to do at plowing time, while now they had no seed and didn't know what crops to sow. They had not been unpleasant or impertinent to Skias, yet this brute grew wild and would not listen to reason. He must not have had a mother or another woman to nurture him at her breast; a she-wolf must have fed him in wild forests. Who, at this point, would dare ask this man to intercede for the conscripts?

There was only one solution: plead with one of the powerful men in the province again to lead them out of the trap. All of them were openly hostile and joyful at their misfortunes, it's true, but on their part the villagers had virtually insulted them by ignoring exhortations and admonitions. But there was no doubt that in the province there was an interest in expelling this new-comer, who'd become a thorn in their flesh, and they would col-laborate as much as possible, so that the Trivaeans must not be judgmental toward their previous tormentors for trying to buy out the village in the past. Except for them, what other recourse did they have? It was better to turn to the most popular of the provin-cial leaders, since he would be more moderate in his demands, an important consideration since after their recent expenditures they had little left.

Such were their deliberations, each person adding his or her own comments, and the decision, after weeping, was unanimous, the execution of the plan being assigned once more to Doudoumis and the priest, with urgings to hasten.

There was only one protest and that from the impudent Tagaropoulos, who had incited all the indignation in the first place.

"First try whatever you agreed to," the young conscript said, "then I'll tell you what needs to be done."

But no one showed the slightest interest in what antidote his hollow bird's brain was hatching. Gloomy, they scattered once more, each returning to his work by a different path, while Papa-Vlasis and Doudoumis, accompanied by three of the more respectable villagers, marched off to the provincial capital to pay a visit to the notable.

The man they preferred was indeed more popular than the rest because, like Sisyphus tirelessly pushing uphill the stone of his effrontery, he would see it, as it neared the peak, roll down to the bottom again, whereupon he would push it back up. As a result, he often dealt with the powerless and used their backs as stepping-stones; they loved him because they considered him a victim of his labors on their behalf. His policies, which were flexible, he adapted to suit any party, waving over his head the Russian, the British, and the French flags at different times, so that in the name of these powers he seemed to develop tornado velocity. But since none of these great powers ever knew that it had a champion in this most significant of provinces, the poor man never received its gratitude. He never spent anything, his own property being fully mortgaged, but used the money of other, more simple folk, whom he had pledged to repay with interest once he had prospered, compounding these obligations and annually adding new debts to the old. The size of his indebtedness did not shake him, since he never tried to pay it off, and he managed to find new and more covetous moneylenders whenever necessary. He was convinced, however, that the three powers, as "great" as they were considered, were unable to know the interests of Greece and to accurately judge the significance of his own power. For this reason, already entering a new phase in his life, that of focusing on his own interests, he anxiously waited for the right time for the Eastern

Question to heat up in his province, and was certain that it would knock on the door of his home.

The home in question was dingy and dirty, out of keeping with the ostentation of his family's elaborate dress and of his gourmand's way of life. His spouse wore so many striking but inelegant earrings, necklaces, and bracelets that she might have made an effective display for a goldsmith as she sat, multicolored and palely fat, on a tattered sofa in her salon. Two benches and a plank table, all shabby and oil stained, constituted the furniture of the verandah, from whose cobwebbed walls hung pale and badly executed copper engravings of the de-Hellenized Telemachus of Fenellon.

But before the Eastern Question managed to approach, Doudoumis, PapaVlasis, and the three envoys knocked on the door of his house.

From time immemorial, those approaching a notable as suppliants bring as gift a lamb whose ears they twist on entering the courtyard so that its bleating will tell him that they have not arrived empty-handed.

Bowing down, the Trivaeans stopped at the entry and, persuaded by the nod of the notable, who sat on the sofa cross-legged, went in, PapaVlasis and Doudoumis sitting on the floor, cross-legged as well, humble and reserved, while the others remained standing.

The great man, with magisterial condescension, inquired after them, interested in all the recent events of the village, pretending to know nothing, surprised that he had not been informed earlier. To his queries, PapaVlasis and Doudoumis gave short responses, since these matters were common knowledge, whose repetition they considered tiresome, though it was unlikely that others would know many of the details. While this interview was being conducted, at times his wife, at times his adolescent son, or his servant, would enter and whisper in his ear, while he listened carefully, smiled, frowned, or shrugged, so that the villagers saw that more weighty matters occupied his far-reaching mind, barely allowing him time to listen to their pleas. Occasionally, he would utter a loud aside that an accursed ministry was asked to tender its resignation. Behold, these intellectuals, these so-called honorable men . . . these luminaries . . . have all been brought to trial . . . tested.

The ministry of Tassos was falling, Doudoumis and the priest understood, nodding to each other. And shortly, the great man, absorbed in thought, after another message, would exclaim, "These are good ministers . . . friends of mine."

After being fully brought up to date by the village representatives, he asked them what they wanted done.

"Save us from this godless man."

"Save you from the accursed newcomer," he replied somberly, "after he's tied you hand and foot? You want to shut the stable after the horse has run off. It's no longer a matter of healing the sick, but of raising the dead. . . ."

"When you notables want it, anything can be done. We'll kneel before you. We're at your mercy. And we'll bless you to the last generation . . . as long as Trivaeans exist."

"Prayers need a censer, and censers need incense, and without incense you can't venerate a saint."

"We understand, Your Eminence. But you know how poor we are, with our souls in our mouths."

"It's not on my account I'm asking. You know me. I've always given, never taken. Even the stones will testify to the sacrifices my family has offered for the Revolution. But up to this moment, even as we speak, what recompense have I had? Persecution. Disdain. Who among those foreigners acknowledges me? We've struggled for the nation's independence, and we're not sorry to have given even our last penny. But if only we could see the nation prosper! That's the frustrating thing! That's what consumes us.

To see you still enslaved after we've gnawed through your yoke with our own teeth. . . ."

"Yes," the Trivaeans sighed and raised their eyes to the heavens. "The Lord knows what we're going through. . . ."

"For myself, I want nothing. I've decided to live on very little. A dry husk of bread. I've said it before and I say it every day to my wife and children. But we'll work for the Motherland."

"May Your Eminence's life be a long one. Yours and your children's. We intend for you to be justly compensated for your efforts. If we free our village, half of it is yours and we'll love you like a father. But what do you expect us to give now, since the scavenger birds of Kapetan Tassos have devoured even our livestock?"

"I've told you, I want nothing. God reigns. After we've freed your village and you prosper, and you wish to give me a token of your gratitude, that's another matter. But now you need lawyers in various courts to invalidate the land auction. There will be legal expenses. Besides this, a report must be submitted to the government and sent to the proper office. Don't be misled that 'knock and it shall be opened' means that doors are opened to anyone who knocks. You have to know how to knock, and for this we must find the proper man. This and the other will require one thing and another. . . ."

Doudoumis and PapaVlasis gave each other a lamenting look. The notable maintained his silence, not curious to learn what was on their minds and, though present in body, appeared to be far away. Doudoumis finally dared to ask what the cost might possibly be.

"Including everything I've mentioned: the report, the trial, and so forth, now, in advance . . . only five thousand."

The wretched Trivaeans were overwhelmed by gloom and bitter tears filled their eyes.

"Yes," he added, "I see that for you it is perhaps a lot, but I quoted the lowest price, the very lowest. . . . God reigns. Perhaps even this won't be enough. For the time being, though, I'll make up the remainder. This is rock bottom. Think it over, discuss it at the village, and if you decide to pay the price, come back and I'll tell you what do to."

The decisive tone of his voice startled them. Believing that there was no other course and unable to ask him to pay in advance from his own pocket, they thought it best to leave and inform the others of the results of their mission. The terror that had overcome them all stifled every mournful outcry capable of expressing their misfortune, but their tragic feelings were clearly depicted in their faces.

At almost the same time, Thanos, alone and unnoticed, was approaching Trivae. He considered the advice of Ayfantis on his trip, but the clarity of his plans was disturbed often by the image of Ephrosyne, with whom his parting was even more powerful because it was wordless. The constant reminder of his ingrat—itude plagued him, and he saw her somber and silent face as a reproach.

"I shouldn't have been so ready to abandon them," he thought, "and so eager to rush selfishly to my own estate. They did everything they could to free me from jail and cared for me when I was sick, as though I were part of their family. Shouldn't I have gone with them to Thessaly to show my gratitude? I should have seen them settled in their own home first. They helped me when I was exiled and made me more happy than I was when in my own cabin. Only then should I have worried about the estate I know nothing about. But I rushed, I rushed. . . ."

Deciding to visit them after he had settled his affairs was not enough to calm his sense that he had been ungrateful. Besides, when could he be sure to have arranged his affairs? Evidence of his gratitude would be considerably delayed. Perhaps by executing the advice of Ayfantis and keeping him abreast of his work, he might afford him the happiness of knowing that he was a participant in a good work and had found someone willing to follow his teachings and to improve the well-being of the many who suffered.

Brooding like this, Thanos arrived in Trivae around sunset. The evening star that emerged from the darkness appeared even brighter, rendering the remaining stars visible. Though he had passed many deserted spots before arriving at his estate, the nearer he got to the village the greater his perplexity that, though the season was well advanced, and after torrential rains, there was no sign that the land had been plowed. His arrival was expected, he supposed, and he hurried his pace, as though a few moments mattered, thinking that the prosperity of many impoverished families depended on him.

Before entering the village he met Skias returning from a stroll with his bodyguards.

"Well, look who's here," Skias strode up to him, addressing Thanos as someone common and ordinary, not as his superior. He ordered Crow to take Thanos to the hut to rest, while he remained at the water hole to count the livestock that had come to drink, having suspected for some time that the peasants were hiding their number.

Thanos, annoyed at the conversation of the insolent Skias, followed Crow and, entering the hut, asked him about what had been happening.

The peasants, he learned, were lazy, deceitful, cunning, and cowardly. They had not sown yet to force Kapetan Tassos to advance them money for seed, but Skias would bring them to their senses.

Despite his outrage, Thanos listened, betraying his thoughts as little as possible, being assured now about the truth of what Ayfantis had said. He questioned Crow, who told him everything, describing the humorous scene at the whipping without noticing the reaction of his listener.

Only one thing remained unclear to Thanos: How valid was the claim of the peasants that the village was bought for them? Crow mentioned their belief to show how far the villains' audacity would go without the saving prudence inspired by the whip. Thanos, however, knowing well the duplicitous ways of his brother, was overcome by suspicions that a scorpion lay beneath every rock. That night, despite his exhaustion, he could not sleep, while the others snored away untroubled.

He was the first to leave the hut, emerging as the sun rose, and met the Trivaeans on their way to pasture their few animals far from the village and the glare of Skias and his henchmen. In the dusk, their faces looked even more gloomy. When they saw someone emerging from the hut, they hastened their pace.

But PapaVlasis and Doudoumis waited as a smiling Thanos, exuding encouragement, approached them. Their side of the story, however, upset him even more than Crow's narration. In their every word, he saw their submission to misfortune—grinding poverty, inability to cultivate, and uncertainty of how the harvest would be apportioned—and he felt a pressure in his heart. He could understand their doubt about his intentions, this self-described brother of Tassos, whose affable manner had tricked them and about whom they dared not express the slightest censure. Thanos's encouraging words may have been just another trap to prevent their seeking the support of someone else.

Thanos wanted to fulfill the promises made to them at once and asked which men in the province would lend them what was necessary to begin cultivation, promising to be unsparing in their support and offering his half of the estate as security. He expected to hear soon from his brother about his administration of the estate, as Ayfantis had instructed. But if Tassos could not understand where his true interest lay, willingly compromising with the interests of the peasants, Thanos would give up his share and leave for Thessaly. Ayfantis would approve of this generosity, he was sure, and take him back into his service after a sacrifice that agreed with his principles and conformed to his instructions.

PapaVlasis and Doudoumis were befuddled. They had just been given permission to offer half the village as security for the loan. What were they to believe: the lashes of Skias or the words of this alleged brother of Tassos, who had appeared suddenly and unexpectedly? If Thanos were really who he purported to be, Skias—as an inferior and servant of his lord—would have received him differently. On the contrary, Skias had given little sign of submission, not the previous day, nor today, because on leaving his hut and encountering Thanos, he did not bow but addressed him in the familiar and continued his morning walk with his henchmen, an absolute master.

The other peasants may have thought them obtuse, but Papa-Vlasis and Doudoumis did not miss these signs. After pondering all these things and drawing conclusions contrary to what they had heard from Thanos, they were unwilling to draw once more on themselves the wrath of the easily aroused Skias. They informed the rest of the peasants about this, but the other Trivaeans, not having the responsibility of PapaVlasis and Doudoumis, replied that Thanos's wish should be executed. If Skias did not like this, let whoever gave the order be held accountable.

Things were tight, the season of year was advancing, and the poverty of the village was increasing daily. The three conscripts were to present themselves shortly, too, and the peasants were not willing to accept many excuses. Expecting nothing good to come of it, PapaVlasis and Doudoumis, yielding to the will of the many to give the oracle another try, traveled once more to the distant capital of the province to negotiate for a loan.

The first visit to the notable had not eluded general curiosity. Those who shared in his altruistic goals toward the village took the hint and began their machinations. Though the neighbors kept careful track of the fox, they were unable to learn anything definite. In competing to snare the prey themselves, they used other villagers to sniff out the secret but failed because the Trivaeans, knowing from experience what value the altruistic cooperation had and how it could mistakenly be changed to opposition, were careful that their project not be betrayed and reach the ear of the satanic Skias.

When the curious, therefore, saw the two village elders, who had been thrashed a short while before, return to openly negotiate for a loan, mentioning a brother of Tassos and his generous offer of assistance, they supposed many things but could come to no conclusion. As was natural, PapaVlasis and Doudoumis mentioned the matter to their chosen protector, whom the skinflint usurers had already consulted as to whether they should consider lending the Trivaeans money. These were the men who, whenever their assistance was required, devoured the revenue and diminished everything, confusing the public so that no one would understand. Instead of paying the stipulated value to the public treasury on time, they deposited the interest on the revenue in their own accounts. Depending on the enriching debtors rather than on the creditworthy, they demanded that PapaVlasis and Doudoumis submit the documents of ownership. This way, their patron said to them, we'll have the means to examine the irregularities by the proper lawyers.

Though the remaining terms of the loan were daunting, the request that proof of ownership be submitted seemed reasonable to Thanos, too. Having nothing else to do until word arrived from Tassos, he wrote another letter, requesting power of attorney and an acknowledgment, in writing, that half of the land was his. Skias's presence was redundant, he noted, for the peasants were docile and submissive. He asked for a speedy response.

Thanos was under additional stress. Writing to Ayfantis he considered improper before implementing his teachings, but to keep silent was to be misunderstood. His only hope, a minor one, was that if he showed no displeasure toward Skias, but praised his zeal and manliness, offering an occasional clever remark about excessive and inappropriate severity, he might be able to appease and tame the savage. It was a vain hope, and he should have remembered the folk adage that "a bent stick can never be straightened."

»»» 18 «««

Return of Ayfantis to Thessaly

Because nothing unusual occurred on the return trip of the Ayfantis family to Thessaly, the monotony of the crossing allowed Ephrosyne to abandon herself to passionate thoughts. Her open, inquisitive, and vivacious nature, once serene and calm, had darkened considerably. She tried to disguise her sorrow, but it worked its way into her every thought, drawing her mind back to it, plunging her once more into apathy. Once this happened, little could arouse her interest and, if something caught her attention, it was only a momentary respite.

Her face no longer had its rosy hue, and her abstracted glances, her perplexed frowns, and her incoherent conversation were clear signs of her confusion and did not elude her father. It was then he understood how deep and powerful her feelings were. It was not possible to stop the decline or to provide a quick remedy. These sentiments were not hard to understand; in fact, shaken by his suffering, she felt an even stronger bond to Thanos, who, while being tested by adversity, had not altered his values.

Certain of his intuition, Ayfantis thought it unwise to ask his daughter to confess her secret, for it is only a beginning player who plucks the strings of his lyre harder than necessary merely to enjoy the clarity of its sound. Modesty would not permit his daughter to reveal her secret, and without prying into what should be unspoken, he often discussed the beloved with her, affording an outlet to her feelings and release from their burden, appearing unaware of the effect of his words. The skillful way he offered spiritual healing revealed the nobility of his character and the tenderness of his paternal love.

Ephrosyne sensed that her father knew she grieved, since what had happened and why was known to those involved. As long as his care and attention did not try to sound the depths of her suffering, it was somewhat reassuring that her secret did not elude him. Strolling with him on the deck of the ship and supported lightly on his arm, she cast her brimming eyes down to the parting waves.

Ayfantis regretted not having paid enough attention to what had been happening between the two, since he might have been able to correct things. He would make every effort to do so and to learn how Thanos was doing when they reached Thessaly.

Ephrosyne, too, was eager to reach Domokos, where there should be letters from Thanos to her father. She had had signs that Thanos, though he may not have suffered as much as she, was not indifferent to her, either: he had been cheerful and happy before, but after deciding to establish himself in Trivae, his mood changed, and when they were leaving, he was agitated and taciturn.

The more she learned about Thanos, the more she saw that there was nothing blameworthy in him. He was a good man, somewhat reserved, perhaps, but this, in her opinion, was appropriate to men, who were naturally acquisitive and in whom self-interest was preeminent. She did not think Thanos greedy for devoting himself to the management of the estate, merely acting in his own interests. Moreover, it was natural that, having received no encouragement from her, Thanos had no reason to act otherwise, bearing in mind his position in life. Suppose he had come to Thessaly: what could he be but a foreman on her father's estate? Suppose he had sensed her feelings toward him and did not wish to see her burdened, did it follow that he liked her? Certainly Thanos himself, considering these matters, could have arrived at similar conclusions and, modest as he was, judged it the ideal time to break off the relationship, unaware that the separation would cause her inconsolable sorrow.

There was nothing more she could expect from him besides knowing that he prospered and that their separation would not be temporary, but permanent. . . . She did not wish him to be a refugee again, to ask for asylum in Thessaly, and to be so impoverished that he needed patrons. . . . It had been a dream and, like a dream, it had vanished. Would that the dream had not lasted so long. . . . Would that it not have been so clear that it resembled reality. . . .

These thoughts, as diffuse as the clouds that loomed on the horizon, roiled Ephrosyne's mind as the ship plowed through the cresting waves. Ayfantis sensed her thoughts and feelings but said nothing. She was his flower, unique and priceless, uprooted by a swollen brook and wrenched into a wide flowing river that rushed toward an uncharted sea, while he, the anguished gardener, ran along the bank, hoping an obstacle stopped it before it was swept into the bay.

Between father and daughter there was something like animal magnetism—because without having spoken, by way of intimate, instinctive feelings—each was aware of what the other thought and felt, but neither wished, because it was unpleasant to the other, that the thought be expressed.

With these concerns they reached Volos and proceeded to Domokos. Their house, broken into and ransacked by the Albanians, was wrecked, but for Ayfantis and Ephrosyne the most lamentable fact was that there was no letter from Thanos, though there should have been several according to his promises. Kioura undertook by herself to restore the relics of their broken and soiled furnishings. Ephrosyne had paled. The wretched Ayfantis was baffled, unable to help his daughter recover her stability and solve the unexpected complication.

Knowing that Tassos was aide-de-camp of the Leader in Hypate, Ayfantis wrote for news of Thanos, assuming that any correspondence would have been forwarded and that Tassos would have waited to hear that Ayfantis had arrived in Thessaly before sending them on. Tassos responded immediately. When the answer arrived, Ephrosyne leaped for joy. Her father broke the seal quickly but, sensing from the thinness of the envelope that it contained little besides a letter from Tassos, was able to moderate the hopes of his daughter.

Tassos was happy that they had arrived safely in Thessaly and felt grateful for Ayfantis's interest in him and his brother. As for his own affairs, he could barely catch his breath from the countless chores and responsibilities, personally overseeing the more significant. Corresponding with his benefactor, however, was a refreshing break for him. Since they were so close by, he hoped to persuade the Leader, who gave him not a moment's rest, to grant him a few days' leave. His brother had reached Trivae in good health, he had learned, and was now diligently running the estate, implementing the instructions of his knowledgeable benefactor. From his brother's letters he saw that the lessons of Ayfantis were most useful to him.

The letter's contents convinced Ayfantis that Thanos had indeed been entrusted with the management of an estate that demanded great initial efforts and that he had little time to attend to anything else. Ephrosyne should have felt reassured that Thanos was making progress in executing the correct principles her father had inculcated, and that the major and complex works of managing an estate, left virtually abandoned, took time, especially when the most effective methods were still uncertain.

Ayfantis knew that if Thanos wished to realize a small part of his teachings, he had not a moment to spare, since he had arrived late and time was of the essence. But once he prospered, he would certainly attribute these results to the man who had taught him these principles. Curious as to how his advice had been understood, Ayfantis often brought his conversations with Ephrosyne around to Thanos. He planned to write to Tassos once more and to offer to explain to Thanos whatever puzzled him. He would thus inform Thanos that he was remembered and expected to fulfill his promise to write to them directly, revealing nothing to Tassos.

Despite the resourcefulness of Ayfantis in inventing ways to provoke a letter from Thanos to ease Ephrosyne's disquiet, things became more complex. She judged by the heart, not the mind, and all the arguments that convinced Ayfantis about the unknown had little effect on her. In her view, the present was obscure and no ray of hope penetrated the gloom. Thanos may have prospered by effecting her father's teachings, but he merely revealed himself to be forgetful and unresponsive, since he had often promised to write, considering this, in his words, a sacred duty. Was this how he would fulfill his promise to visit Thessaly and those he considered his benefactors once the affairs of Trivae were settled? Perhaps he had some justification, having no reason to believe that they longed for his letters and cared whether he fulfilled his obligations or not.

That thoughts like these might have occurred to him was, in her opinion, understandable. Deducing Thanos's motive, on which she relied, from what she knew of his ideas, she began to see her father's calculations as cold and his conjectures as forced and irrelevant. It was not essential that simple gratitude be expressed as, and when, her father expected. She did not go so far as to consider Thanos ungrateful, since she found justification for his not fulfilling his pledge; rather, she listened to the voice within herself that argued Thanos's case. Her father also supported him, but for other reasons, and between them there was a great difference. If she were correct that Thanos, despite his promise, did not understand that he was upsetting them by not writing, one could conclude that as time passed and he became engrossed in his work, he would no longer think as he had; the vivid memories of the past would dissipate, and he would become indifferent. Perhaps that had already happened?

Whoever suffers psychologically punishes himself and is most resourceful in uncovering whatever is hurtful and makes him suffer.

Ephrosyne, though she said nothing, disguising her feelings by a mask of indifference, offered her observant father enough signs to show that she was troubled.

Ayfantis was alarmed when Tassos did not hasten to reply as he had to the first letter. Ayfantis's neighbors and Ephrosyne's contemporaries tried to explain, according to each person's reading of the situation, the obvious change in the family's appearance. Some supposed that Ayfantis had suffered huge losses and only with great difficulty would bring his affairs back to their previous fine condition, or that having savored the joys of life in Greece he wished to establish himself there but encountered insuperable obstacles in liquidating his property, or that he foresaw unpleasant developments menacing Thessaly, probably because of more accurate information from newly acquired friends. Ephrosyne's peers, by and large, attributed her uncommunicativeness to pride, brought about by the fine air of Athens. Having been introduced to more genteel ways and having attained a higher style, she was no longer pleased by the traditional simplicity.

None of them divined the truth. Ayfantis had indeed suffered many losses, but all of his employees had been steadfast in his absence, so that his fields continued to be cultivated and his livestock, herded to safe pastures, had survived. The only damages sustained were in the looting of his residence and his loss at the trial. When the family returned, he resumed the management of his affairs, though now, concerned over his daughter, he paid less attention to the oversight of his estate. He had nothing more to hope for from Greece, judging agriculture in Thessaly superior, so that only his daughter's plight might possibly draw him back to the Greek kingdom.

It would be unnecessary to note how long it would take to discover what dwelled in Ephrosyne's heart. Her face revealed her submission to an affliction without remedy, which added gravity to her other attractions and provided a sweet glow that moderated the sadness of her disposition. Only her father, who knew how to interpret all of her gestures, could see the quietly smoldering flame hidden by her maidenly modesty.

The nourishing rains of winter revivified the exhausted power of the parched soil with the green mantle of rest. Though at this time of year Ephrosyne usually took on many projects and invited many of her girlfriends to help her, nothing came to fruition now, but whatever she prepared she shortly abandoned, unable to persevere. The life of retirement did not free her mind from the exhausting powers of concern, while her imagination, willfully following the inclination of her feelings, magnified and made monstrous her sorrow. Only her religious principles, pure and deeply rooted, resisted this inclination, but because of their force they rent her heart, unable to offer sacrifices to her unjustifiable and overpowering impulses. She eagerly went to church and her prayers were emotional, but she continued to feel the pressure of their weight when she returned.

After this passage of time, a letter from Tassos finally arrived, explaining his tardiness by blaming his many occupations. He'd had more letters from Thanos, he claimed, which indicated that he was succeeding marvelously in implementing Ayfantis's agricultural principles, but that he now had many things to attend to and innovations to introduce. Since he was no clearer than that, the barb Ayfantis had aimed did not strike home. The letters offered few details and, because they were vague and trite, provided no illumination.

Ayfantis interpreted it in the way that satisfied him, but he also saw that it did not contribute anything new. Hoping for a more favorable result, he would seek another path, which he had yet to discover.

Tassos, Aide-de-Camp to the Leader

At that time Tassos was serving in Hypate, where the Leader, for whom he was aide and right-hand man, had established his headquarters. The Leader had been assigned the administration of border control and the suppression of brigandage, but the entrepreneurial workshops of Tassos did not limit themselves to this charge.

The Vlachs, also called *Karagounies*, had not changed their nomadic life and annually descended from the mountains of Pindos to winter in the fertile valleys of Phthiotis and nearby districts. Once the pastoral tax replaced the land taxes imposed by the provinces, these shepherds, as well as all the local livestock breeders, had a major economic interest in taking over the glens, where the grass grows dense and rich. These decisions are made, at a preliminary stage, by the mayors and the presiding officer of the local councils consisting of the nomarch, the provincial governor, and the magistrate. By rights, the Leader had no role in this highly prized procedure, but Tassos managed to find a way to involve his armed force without being perceived. For this purpose, all the mayors and demotic councils had to be composed of his own men.

The affluent shepherds, the so-called *tzelengoi*, having understood who had the power, immediately began to address themselves to Tassos, who received their customary offerings and let his wishes, accepted as orders and never ignored, be known to the subordinate ranks. Tassos did not limit himself to leeching off only the chief *tzelengoi* as soon as they arrived but on all shepherds, as long as they wintered there. Since they had no alternatives, they were thus subordinated to him.

These nomads, completely isolated from the good things of social life, wanted even more to be isolated from the bad. Whatever social problems did not concern them they ignored or were indifferent to, caring only that they not suffer themselves. They lived a patriarchal life of age-old simplicity, sharing their milk and cheese and lavishing aid on whoever visited them. In their opinion, the brigands, because they were hunted down and struggled to survive, were even more worthy of aid, and to them they gave aid and comfort. Returning the favor, the brigands never attacked them, as long as they were willing to hide them and even to identify certain opportunities for them.

But toward none were the brigands so savage as to shepherds who betrayed them and whom, in the wild, remote from human habitation and especially during winter, they approached in complete trust for food, weapons, and information to guide their actions. The nomads did not create brigandage but found the institution existing with society, an inseparable element of it, and so they felt no obligation to help in its reform. They guided themselves by the customs of the country and because, according to their pantheistic creed, God was everywhere, so were the brigands; thus brigands were a part of divine providence.

God sends the stranger, the shepherd believes, and whoever does not receive him, sins. God sends the shepherd, the brigand believes, so that he, too, could have a place to hide from those who want to keep everything for themselves.

Tassos did not see things this charitably. For him, brigands were the great lever of his intricate machine, while for them, it was his hand that could reach into all municipal ballot boxes from which the names of mayors and members of the municipal councils emerged. Using the brigands, Tassos could keep the nomads under control by whispering into the head shepherd's ear that the *tze-lengata* must not fall out of the grace of the all-powerful Leader. In this way, the brigands themselves became mere tools of Tassos, fearful of being punished for insubordination, for which they had examples, and thinking and acting as he wished. Tassos involved himself not only in municipal and electoral matters but extended his authority everywhere, providing benefits and profit to the leaders who submitted to him. Everyone did whatever was demanded and dared not complain.

The brigands had reasons for working with Tassos. He knew all their hideouts and meeting places and was in charge of their pursuit, which, though bloodless, because they had been warned in time, was carried out with great military display. His failure to capture the brigands was easily explained, for the borders beyond which the brigands escaped could not be sealed and the brigands could always find refuge in the neighboring towns.

Those who took hostages for ransom were not as well satisfied working for Tassos, because those who deserved punishment within his system were not among the most affluent. If this occurred, again after Tassos gave his permission, the brigands selected victims valuable enough to make up for their times of idleness, or at the behest of those who directed their efforts. Grateful, in fact, for these furloughs, they gave Tassos his cut, awarding him the lion's share. There were other benefits to this, since through him they could fence their stolen goods and approach their value; otherwise, these goods would be worthless to the brigands, who preferred gold. Incalculable profits were created by Tassos as manager. Although he had many partners and middlemen, depending on the operation, he formed his own flock of sheep, acquired many valuable objects, and amassed a great deal of wealth in a short time.

Of the principle of the newer economic theorists that capital, the fertile and productive income, is the surplus after consumption, Tassos was hardly aware, but he espoused the idea that capital is always that which, locked securely away, is not subject to decay.

But there was another, more convincing reason for keeping his wealth a secret, and that was to avoid public attention and outcry. If those who knew him as poor and insignificant had suddenly learned that he was wealthy, they would doubt that this abrupt change in fortune had been effected by legitimate means. Try as he would to conceal his success, he could never deceive the sharp-witted who did not share the spoils, but were harmed instead, and who referred in whispers to his "headquarters" as the "brigand's quarters." But these malcontents were written off as opponents of the political regime and anarchists, always censuring whatever happened and following the unattainable pie-in-the-sky reformers. Seeing how futile their observations were and how dangerous to their own interests, besides, these not being secured under the clearly defined protection of the laws, they lost their courage and confessed their beliefs only when certain that their comments would go no further.

On the contrary, the majority of notables flattered Tassos and publicly proclaimed him tireless, forceful, a bastion of public order, and a laborer for the common good. His favor provided security to some when he visited their estates, though they themselves dared not live on their land, or engaged in commerce regardless of the danger and grief, or collected taxes, and allowed others to maintain their political strength and importance, either during municipal or parliamentary elections, defeating and neutralizing their political opponents. Thus, if not the majority, then certainly the most active found Tassos's system useful and, besides being his collaborators, provided him the moral support of their good opinion.

Tassos did not limit his attentions only to those around him but directed his tireless gaze to distant Athens. The headquarters, which housed the treasury and the office of the Leader, was administered by two scribes occupied in sending reports to the government wherein everything illicit was presented as licit and everything that had occurred was claimed to bear some relation to what had been lawfully ordered. It was this office that confected all the elegant praises that filled the newspapers of the capital and that refuted in thundering terms the allegations of prattlers. The office was kept totally ignorant of those who were on the payroll, but the payroll, which Tassos controlled, gave orders to the office through the mouth of the Leader.

Preoccupied with these great and incalculably profitable matters, Tassos had little time to consider Trivae and the revenue from the village. According to his thinking, though, the money would arrive with no out-of-pocket expense on his part. How then could he understand about crops being harvested from land not yet plowed, about a new way of dealing with peasants, about setting aside land for them to own, about offering half, or the entire, village as security for a loan so that the peasants could sow for their own account, after which, all from his own funds, the peasants would work to sow his land?

He respected and honored Ayfantis, whose suggestions his brother continually repeated, but Thanos might have misunderstood him or, because he did not know how hard money and possessions were to come by, fell into excesses out of youthful emulation and frivolity. Tassos did not believe that Ayfantis became rich by turning everything over to the peasants. Only when he had attained great wealth was he able to devote a generous portion of his fortune to benefactions, because this is what he was inclined to do.

To each his own, but each must also know his own limitations. At this point, Tassos himself did not have the means to follow the example of Ayfantis, which had rattled his brother's wits. Thanos would learn his lesson, he hoped, and understand at last that whoever wanted to become rich had to function in the world without needing others. But Thanos kept wearing blinders even after his fate had changed. After his hayracks had burned, he found refuge in Thessaly and a generous patron, through whom he was able in a short while to recoup all he had lost. Then, released by the courts, he learned that he was part owner in a large estate.

As a result, it appeared to Thanos that the change from great poverty to wealth was not at all rare, unaware that the opposite is much more common and that poverty is a permanent condition from which the mass of people never emerges. Just as Thanos received half of Trivae without any effort on his part, so he was himself ready to give it away to make happy the peasants he saw for the first time, and thus knew nothing about, and whom he trusted would be grateful and return the favor more generously. How wrong could a man be? With a little experience he would understand that once the peasants became independent and affluent, they would turn on him first to expel him completely from the village. That was natural. No one could be happy when he did not possess something in its entirety. When a man has nothing, he is humble and subordinate because he understands that there are things he cannot possess.

These were his thoughts on receiving Thanos's first letter. From what his brother had written, Tassos knew he had made a mistake in accepting the suggestion of Iapetos. Thanos was not the right man for the job. Nor could he change his brother's mind, stirred up as it was with Ayfantis's teachings. Not wishing to renege on his promise, though, Tassos decided not to respond at all and to give no orders. What he had told Skias would not threaten his ownership of the property, while Thanos, deprived of documentation and with no resources of his own, would be powerless to act.

The letters from Thanos that followed reinforced his opinion. There were descriptions of wretched peasants and depictions of their great poverty, bereft of material for sowing; there was the despair that replaced the promise of Tassos's sudden appearance; there was the intention to offer his half of the village as security for a loan; there were subtle hints that the services of Skias were unnecessary, that the man, by inappropriate harshness, had inspired fear in the humble and downtrodden people, discouraging them about their hopes for the future. All these comments achieved a result opposite from the one Thanos had intended.

The conclusion Tassos drew was that he would be greatly harmed by responding to Thanos's letters. His brother had yielded to compassion—in his opinion, a youthful and thoughtless thing—but Tassos ran the risk of being expropriated if he admitted in writing that the brothers shared in the ownership of the estate. The offer of co-ownership had been made not in earnest but to motivate Thanos, because he was a knowledgeable agriculturist who would augment the estate's income. After some time, if he wished to withdraw and there was a little money left over, Tassos planned to inform Thanos about how things stood and to give him some money to get by on. But Thanos upset this plan from the start, demanding a document certifying to his rights to half of Trivae. What Thanos said about Skias, moreover, assured him that Skias's presence in Trivae was indispensable, lest the peasants' minds be swayed and their foolish hopes develop into claims. The despair of the Trivaeans was necessary so that they would submit to their lawful master. Once they stopped dreaming of a change in their condition, they would bow their necks to the yoke and become willing laborers, expecting to be recompensed for their efforts according to their devotion, and not led astray by other illusions.

Thanos, having received no response and not knowing to what he should attribute the ruinous silence, may have been indignant, but Tassos, seeing the solution develop according to plan, was satisfied. Finally, disinherited, Thanos would decide to leave Trivae, allowing

Tassos to manage the village as he wanted. "Let Thanos go back to being Ayfantis's servant again," he thought, "since that seems to be his lot. He doesn't know how to benefit from circumstances and live independently. I can't afford support him indefinitely."

Thanos tried every way he could to assure himself that Tassos was receiving his letters. He was convinced of this when he wrote to his mother, asking her about Tassos and enclosing a letter to him in the same envelope. Her response, written in the hand of a scribe, implied that she had had letters from Tassos, for Barbara blessed her firstborn for his progress as aide-de-camp, saying that she heard his name praised daily, and censured Thanos for having accomplished nothing. Here he had a large estate under his control, yet depended on his brother for orders, annoying him who had many other things to attend to.

After this letter there were no doubts that he and his brother had different attitudes and that trying to persuade Tassos was wasted effort. This failure he attributed to his brother's usual indifference to domestic matters and his preoccupation for promotion and honors. Besides this indifference, he saw that his brother ignored his exhortations, dismissing them as of little value, perhaps, and not seeing things the way he did. A sensitive man would have been moved by the descriptions of the peasants' plight and would want to improve the lot of people who could prove valuable to him. Since neither self-interest nor empathy seemed to affect him, he needed something else to arouse him from his lethargy.

For this purpose Ayfantis might be a good mediator. Tassos seemed to respect the man, and benefactions and exhortations directly from him would be decisive. Besides, writing to Ayfantis would simultaneously fulfill his promise. In a way, he was reluctant to write before having put his teachings into effect, but he justified himself by providing a detailed report of matters and explaining how he had tried to convince Tassos. He said nothing critical about his brother but attributed the reason for his neglect to the small regard he had, justifiably perhaps, about the proposed measures Thanos had planned to implement. He requested that Ayfantis support him by writing an admonitory letter saying the right things to enlighten Tassos about his true interests, the neglect of which was not merely harmful to him but to many others.

This was Thanos's last attempt. After this, there was nothing else he could do and his presence in Trivae would be superfluous.

Thanos's letter, so longed for, finally arrived to put an end to the perplexity of Ayfantis and Ephrosyne. Often read and commented upon, it provided material that could be interpreted in a way that supported the wishes of each.

For her part, Ephrosyne found sufficient cause to justify her excessive concern. Even though it seemed that Thanos's luck had changed for the better when he became half owner of a village and was on his way to riches, he was not quite there. Obstacles had a way of springing up unexpectedly that rendered his future uncertain. What could he accomplish without means and surrounded by destitute people who, unable to recompense him, would naturally consider him an enemy? His silence until then, thoughtful because it spared them worry, revealed his gentleness and nobility, traits of which she was fully aware. Wishing, as her father had taught him and as his own spirit desired, to make his own way, not from common misfortune but from common prosperity, he refused to write before accomplishing something worthy of note. But how could he surmount these obstacles, the highest of which was his brother's indifference?

Ayfantis, certain that such a good student could not forget his teacher, explained Thanos's silence by citing the concerns of managing an estate. The resistance of Tassos did not strike him as exceptional, either. Someone brought up according to other principles could not believe that he could become rich if his employees prospered as well, because he could not understand that profits could sooner be made from the haves than from the have-nots. Tassos, Ayfantis knew, would view the advice his brother expressed as moral precepts merely, not really useful for attaining wealth. These ideas Tassos claimed to accept gratefully, as well as his brother's busy implementation of them, but he would abstain from supporting what he believed was condemned to failure. The mediation, which Thanos sought, might result in the desired goal, but for this Ayfantis would need to speak to Tassos face to face so that he would not have the slightest escape. Since he had admitted, in writing, that he accepted the advice of the older man, Tassos could not express the contrary now. By changing the terms of the discussion, therefore, and by person-to-person conversation, Ayfantis would unexpectedly ask that Thanos be provided with written confirmation of his rights.

When the morning swallow's return announced the flowery spring, Ayfantis set out for Hypate with Ephrosyne, who was easily persuaded to go along, for she wanted to be with Thanos, especially now that her father would be interceding for him.

Domokos was not far away, and Ayfantis could say that he wanted to purchase livestock to supplement his flocks. The presence of brigands was of no concern to him because he had befriended many, and the shepherds, too, were well disposed toward him because of his many benefactions.

Iapetos, after his release from jail, was in Hypate a few days before their arrival, exploiting his friendship with Tassos and staying at his home. Without an income now, having exhausted his few funds and the generosity of friends, toward whom he had already become a burden, he thought it wise—at least until the scandal of "the juicy olive" had been forgotten—to remove himself from Athens for some time.

He had learned of Tassos's great success and had a general idea of his business affairs. From Tassos he had a right to expect something. After all, he had played a major role in securing Trivae for him. But his efforts to ingratiate himself seemed to prove the adage that when grace is hoped for it is already dead. Iapetos possessed letters, however, and from these the means Tassos used to defraud the peasants and the government were incontrovertible. Though pressed by great need, he used no threats, unwilling to reach the breaking point before exhausting every recourse. He wrote to his inattentive friend, tactfully informing him with pleasantries about his woes and occasionally observing that under these circumstances he would learn who his real friends were, that he expected nothing from Tassos though it was within his power to be extremely useful. Tassos did not respond.

Whenever as few as two people were present to listen, he sang the praises of Tassos to the point of tedium, hoping to attain his objective, willing, instead of money, to accept a share in the many enterprises. That he might succeed was not unlikely, and he knew that whoever takes the initiative to mix into, penetrate, and spy upon everything acquires handholds and achieves his objective more quickly than one who merely requests.

Tassos joked with him, skillfully parrying his thrusts and hiding the clues, so that Iapetos would not be able to have things his way. This presented a danger, because Iapetos would not limit himself to minor matters but might with his ability immediately draw public attention to Tassos's business. Nor would he dare repulse Iapetos and throw him to the vultures, fearing the man's Athenian contacts, through whom he could give voice to the hundred mouths of rumor. Thus there was constant shadowboxing between the two friends, in which the one was venturesome and attentive, while the other countered and retreated.

Iapetos no longer had that arrogant and frivolous air, so esteemed in Athens. Human affairs were a wheel, he understood, and he had fallen off. His quick glance now wavered and seemed frightened, as though he peered at something dark and secret and wished to divert the attention of others, assuming that they were observing all his moves. But his preening ways had not changed at all, and he continued to be ornamented and mincing. He scurried to and fro all day, prying into confidential matters and acting as though he did so under the orders of Tassos, who cleverly sent him off, exhibiting indifference, as though preoccupied with other matters. Though he had taken all the byroads, Iapetos always seemed to be on the wrong track and starting afresh. As on other occasions, it was he who first learned of the arrival in Hypate of Ayfantis and Ephrosyne, and he who first received Ayfantis as he entered Tassos's residence.

Meeting this man was not pleasant for Ayfantis. Unable to forget what had happened in Athens, he did not wish to renew this disagreeable relationship and, learning that Tassos was not at home, he turned to leave, pretending not to have recognized him. Iapetos tried to convince him to stay, hoping to learn what he wanted so that he could pass on his wishes to Tassos, since there were no secrets between the two friends. But he did not succeed in changing the mind of Ayfantis, who did not even thank him for his friendly reception but coolly responded that it was nothing urgent and turned his back.

In the meantime, the long-awaited Tassos arrived, expressing surprise at the unexpected visit. Ayfantis said that he was there to purchase livestock.

Even with Tassos present, Iapetos took the liberty, which exists between the closest of friends, not only to remain, prohibiting a private dialogue, as Ayfantis wished, but insisted on participating in the conversation, cleverly turning it into light and witty banter.

"Phthiotis," he broke in, "is noted more for its brigands than for its livestock."

"That's why it is worthy of pity, but I believe Mr. Tassos is making every effort to free his homeland of this terrible scourge. It's a serious reproach to Greece, which is capable of civilization, not to be able to act any more effectively than Turkey. And this cannot be disputed."

"I execute the commands of the Leader who is willing and tireless," Tassos replied. "Against brigandage, however, the Turks have more effective means, believe me. They don't have our responsibilities. They're not bound by forms and laws. They are not hampered by courts demanding evidence, thanks to which time is wasted on investigations in order to prove what everyone knows but which unfortunately succeed in making everything seem unverifiable."

"Yes," Iapetos agreed, "responsibility and control have paralyzed the strongest of arms, as the finest singer is silenced when he suspects that the audience won't like his song. That's why applause beforehand is encouraging to him."

"I don't know what your singers need. But as someone who lives in Turkey and is, in fact, a subject, I can speak from experience about the evils of irresponsible power. Look, for example, what occurs in the course of our guarding the borders. The current *derven aga* receives wages, or, as we say, *hartzia*, for three hundred soldiers. He maintains only fifty, though, and I doubt that even these fifty have weapons. Perhaps you've learned about the treaty he's drawn up with the pasha?"

"No," Tassos said, "we're not aware of it."

"It is, in fact, hard to believe. The *derven aga* is obligated to recompense every act of brigandage committed by bands containing fewer than twenty-five men. But since all raids against us are perpetrated by large bands that do no harm to his reputation, he provides asylum to all your Greek brigands, because as a good friend of theirs he always gets his cut."

"As far as we're concerned," Iapetos resumed, "many sharp-witted politicians who see into the future maintain that it is not in the nation's interest that the seed of brigandage be expelled."

"From all I've seen and heard, I believe that there are such politicians in Greece. But I prefer the myopic to these sharp-sighted men who wish to solve the present problems. I confess that I don't know how good can possibly emerge from evil."

"How so?" Iapetos asked, smiling and glancing at Tassos. "Do you deny that brigandage has its value and that it is not like other evils? Do you deny that by following this life, the brigand maintains the warlike and manly spirit, which may well become useful to us? Do you deny that our Revolution and independence are owed to these so-called klephts? . . ."

"At that time, perhaps, that way of life was useful to the Greeks, who were under the yoke of slavery, and it may prove to be useful once more to us. But since in Greece you're already free, you should no longer bear arms except to maintain law and order. But you must be complete cowards if your only manhood consists of brigands attacking the unarmed. The klephts of the revolutionary era were not such villains and bloodthirsty plunderers; you dishonor them by comparing them to these monsters."

As much as Iapetos repelled him, Ayfantis took part in this discussion to censure the ideas he knew Tassos shared, which led him to behave with cruelty toward the Trivaeans and with insensitivity toward his brother. By entering into the spirit of Tassos, he hoped to shame him into being better than he actually was. Iapetos cheerfully joined in, needling Tassos for his deceitfulness and ungratefulness while exhibiting the quickness of his mind, though all he did was embellish the trite values of those who were considered men of experience.

"I grant you," Tassos said, "that all brigands aren't the same. That's why we hunt down the bad ones and punish them, while the heroic klephts, whose lineage goes back to the old days, we respect and honor greatly. A day will come when we'll know what these men are capable of doing."

"I can't distinguish between the two," Ayfantis replied, "but I assure you that if I ever saw you coming toward me accompanied by such brigands, I'd be terrified and would want to flee to safety from the hands of such 'saviors.'"

"You'll find me running away, too," Iapetos added, "so you'll be inspired with courage and a sense of safety."

Ayfantis, not deigning to reply to the braggart, turned to Tassos, who was silent. "I stopped by today just to pay you a visit. We'll talk about another matter some other time."

Both accompanied him to the courtyard. The next day Tassos visited Ayfantis alone so that Iapetos would not be able to learn their business.

Ayfantis started off by inquiring about the local livestock breeders, then mentioned what he had learned about Trivae and Thanos. Caught out in a lie by a person he respected, Tassos did not know how to react, but Ayfantis avoided pointing out the contradictions between what he had written and what he had done. He spoke calmly, assuming the role of the sincere friend of both brothers, asking his permission to intrude, as an adviser, into the situation for their welfare, explaining how he himself had always benefited by behaving moderately toward employees. Others, small-minded and ambitious, afraid lest anyone obtain any of their profits, did not make as much money as he. This point he stressed, aware that Tassos had not been convinced by his brother's arguments.

Ayfantis's sweet and avuncular manner was successful. By not stressing his contradictions, he reassured Tassos that he could once more pretend to be a cordial and trustworthy person. Tassos acknowledged everything and, justifying the past, admitted that the concerns of his work had kept him from paying the requisite attention to Thanos, to whom he would write immediately and give him complete authority to do whatever he thought best.

Ayfantis used the same excuse of overwork and suggested that Tassos write the letter at once and that he would undertake to post it to Thanos.

This unexpected intrusion, changing Ayfantis from the role of adviser who offered suggestions to that of mediator who applied pressure, was upsetting to Tassos; if he concurred, Thanos would use this to act in a way completely antithetical to his interests. Tassos promised to write, on his soldier's honor, so that Ayfantis would no longer need to worry.

Now the time was right. Tassos was entangled and could not go back on his word without exposing his deception.

He was planning to leave soon and did not want to be burdensome, Ayfantis said, and Tassos was a very busy man, but since he'd been asked to mediate, it would give him a great deal of happiness to present Thanos with the agreement. Would Tassos deny him this pleasure?

There was another reason for the letter to be written in his presence, Ayfantis said, wishing to provide some cover for Tassos, whose evasions had been exposed, and that was that he had a few more suggestions to include.

As Ayfantis dictated, Tassos wrote that he fully agreed that Thanos owned half interest in Trivae and had authority to do whatever he wished. He seconded the older man's admonitions and even added to them magnanimously, amazing Ayfantis with his great success.

But Tassos had thought of a way to stop what was to happen. Ayfantis would send the letter by post and it would be a simple matter to seize it.

After Tassos left, Ayfantis showed the letter to Ephrosyne and read it over often to convince himself that he'd sorted out all the problems.

But Tassos was uneasy when many days passed and no letter to his brother showed up at the post office. Perhaps Ayfantis planned to send the letter off another way? He needed to be sure, before Thanos had acted in a way that could not be undone. Iapetos, inquisitive as always, was also uneasy, especially when he learned that Ayfantis was planning to leave.

It was, in fact, while preparing his departure that Ayfantis was visited late that evening by Ghikas Tramersis, the shepherd who had interceded for help for Tassos when he was wounded, and for Thanos when he found service with Ayfantis.

Tramersis entered not affably, as was his wont, but as someone diffident and irresolute. Ephrosyne received him and announced him to her father, who made it clear how happy he was to encounter him in Hypate and assured him that he would have been even happier if he had known days before that he was there.

"It was only today that I learned you are here," Tramersis said, "and came to ask about your health and when you are leaving so that I may wish you a safe trip."

"We may be leaving in two days."

"You'd do well to leave tomorrow so you could have us as company. We're leaving, too."

"Why don't you delay? We'll be ready to go soon."

"There are many reasons. It's not necessary to go into them now. But I suggest that you leave tomorrow, too."

"I don't see why."

"Pretend that you do. But if you listen to me, you won't be sorry."

The serious manner of Tramersis, the admonitory tone in his voice, and the mysterious something in his words piqued Ayfantis's curiosity, and he gestured to Ephrosyne to leave so that the man would have more freedom to explain himself.

But Ayfantis did not learn any more about what was happening when they were alone. It was better to leave the next day, Tramersis repeated, and that he would not be sorry.

"But . . . you think there's a danger if we delay?"

"That I don't know. You are your own master and can do as you wish. But I ate bread and salt in your home and say this to you: leave tomorrow."

"Fine," Ayfantis agreed. "I hear you and don't doubt that you give me good advice. We leave tomorrow morning. But Lamia is our destination, and that's where we'll go."

"Once we arrive in Lamia, I'll tell you what to do. But tomorrow morning, we'll be waiting for you outside Hypate."

"Yes, without fail, and we'll say nothing to anyone."

Tramersis, with a sober look, glanced at Ayfantis. "Before dawn," he bowed. "We'll be waiting."

The dangers of which Ayfantis was ignorant, which threatened him from every side, were many. Tassos, not finding the letter for Thanos in the post office, decided to appoint a band of men to stop Ayfantis when he left Hypate and, without any rough treatment, take all his documents. By good fortune, the shepherd nearest to Hypate happened to be Tramersis, who had learned two days before that Ayfantis was planning to leave and was ordered to prepare for his overnight stay. To what end the trap was being prepared, Tramersis did not learn, but being devoted to Ayfantis and knowing that he was planning to leave Hypate around then, he had an evil presentiment that something might happen to him along the way. Perhaps he might not have suspected if Tassos had given him a command, but he had been notified by a subordinate and, not daring to question the order further, did not know if the brigands had their own purposes or if they worked for others; but he could never believe that Tassos would show such ingratitude toward a man who had done him so much good and whom Tramersis himself had introduced.

Another factor increased the dangers to Ayfantis. Iapetos, being idle and unable to make progress through Tassos, who kept slipping through his grasp like an eel, thought he would succeed in Hypate to accomplish what he'd been unable to do in Athens. Ayfantis planned to leave with Ephrosyne soon, he'd learned. By abducting her, Iapetos would teach the man how to distinguish between one brigand and another. The good father would then suggest conditions and terms but nothing would come about if there were no wedding.

He approached those who lurked around Tassos's door and promised them much if they would help him out. They passed this matter on to Tassos confidentially, and he approved, but he had his own reasons. Iapetos would be useful as a cover. Once he had Ayfantis's documents in hand, he would arrest Iapetos and abandon him to the mercies of the courts, ridding himself of a problem and simultaneously rendering Ayfantis obligated to him. For this reason, pretending ignorance, he allowed Iapetos to execute his plan.

Iapetos, assuming he had tricked his friend, did not tell him of his plans because he suspected that Tassos would oppose him. For this event he had a costume tailored, which he tried on before the mirror, considering the impression he'd make on the abducted girl when he appeared before her, bearing his light weapon gracefully, girt with his sword and dagger. His imagination soared as he saw himself in the mirror and he lunged in fencing gestures.

Ayfantis took Tramersis's advice seriously, knowing from experience both his friendly disposition toward him and the mores of the shepherds, who, in these circumstances, were afraid to confess all they knew. Preparing and predisposing Ephrosyne, they rested only a few hours and left Hypate on horseback before daybreak, accompanied by two servants.

In absolute silence and while everyone slept, they descended to the Frantzis Bridge. Tramersis was overjoyed to see that they had taken his advice and started off at once along the right bank of the Spercheios straight for Lamia, from which they would leave again as quickly as possible. They continued on to Stylis because Ayfantis planned to travel with Ephrosyne to Trivae, bringing Tassos's letter along with him, to arrange matters to his liking there.

Tramersis's advice ruined the traps set by Tassos and Iapetos. Learning of the escape, both were devastated, each for his own reason.

The Final Events

Matters in Trivae were getting worse by the day.

Seeing that the mild and meek ways of Thanos had led to nothing and that his benevolent arrangements were in vain, the peasants began to hold him in contempt. Because he also behaved courteously toward the implacable Skias, Thanos suffered what happens to those who believe they can reconcile the irreconcilable, and, since no middle ground was possible, he succeeded in accomplishing the opposite. He praised Skias for his steady will and unrelenting strictness, believing in this way that he would make him more tractable, for there was clearly no need for another's presence, and he nurtured the withered hopes of the peasants, exhorting them to patience because he would shortly have the means to bring about the desired remedy. To Skias, who believed that once strictness ceased, so would submission, he appeared childish and ludicrous, while to the peasants he appeared, like his brother before him, to be a fraud and a deceiver, or as a worthless and runaway horse or—to use their expression—a fifth wheel on their wrecked carriage.

Their indignation became intolerable because they had sown too little and too late and the crops would not last them beyond midwinter. They could ascertain to the day when they would be without livestock, except for the animals they kept for food, the rest having been slaughtered to provide the necessities for the Man with the Whip and his henchmen to devour.

Among the peasants Thanos distributed the little money he had brought with him, insisting that the food allowance not be increased on his account. But no relief came of this.

During this turmoil, the more violent came into the ascendancy and the words of the milder no longer carried any weight. Papa-Vlasis and Doudoumis were discounted as totally inept. How much the importance attached to their arguments had diminished could be seen when the demarch requested, following his superior's orders, that the conscripts be handed over. The two notables employed all their eloquence to convince the Trivaeans that it was to their interest to appear submissive to the authorities so that, while they worked to change its decision, they would not incite the government to use countermeasures. Only old Lahanopoulos assented, but Asimina gave him abrupt retort and helped her son escape. Tagaropoulos got away, too.

The leaders of the province were pleased to see confusion increasing and aggravation intensifying, a blaze they augmented to hurry the confrontation. By showing the peasants that the only way out of their dilemma was to abandon their village, scattering hither and yon, they wanted to provide an example to others not to trust newcomers. This scattering would also deny Tassos the means of cultivating his lands. In the eyes of all, he would be viewed as a common enemy, unable to do anything on their behalf.

The peasants did not hate Thanos as much as the rest, but he could not ignore the rage that boiled within them. Their anger was just and, though he knew that he would not be able to change things, he struggled nonetheless. Pale and silent, he avoided the society of men, counting the days during which he had to stay in Trivae, assuming Ayfantis offered his mediation and it was successful. He should have had some response, but he hadn't discerned the slightest glimmer from the profound darkness on the horizon. He was ready to abandon everything, having drunk to the final drop the bitter potion given him by his brother.

The destruction of his plans was as tragic as their success would have been gratifying, for not only his own happiness but that of many others would have been achieved. Everything he had wanted to rescue was going down around him in the same shipwreck; his benefactor had forgotten him, perhaps considering him unworthy of attention, since he had accomplished nothing; because of his brother's ruthlessness, Ayfantis probably wanted to avoid him as well, and he would no longer have the freedom to be speak openly before him; what recourse did he have but to make his way back to Thessaly and serve him? Seeing everything around him hateful, repellent, and wild, he finally accepted everyone's opinion of him.

Thanos did not know that Ayfantis was as interested as he in the success of his goals and that the happiness of another person was involved with this. And because he was planning to go to Trivae to help restore conditions there completely, it did not occur to Ayfantis to write to Thanos that he was coming to Hypate with the letter from Tassos.

He was already on route to Piraeus. Arriving in Athens, he has-tened toward the Isthmus to fulfill the wish of Ephrosyne, whose countenance grew more joyful as they neared their goal and the certitude increased that they would assuage the unjustly suffering Thanos. Beyond this, her hopes did not extend, suppressed by her natural reticence, as rushing waves withdraw after surging onto a sandy beach. Her father's care quieted her heart and calmed her agitations. As the fern requires the shelter of rocks, she needed her father, lavishing attention on him and attentive to his needs so that their trip would be less tiring. But hurry as they did, the road along the Isthmus had many treacherous spots, and many days were to pass before they reached Trivae to learn what had happened there a short time before they arrived.

While the threat of being liable to criminal proceedings for not producing the two conscripts shook the peasants, the challenge of feeding and otherwise satisfying Skias and his henchmen completely stymied them. Skias, however, had begun to suspect that the Trivaeans were hiding their livestock to plead poverty and to evade their obligations to him. To assure himself, he went out to inspect the surrounding countryside, searching—as an expert in these matters—all the dry torrents and hollows. Instead of livestock, however, he discovered Tagaropoulos in a ravine and, in an uncontrollable fury because he had found no animals, he whipped him from his hiding place and ordered him to give himself up at once to the proper authorities. Thus barred from every hope of evading prosecution, for even Skias worked against him, Tagaropoulos rushed back to Trivae like a madman.

"There's no way out," he said, fanning the already burning anger of the villagers' despair. "It's either him or us. Either we all scatter to hell and gone, or this beast must be wiped off the face of the earth. Whoever has the nerve let him follow me."

His ravings, the fever of his murderous face, his bloodshot and fearful glance, his wild hair, the power of his words, and the fearlessness with which he spoke electrified his listeners and inspired them with strength and spirit.

"This is the time!" he roared. "Let's go!" Turning, he set out with a steady pace toward the cabin of Skias, followed by everyone.

The courage of his followers strengthened his resolve as they entered Skias's cabin and seized his weapons, which they would turn on him.

Skias saw the mass of peasants leaving the village but did not understand where they'd come from, and he angrily proceeded toward them himself swinging his whip.

"Let him get a little closer," Tagaropoulos shouted, loading the weapon and hiding it under his overcoat.

In the meantime, Thanos arrived and understood at once that a bloody confrontation was in the offing. Having no hope to mollify the savagery of Skias, he turned toward the peasants to plead for them to withdraw.

"Yes," said Tagaropoulos, "we should bend our backs so that you can step on us. . . . Sweet words from one, and the *falanga* from the other. Honey and vinegar. . . . Get out, snake! . . ."

"Get out, snake!" all repeated.

His pleas were in vain, though, for Skias and his men hurried their pace and virtually ran toward them. Thanos, his hands raised, continued to implore the peasants to withdraw, assuring them that things would quickly improve, that he expected a letter that would gratify them all, and that Skias and his men would be sent away.

The henchmen charged furiously toward the peasants, still assuming that they were unarmed.

"What're you waiting for?" Tagaropoulos shouted. "Fire away!"

In a moment, they had emptied their weapons and wasted no shell. Thanos was first to fall. Wildcat, who turned immediately to flee, was the only survivor.

The peasants leaped joyfully and rushed toward the bodies to assure themselves that the job had been done.

Tagaropoulos neared the corpse of Thanos. "The snake can't bite any more."

The peasants exulted. "No, it can't bite."

Then Doudoumis and PapaVlasis arrived. "What have you done?" they cried, seeing the gore. "You've ruined us all."

"If you like being whipped," Tagaropoulos replied, dancing. "Look, nothing happened to this one," and bending over, he took the whip from the hands of the supine Skias, who was breathing his last.

"And this fine young man," Doudoumis said unhappily, "what harm did he do to you that you should kill him?"

"You liked his sweet talk? His fairy tales? Let all the Christians die of hunger as long as Doudoumis can listen to sweet talk."

"The poor lad," Doudoumis replied, "the bullet got him in the neck and you'd think that he sleeps easy, without a troubled conscience."

"Rest in the Lord," the priest added. "His face shows that there was no evil in his spirit and always a good word on his lips. The Lord knows, who examines the hearts and kidneys. . . . May those responsible beware."

"We," Tagaropoulos cried out, "we'll give accounts to God and to men."

It was later that the peasants began to consider the consequences. Though for some time they'd been spared the yoke, they still had its marks around their necks. The authorities and courts, they knew, would demand that the criminal act be punished. Talking among themselves, they began to criticize what had happened and the tide of reaction turned. To show that they repudiated the act, separating the fate of the perpetrators from that of the bystanders, they decided to inform the authorities of what had happened and to bury the dead afterward.

The news spread immediately. Ayfantis, a little later the same day, heard it on his way. He did not learn precisely what had happened, only that there had been murders in Trivae. Because the news was broken in her presence, he was unable to keep it from Ephrosyne.

Shaken, they arrived in Trivae the following day.

Ephrosyne, seeing the body of Thanos lying in front of the church door, fell from her horse before anyone could catch her. Either the fall was heavy and her injury was critical, or the shock of the unexpected sight was so great, but Ephrosyne did not get up.

The peasants rushed to aid her afflicted father, but nothing could recall her to life, for she had given up her spirit.

The grief of Ayfantis was shared by all the peasants. Despite his stammer and incoherence, they learned why he had come to

Trivae and what the noble heart of Thanos had intended for them, about his efforts toward his brother on their behalf. Worst of all, they had ruined everything by this terrible act and could no longer hope to see an improvement in their lives.

Their curse on the perpetrators could not resurrect the dead, nor could they soothe the irremediable wound in Ayfantis's heart. The murderers bolted, convinced that they had done an evil thing and frightened of the mob's rage and the law's punishment.

Ayfantis wanted the funeral of Thanos and Ephrosyne to be held jointly, and all the peasants, with groans and lamentations, attended the rite. The two were buried far from the defiled village, along the banks of the Alphaeus, under the forest shade. A marker from an ancient memorial found nearby was set there.

PapaVlasis wrote *Thanos and Ephrosyne* in charcoal and, though the letters were immediately worn away, they remain fresh in the memories of the peasants, who narrate the suffering of Thanos and Ephrosyne as an episode out of their own misfortunes. Sometimes, they insist, when all is quiet and only the babbling of the river can be heard, around matins, before the sun's rays have dispersed the shadows of the night, a melodic voice singing hosanna can be heard within the trees.

The visitor to Trivae can ask the peasants to direct him along the banks of the Alphaeus to the monument to Thanos and Ephrosyne. "Around them," as Sappho writes, "cold water babbles of the fragrance of apples." There, listening to the peasants' naive story of the lovers' unfortunate end and seated upon their grave, cooled by the waters of the Alphaeus, under the forest shade, he may recite the words of Virgil: "Offer lilies with full hands."

Chapter 1

5   *of iambs . . . of reeds*   These had a liturgical function in the worship of Dionysus by his bacchants.

7   τύμβος σᾶς ἀλόχου . . . σέβαζ ἐμπόρων . . . *butter is churned* τύμβος σᾶς ἀλόχου . . . σέβαζ ἐμπόρων means not "merchants and grocers wish to worship" but "merchants reverence the tomb of the spouse," and ἐπὶ χθονὶ πουλυβυτείρῃ actually means "on the fruitful earth."

7   *Hippocleidis*   Hippocleidis, a rich and handsome Athenian, went to Sikyon with a friend to compete for the hand of Agaristes, the beautiful daughter of Kleisthis, who wanted the best of all Greece for a son-in-law. All the suitors stayed for a year and were tried in various contests, including symposia. The local people all wanted, and admired, Hippocleidis, but when it looked as though he had the prize, he danced, then demanded a table be brought, and did what seems to have been a headstand, legs high in the air. The staid Kleisthis got up. "O son of Teisander," he said, outraged, "you've lost the bride with your dance." The young man responded, "What does Hippocleidis care?" (Herodotus, *Histories* 6.129).

Chapter 2

10   *Astydamas*   Astydamas was an Athenian tragedian whose 240 theatrical works won fifteen contests. His *Alkmeon* was praised by Aristotle (*Poetics* 14) for its use of plot.

11 *Shield pressed on shield . . . man on man* A quotation from Homer's *Iliad* (13.131).

12 *The Church is held in contempt . . . property is consumed daily* Papa-Jonas here refers to the autocephaly of the Greek Church. See "Historical Background" (page xx) for further discussion.

Chapter 3

16 *Skiron and Pityokamptes* Theseus slew the brigands Skiron and Pityokamptes using their preferred method of killing their victims.

17 *Stygos and Typhon* Stygos is a tributary of the Krathis in Kalavryta. Its source is the highest reaches of the Aroanian Mountains, from which the notorious waters of Stygos flowed. In the past, the water was considered deadly and capable of dissolving metal. Typhon is the god of winds.

18 *Catalans* Kalligas notes that this word appears to have been retained since the Catalan depredations.

Chapter 4

28 *Either a Caesar or a Nobody* *Aut Caesar aut Nihil.*

28 *a furrow . . . from which an abundance of good counsel springs* Line 593 of E. D. A. Murshead's translation of Aeschylus's *Seven against Thebes* reads "And in his heart he reaps a furrow rich wherefrom the abundance of good counsel springs."

28 *derven aga* An Ottoman military rank; a leader of an armed force charged with the security of public roads and mountain passes.

Chapter 5

31 *Portaria* A town north of Volos that is the seat of a score of villages known for their agricultural produce and manufacturing, especially of ribbon, cloth, and silk.

31 *Myrmidon* A region surrounded by the Pagassaic, Euboian, and Malaic Gulfs.

32   *piastres . . . florins* Piastres (*piastre d'argento,* "plate of silver") are Turkish coins of slight value. In 1877, two silver piastres were worth about five English pence. Florins are gold coins, initially stamped with the figure of a lily, issued in many countries.

33   *koufeta* Koufeta, Jordan almonds, symbolize the bittersweetness of married life and are given as favors at Orthodox weddings.

35   *kaim makam* From the Arabic. In Ottoman administration, a governor of a district, locum tenens. In military rank, a lieutenant colonel. Greek form, *kaimakamis.*

35   *imam* A Muslim cleric.

37   *no longer trusted the gifts of the Greeks* *Timeo Danaas et doni Ferentes* (Virgil, *Aeneid* 2.49); translated literally, the phrase means "no longer trusted the Danaans."

Chapter 6

40   *Psomathia* Psomathia (Turkish, *Samatia*) was a neighborhood in Constantinople near the Boulevard of the Seven Towers that at the time was almost exclusively Greek in population.

40   *rayah* As an Orthodox subject of the Ottoman Empire, a *rayah* did not fall within the Greek ambassador's responsibility or authority.

43   *The Panaghia . . . at Tinos* The icon of the Virgin of Tinos, discovered by a farmer in 1823 during the War of Independence, became an object of pilgrimage because of the miraculous powers attributed to it.

Chapter 7

52   *Aristippos* The founder of the Cyrenaic school, Aristippos stressed that the sovereign good consisted in pleasure and himself indulged in luxury. His philosophy was the forerunner of Epicureanism.

53   *flows from above like oil* quotation from Homer's *Iliad* (2.754).

53   *Nikos Tzaras* Nikos Tzaras (1768–1808) was a famed *armatolos,* then a klephtic leader, of Thessaly. Later, as a corsair, his marauding exploits, with seventy craft, near the Hellespont (Dardanelles)

created havoc among the Turks. He fought for the Serbs under Karageorge and supported the Russians during the Russo-Turkish War of 1807 but was abandoned by them when they signed a treaty. He was killed in an Albanian trap at age thirty-six and buried on the island of Skiathos.

53   *mourte*   An infidel.

56   *the accursed hunger for gold*   *Auri sacra fames* (Virgil, *Aeneid* 3.56–59).

Chapter 8

59   *sheep who bore fleeces but not for themselves*   *Sic vos non vobis vellera fertis, oves* (Virgil, *Appendix Vergiliana*).

60   *Themis . . . Asklepios*   Themis was the personification of laws, custom, and equity. Terpsichore was the muse of choral dance and song, and Euterpe of lyric poetry. Poseidon, of course, was the god of the sea, and Asklepios was the god of medicine.

65   *nomarch's*   A nomarch is a governor of a prefecture; a prefect.

65   *five of the thirty-five lepta*   At five drachmas to the dollar, this was worth about seven cents at that time.

Chapter 9

69   *a Karamanian sheep's tail*   A sheep with a broad tail; Karamania was a region in Asia Minor that included Cappadocia and Phrygia.

70   *What ails . . . ailed me*   A folk adage.

Chapter 10

85   *the colacretan's milk*   A κωλακρέτης was a financial officer in early Athens; this phrase is used comically and disparagingly (Idomeneus, *Historicus* 5.724).

85   *I saved you, as all Greeks know*   A quotation from Euripides' *Medea* (2.1.476).

86   *Trophonios*   Trophonios, the son of Apollo and Epikaste, or of Zeus and Iokaste, was an architect of many temples. He disappeared in a crevasse, which thereafter was called the dungeon of Trophonios, later the site of the famed oracle.

87   *Doubt all you want* Νᾶφε καὶ μέμνησ'ἀπιστεῖν, ἄρθρα ταυτα τῶν φρενῶν (Epicharmus, *Comicus*); the phrase literally means "Beg but remember to disbelieve these twists of the mind."

Chapter 11

95   *Tithonios*   Tithon was the son of Laomedon and Stryo and the brother of Priam. Because of his beauty, Eos loved him and asked for his immortality. She forgot to ask the gods for his eternal youth, however, and he became very old. The gods, horrified, turned him into a cicada.

96   *Ambassador Tade or Deina*   "Tade or Deina" (Τάδε Δείνα) is the Greek equivalent of the English "so-and-so."

Chapter 12

102   *hurrah*   "Hurrah" is meant to represent τήνελλα, a word formed by Archilochus (*Lyricus* 119) to imitate the twang of a guitar string: he began a triumphal hymn to Heracles with τήνελλα, ὢ καλλίνικε χαῖρε; hence the words τήνελλα καλλίνικε became a common mode of saluting conquerors in the games.

102   *Marsyas*   Marsyas, the legendary Phrygian satyr, challenged Apollo to a contest in flute playing with the condition that the winner could do what he wished with the loser. But he used the flute that Athena had thrown away because her features were distorted while she played it. The Muses decided in favor of Apollo, who tied Marsyas to a tree and flayed him alive.

102   *Persian tongue*   Datism, from Datis, was a Persian general at Marathon who spoke broken Greek.

102   *Asiatic tendencies*   To speak with Asiatic tendencies is to speak with mistakes.

103   *Men are selected through trials*   A quotation from Pindar's *Ode* (4.18).

104   *Elpiniki*   The daughter of Miltiades, the Athenian general at the Battle of Marathon, and the half-sister of Kimon, an admiral and a statesman, Elpiniki is apparently meant to signify an aged maiden here. Historically, however, Elpiniki was married to Callias.

107   *Hephaestus and Harmonia*   Hephaestus was the Greek god of fire (Vulcan to the Romans). At the wedding of Harmonia, the daughter of Ares and Aphrodite, and Cadmus, the bride was given a necklace made by Hephaestus that brought disaster on all its owners.

109   *Pelops*   The father of Pelops killed his son in order to feed the gods at a dinner, but only one, Demeter, was deceived by the fare. She ate the shoulder. Hermes, on orders from Zeus, restored Pelops but could not find the shoulder, which was replaced by one of ivory.

109   *Apollonius the Difficult*   Apollonius Dyskolos ("the Crabbed" or "the Difficult") was an Alexandrian founder of scientific grammar in the second century A.D. Four of his treatises survive: *On Syntax, On Pronouns, On Conjunctions,* and *On Adverbs.*

Chapter 13

112   *Teutonia*   The reference is to Bavaria.

112   *These potato eaters . . . an acre*   This is a reference to the homestead principle. Since it was believed that the freeholder was a better citizen of a democracy than a tenant and was a natural supporter of popular government, public lands were acquired for the United States in all territories except for the original thirteen and several others, namely Maine, Vermont, Kentucky, Tennessee, and Texas. "For a time they were regarded chiefly as a source of revenue, but about 1820, as the need of revenue to the payment of the national debt decreased and the inhabitants of an increasing number of new States became eager to have the vacant lands within their bounds occupied, the demand that the public lands should be disposed of more in the interest of the settler became increasingly strong, and the homestead idea originated." The homestead principle, with some exceptions, was not applied by Congress until the Civil War, and the act of 1862

"provided that any citizen of the United States, or applicant for citizenship, who was the head of a family, or 21 years of age, or who, if younger, had served no less than fourteen days in the army or navy of the United States during an actual war, might apply for 160 acres or less of unappropriated public lands, and might acquire title to this amount of land by residing upon and cultivating it for five years immediately following, and paying such fees as were necessary to cover the cost of administration" (*Encyclopaedia Britannica,* 14th ed., s.v. "Homestead Acts").

112   *small-minded squatters*   Kalligas's own word; he puns ἔφεδροι ("squatters") with εδραῖοι ("established" or "strong").

113   *During a dialogue . . . than this*   The source of this passage is lines 462 to 465 of Aristophanes' *Plutus.*

113   *stremmata*   A *stremma* is about a quarter of an acre; 240 *stremmata* equal about 60 acres.

Chapter 14

126   *forcing the husband . . . the lover*   Kalligas calls the husband Amphitryon, the Theban king cuckolded by Zeus while away at war, and the lover Paris.

128   *Eratosthenes*   Eratosthenes was one of the Thirty Tyrants, not the Alexandrian mathematician.

129   *Anakyndaraxus Sardanapalus*   Anakyndaraxus Sardanapalus, the last king of Assyria, was considered an effeminate voluptuary who, when attacked by Arbaces, satrap of Medea, gathered his wives and treasures and burned them, with himself, in his palace.

Chapter 15

130   *spachis*   An Ottoman noble who received a grant of land, a military fiefdom, for which initially he had an obligation to outfit and lead his own cavalry unit. During the Ottoman decline, a *spachis* was simply the owner of a small parcel of land who, by practice, also taxed his tenants.

131   *the Fallmerayer thesis*   J. P. Fallmerayer's thesis, expressed in the two-volume *Geschichte der Halbinsel Morea wahrend des Mittelalters* (Stuttgart and Tubingen: J. G. Cotta, 1830–36), questions the continuity of the Greek people and asserts that massive Albanian and Slavic incursions in the Peloponnisos and central Greece had major impacts on the ethnic and linguistic character of the modern Greeks. Pavlos Kalligas adds a wry footnote: "I recall a fellow citizen of Fallmerayer in Munich asking me privately and confidentially to tell him frankly if I were a modern or an ancient Greek. Liebig had not developed organic chemistry yet." Justus Liebig (1803–73) was one of the founders of agronomic chemistry.

131   *a donkey's disaster*   A Greek idiom (τοῦ ὄνου συμφορὰ) that concludes a folktale.

132   *Thus says Brutus . . . honorable man*   In act 2, scene 2 of *Julius Caesar*, Marc Antony says "yet Brutus says he was ambitious and Brutus is an honorable man."

132   *the tax contractor . . . tax confiscator*   An untranslatable pun (ἐκλήπτορας, ἐκλάπτορας).

135   *from a distant land*   ηλόθεν 'ἐξ ἀπίης γαίης (Homer, *Iliad* 1.270).

140   *kokoretsi*   An appetizer of skewered innards.

Withdrawn

Chapter 16

147   *be generous with grain . . . a nuisance*   The quotations in this passage are from Lattimore's translation of Hesiod's *Works and Days* (2.604–5, 2.441–43, and 2.602–3, in order of appearance).

Chapter 17

150   *oka*   An *oka* is 1,282 grams in the Turkish system, or about two and a quarter pounds.

152   *I'll bow before you . . . this dummy*   A folk adage; κόπανος ("cudgel" or "pestle") is the word used for a fool or an idiot.

156   *the Russian . . . French flags*   At the time, the Greek political parties